10/02

KELLY

THE THREE-TOED HORSE

Also by Peter Bowen

CRUZATTE & MARIA

THE STICK GAME

LONG SON

THUNDER HORSE

NOTCHES

WOLF, NO WOLF

SPECIMEN SONG

COYOTE WIND

IMPERIAL KELLY

KELLY BLUE

YELLOWSTONE KELLY

KELLY AND THE THREE-TOED HORSE

A Novel Featuring Yellowstone Kelly,

Gentleman and Scout

PETER BOWEN

ST. MARTIN'S PRESS

NEW YORK

www.stmartins.com

Designed by Kathryn Parise

LIBRARY OF CONGRESS CATALOGING-IN-PUBLICATION DATA
Bowen, Peter.
    Kelly and the three-toed horse / Peter Bowen.—1st ed.
        p. cm.
      ISBN 0-312-24106-2
    1. Kelly, Luther S. (Luther Sage), 1849–1928—Fiction. 2. Fossils—
Collection and preservation—Fiction. 3. Horses, Fossil—Fiction.
4. Wyoming—Fiction. I. Title.
PS3552.O866 K43 2001
813'.54—dc21

                                                        00-045961

First Edition: March 2001

10 9 8 7 6 5 4 3 2 1

For Russell Hope,
horseman, eccentric, and autodidact,
who is never, ever sarcastic . . .

KELLY

THE THREE-TOED HORSE

CHAPTER

1

We was all drunk that day.

After years of graft, corruption, chicanery, double-dealing, theft, death, and all them other exercises in basic American character the two mobs of thieves had finally met in Utah, and the railroad stretched from coast to coast.

"I'm so happy I don't know whether to puke or go blind," says 3-Card Thurman. He had gotten fairly rich from the fool laborers on the Union Pacific, whose callused fingers couldn't feel his shaved decks of cards. 3-Card could gamble honest if he had to, and he only had to if some smart feller had an assistant stick a gun in his ear.

We was back a ways from the big party, around the spot where the two tracks met, what with all the nobs and speculators and politicians and journalists clubbed up close to where the Golden Spike was to be drove home. Me and 3-Card was on top of a water tower, and we could see good right down to the spot where Durant and Crocker was going to symbolically nail the nation together.

It was quite a ceremony.

After some speechifying, Durant staggered over to the tie that binds and a flunky handed him a sledge. He was grass-grabbin' drunk, and he swung the sledge up, damn near busting the jaw of some scribbler, and he dropped the head wobbly-like and it hit the tie and bounced off and got a politician in the knee.

"This ain't as bad as it could be," I says to 3-Card. "A couple of 'em might die."

A couple of Durant's toadies lifted him off the ground he'd folded up on and one of 'em held the sledge up high and the other wrapped Durant's fingers around the handle.

Durant hit the dirt and fell over, nose down on the rail.

He didn't move, and the flunks lifted him up and a feller in rough honest workingman's clothes drove the spike home. Durant's head was lolling.

Then Charley Crocker of the Central Pacific lumbered forward to take his swings at the spike the sledgeman had set. Charley was so damn fat he couldn't see the spike over his belly, and time he bent over far enough to tell where it was, he'd missed it again.

He did manage to get a lawyer's foot, though, with his last swing.

"How the hell can you tell it's a lawyer?" says 3-Card.

"He was tryin' to pick Crocker's pocket," I says. "What else could he be?"

The lawyer's foot was poorly for it. He was writhing on the ground and screaming.

Finally, Charley Crocker wore hisself out swinging, and he dropped the sledge and gasped and put a hand to his chest. I was hoping for him dropping dead, but after a few heaves he seemed fine, damn it, and he stood with Durant, while Durant's flunks held him up, and photographers set off a lot of flash powder and everybody hurrahed, everybody near 'em, anyway. A lot of us on the outside had a different opinion.

"More riffraff," says Blue Fox, a Cheyenne acquaintance who'd gone through Dartmouth College and didn't think much of it. I sorta suspected he was the Indian who come up to one of General Grenville Dodge's sentries three years before and asked in a plummy English accent for directions; it seemed his hunting party had got lost. The poor soldier got all helpful and ended up dead and scalped and all Dodge's horses were stolen.

When I asked Blue Fox about that he got all horrified-looking and said he was desolate that I could think such a thing of him. Well, it was goddamned easy. The horse thieves had been Cheyennes and I purely couldn't think of one of them had English good enough to pull that off, but . . .

There was a boom toward the west, and a big cloud of smoke with timbers flying everywhere and I even saw a couple bodies flopping through the air. Some Irish lads had set off fireworks by way of celebration.

"Shit," says 3-Card, "there's that goddamned Luke Gooding. I will see you boys around," and he slid down the timbers and rode off casual-like. Luke was a Federal Marshal, and if he wished to speak with 3-Card, it was a sure bet 3-Card would really not like to speak to him.

Luke was sort of not looking but looking and finally he seen me and he began to mosey over toward the water tower me and Blue Fox was on.

"As concerned citizens," says Blue Fox, "perhaps we should have made a citizen's arrest."

"You ain't a citizen," I says to Blue Fox. "And besides, Luke is a good man and maybe he'll just shoot you by way of the public good."

I couldn't help liking that Cheyenne son of a bitch. And I sure as hell couldn't blame him for killing every soldier and track layer he could manage. This damn railroad meant the end of his people, and he knew it.

Luke was gettin' closer, slipping through the crowd, never looking up. He went round the back of the water tower, to cut off escape, and I heard him cuss a little and then he clambered up.

"I'd like to swear out a complaint," says Blue Fox.

"I'll goddamn bet you would," says Luke. "Likely arrest and hang everybody here."

"What a wonderful idea," says Blue Fox.

"Kelly," says Luke, keeping an eye on Blue Fox, "I know damn well you been with 3-Card. Now where is he?"

Luke was a good man, but not a real patient one, and if I hemmed and hawed, he'd throw me off the tower, see it improved my memory.

"Left when he seen you," I says.

"3-Card cut a whore over to Rosie's couple days ago," says Luke, "for no more than laughin' at his pecker."

"CUT A WHORE!" me and Blue Fox bellers together.

This was one of them things just ain't allowed out here. Whores is just as good as anybody else out here, and that is that.

"That bastard," I says.

Blue Fox had stood up on the timber.

"Rosie's is a good place," he says.

Was, too. You come in, you take your bath and put on clean clothes, you go to the big parlor, pick your girl out, and go on upstairs. You behave. You don't, Rosie's bouncer, a four-hundred-pound Kraut named Wolf, beats hell out of you and then throws you out the third-floor window. A couple of drunk drummers pulled guns on him once, shot him five times. He smashed their heads together so damn hard Rosie had to put new wallpaper in the room, since the old wallpaper was covered in spatters of brains.

"Cut her and left her tied," says Luke, "and sneaked off."

"Didn't know Luke had them habits," says Blue Fox. This from a feller once slowly skinned a couple soldiers, for three days, while sixteen of us was bottled up in a blind canyon, just to make sure we didn't sleep so good.

Us whites was just as bad, and you don't hear the stories because we won, whatever that is.

"Well," says Federal Marshal Luke Gooding, "I expect I'll just have to go after him."

"Stuff and nonsense," says Blue Fox. "Kelly and me are headed that way. 3-Card's a good cheat, but he ain't what you'd call a plainsman."

Christ on a stickhorse, here I was being volunteered to ride with one of the worst cutthroats I ever knew, and I knew plenty, after goddamned 3-Card. Still, cutting a whore was about as bad a thing as you could do out here.

"When you catch him," says Luke, "arrest him and bring him to the nearest stop on the railroad."

"Guaranteed," says Blue Fox.

"I mean it," says Luke.

"Of course you do," says Blue Fox.

"This all right with you, Kelly?" says Luke.

"No," I says, "but it'll have to do." I had business on toward

Cheyenne, and Blue Fox would be a handy companion. He wouldn't kill me because he was smart enough to know I might be of use to him some day.

"I got to go west a little," says Luke. "Them damn Loper brothers robbed a train a hundred miles west. Thing ain't even been built all the way through, and they're at it." And he slid down to the ground and went off to kill the Loper brothers. Thing about Luke was he hated paperwork, and it was a rare time when whoever he was after survived. I'd seen a report of his.

"Whun i fend hem he's shotted," it read.

Blue Fox and me was sober, maybe the only ones in the ten thousand or so celebrants all clustered around the Golden Spike. We got some grub on our way east and settled into a lope along the old trail. 3-Card would stay on it till he got over the mountains, at least.

We come on his tracks soon enough, and long before sundown we caught up to him. He was maybe a half mile ahead, bouncing along in the saddle like his ass was india rubber.

Blue Fox was riding along beside me easy as you please, and then I looked south for a moment—something had moved—and he tore the reins out of my hand and slipped the headstall off my horse just like that and spurred his horse and left me. Mine slowed down and looked at me, not knowing what to do.

I watched. Blue Fox held close down on his horse's neck, and he come up behind 3-Card, and I saw his war club, a stone in a rawhide quirt, whirl up and come down. 3-Card threw his arms up and fell back, his skull smashed.

Blue Fox had tossed my headstall onto a greasewood bush. I got down and put it on my horse. Time I was back up Blue Fox was gone.

I rode past 3-Card, facedown, blood leaking from his head. His horse was rearing, scared bad, but the gelding calmed when I grabbed the reins. I got down and made a hackamore out of my rope and slipped off 3-Card's saddle and left it by him and went on.

I needed a spare mount, and there wasn't a thing I could do for 3-Card.

CHAPTER

2

I got back from the trip to the East with Sitting Bull & Company* and what with one thing and another it was the middle of the fall before I found myself in Pignuts' saloon, the sort of low-class place in which I have always felt most comfortable. Pignuts was a half-addled Rebel with a great white scar on his forehead, got, he claimed, at Ball's Bluff. I suspected there was less to the story than he told, but the West was full of heroes of the War then, and it went on in drunken fights when the arguments about who was right got out of hand.

Pignuts had bought one of them three-story railroad cars the Union Pacific had made for bunkhouses for the gang laborers and after a little fine handiwork with an ax and a sledge

*See *Kelly Blue*

and some spikes he opened for business. The bar was a slab from a cottonwood tree set on stacks of cracker boxes. Pignuts had a pal, some cracker from the swamps of Alabama, who made whiskey out of just about anything up Deadman's Gulch. The house booze was piss yellow with an oily film on top and them as drank enough to get the horrors sometimes died. Pignuts had set up another smaller railroad car about a quarter mile back from his establishment for folks to stagger off to and maybe die in, and the local sheriff left him alone, having a lot of work in Laramie.

I bought a bottle and I carefully looked at the seals to make sure Pignuts hadn't diluted my whiskey with his gopher poison, and they seemed all right.

Since I had last been here Pignuts had invested in decorations, I suppose to give a little class to the place, which was damn hard. He had the usual plump woman a-layin' back on a red-velvet couch, draped just a little by filmy scarves, in a big fat gold frame, and decks of French postcards of women screwing donkeys and goats.

Right in the middle of the bar Pignuts had this glass case with a funny little skeleton in it, which try as I might I could not make into a critter that I knew. It was about the size of a spaniel and there was little pieces of yellow-brown rock stuck to the bones.

"What the hell is this?" I says to Pignuts. He had a walleye and it floated around a while before settling on me.

"Feller needed a drink bad, and he traded it to me," said Pignuts. "I give him the drink and he sorta stiffened up and fell over dead. Too bad, he had another five comin'. Nobody knew him, so we buried him out back. Well-dressed feller, and he talked educated."

Another black sheep sent here by a shamed family. The West

was a great place to send the family drunk and claim they was ranching. Often they was all down to the telegraph station first of the month, waiting on the money they got paid to stay here.

"It has three toes there," I says, looking at the front feet. "Damned if I know a critter we got has three toes."

"Well," says Pignuts, pouring himself a drink of my whiskey to hold his shakes back, "we got Sorefoot."

Sorefoot was a feller who, havin' drink taken, bet he could hit his own toes and he shot off four of them and felt no pain until he sobered up. That god-awful whiskey Pignuts sold would get a man so damn drunk you could shoot him in the *brain* and he wouldn't die till he sobered up.

The West was a good place to have fun in, for sure.

A couple of cowboys was sleepin' it off facedown on one of the tables by the wall. Their hats had come off and rolled to the floor. Flies buzzed and settled on them.

A quiet day in Pignuts' Emporium.

"Luke Gooding was by asked where you was," says Pignuts. "Said if I seen you, tell you it warn't what he had in mind. I dunno about what."

"Well, it warn't what I had in mind neither," I says, which was some true, though both me and Luke knew the moment that Blue Fox was more or less deputized 3-Card was dead. I suppose I could have done something about it, but 3-Card had cut the whore—it was worse than we knew, the whore was 3-Card's sister and he had done it for the family honor, which is rich for a tinhorn gambler, and the whores especially at Rosie's tended not to work long before marryin' and there's a lot of First Families of Wyoming would like me to keep my damn mouth shut so I will.

A couple shiftless Irish come in, muddy to the knees.

"We got your damn skeleton in the coffin out there," says one of them, a broad short man with a coat so ragged I could see white skin in places.

Pignuts nodded and he walked round the bar and give them a little money and they left.

"Skeleton?" I says, wondering.

"Feller I got this varmint from was from a rich family back East and they offered a re-ward for the body, so I had them Paddys dig up some bones."

"The right bones?" I says.

"Feller ain't been in the ground long enough," says Pignuts, "He'd be kinda ripe. Out of consideration for their feelin's I thought some cleaner bones would do."

Pignuts was a thoughtful man, and his kind heart shone through.

"How much you make on this?" I says.

"Thousand," says Pignuts. "There's a teamster on the way, haul the coffin down to Laramie."

Someone come in, lifting the buffalo robe served Pignuts' establishment for a door. He stood there blinking in the dim light a while and then he sauntered over to the bar and he looked at the skeleton in the glass case. He nodded.

"My good man," says the dude, "I will pay a hundred dollars in gold for that."

"I ain't a good man," says Pignuts. "I'll take two."

The dude nodded and fished some double eagles out of a purse and counted out ten.

"Case is extra," says Pignuts. Nothing a bit bashful about him.

The dude lifted up the case, and the skeleton stood on the wood slab, wired here and there to hold it up. The dude took out some snips and he cut the wires and one by one he put the bones in a silk bag he took from a pocket of his fancy coat. His silk vest was all roses and violets.

"I do not," says the dude, "require the case."

He looked at me thoughtfully. I was overdressed for the place, having on my beaded and quilled buckskin coat and big fancy new hat and a silk kerchief. My custom boots was new and barely muddy.

"Are you Yellowstone Kelly, by any chance," says the dude.

"Bad luck, but I am," I replies. I smelled trouble, and I hoped there wouldn't be any.

"I am putting together an expedition," says the dude, "and I will pay you well to be the scout."

"Where and how long?" I says.

"Wyoming," says the dude. "In two weeks."

"In the winter?" I says. "Not a good time."

"Haste is essential," says the dude.

"Haste is expensive," I says.

"Five hundred a month in gold," says the dude. "First two months in advance."

"Always was a hasty man," I says. I could buy a tent, flunks, and a couple whores to keep me warm for that money and have enough left over for serious debauchery when I went East. I go there for the ice cream.

He languidly held out a paw, and I took it. His grip was hard and so were his eyes.

"You don't mind," I says, "what the hell was that thing you just bought?"

"It's a horse," says the dude.

Pignuts started to gasp and wheeze with laughter. The dude ignored him.

Least I could do was be polite to the feller. It did cross my mind that I maybe ought to take the gold and run.

Pignuts was slobbering onto his folded arms, head down.

"You familiar with Darwin?" says Cope.

I nodded. A British feller pissed all over the Bible, some said, though I wasn't sure exactly what it was the man said.

Conversation come to a halt just then because the buffalo robe was thrown up so hard it got caught on a nail in the wall. A cold wind blew in, and a beautiful woman stomped across the rough-plank floor, spurs jingling.

Pignuts looked up, puzzled.

Tall she was, with a pile of blond hair in a silk scarf and a pair of blazing blue eyes.

"Um," said the dude, just before the woman slashed Pignuts across the face with a riding crop. Pignuts yelped and cowered. The woman had a dainty silver-chased pistol in her other hand, and it was quite accurately pointed at Pignuts' forehead.

"You smelly bastard," says the woman. "The bones in that coffin are *not* those of my brother. Who was six-foot-four, not five-feet-two. Now you get a shovel, you son of a bitch, and we are going to go and get what's left of my brother."

"He's all rotten!" Pignuts screamed.

"You have a serviceable kettle out back," says the woman. "I saw it."

Pignuts started to work his mouth, and the woman fired one shot that put a neat hole through Pignuts' left ear. The hole welled blood and Pignuts screamed.

"Move," says the blond woman.

Pignuts was blubbering and scared enough to do as he was told. He got a slicker and some gloves. The woman never took that pistol's eye off Pignuts' forehead.

"Good afternoon, Alys," says the dude.

"Delighted," says Alys. "Always good to see you, Jonathan."

Just for a moment her blue eyes met my black ones, and I

had a jolt run through me. It was like you saw yourself when you were not expecting to.

"Mr. Kelly has agreed to accompany us," says Jonathan.

"How nice," says Alys.

Pignuts was shuffling toward the front door. Alys wasn't far behind.

"Sad about your brother," says Jonathan.

"Hell it was," says Alys. "That poor sick bastard was so unhappy he's better off dead."

Alys and the gibbering Pignuts went on out. I heard a team lean into traces, then a wagon rolled. The wind was picking up and smelled of snow.

"Professor Jonathan Cope," says the dude, "and we have much to do. I have business in Salt Lake. I propose you ride there with me at my expense. It will take only three days."

I heard another shot. Maybe Alys had found the right grave, I thought, and didn't need Pignuts anymore.

CHAPTER 3

Cope had a blooded horse tied to the rail next to my big bay, with one of them funny pancake saddles on him, and we swung up and headed toward Laramie. I looked off toward Pignuts' boneyard and saw dirt just-aflyin'. Alys had done convinced him she'd kill him 'less he did something mighty pleasing. A couple men was building a fire under the big kettle she'd spoke of—it was used to boil clothes, to get rid of the lice. That worked well enough, but I learned long ago it's better to find a good anthill and kick it open and lay your clothes on it and let the angry ants hunt down the lice. They get the egg cases, too.

Cope set off, and I followed. Silly his saddle might look, but the man was a horseman, setting easy as he was on his porch in a rocking chair. The wind began to howl overhead, a banshee scream. Wyoming wind is a thing, like the mountains. Some folks went mad and put rifle or shotgun barrels in their mouths and pulled the trigger. If you had an uneasy soul, the wind could draw madness out of you and show you its face.

Laramie wasn't far, and turned out Cope had a couple private cars—nobs traveled in 'em, homes on wheels, right down to paintings on the walls and four-poster beds.

A manservant met us at the door, and Cope bade him show me my rooms. They was in the other car, and an Irish girl was carrying kettles of hot water to a bathtub. I hadn't had a bath in a while, and I took the hint. I stripped down and put on a silk bathrobe was on my bed and I went behind the screen and sank into hot water plain stinking of lilacs. I thought this better wear off before I come back to Laramie or the saloons would be a bad place to go, what with the sort of friends I got.

Whooooooeeeeee, they'd holler, smell that fine feller. And they wouldn't rest till I had been cut down to size.

But the bath felt wonderful and I soaked a long time and I scrubbed and there was even a little brush for my teeth which did as good a job as a willow twig and salt did.

Time I got back to the room, there was my clothes that warn't leather all white and even pressed. They smelled of bluing.

I got dressed and buttoned my shirt and left my heavy beaded coat on a rack and I sauntered back toward the main car. Cope was in what was the parlor, sipping brandy from a snifter and smoking a long cheroot. He nodded toward another snifter and another cigar and I nodded and he clipped the end and held out a match for me. He had them good manners you get only in the blood. He waited till I had a few puffs and a few sips and then he nodded and bent forward.

"When we return," says Cope, "I wish to have you engage the services of some hardy men who know Wyoming. They must have excellent eyesight and be fighters. Offer them whatever the going rate is, plus forty dollars a month."

Going rate was about twenty, so I doubted I'd have trouble recruiting.

"I am a paleontologist," says Cope, "and there are reports of rich fossil beds in Wyoming."

I nodded. He was talking about what the Sioux called Thunder Horses, giant bones weathering out of the earth belonging to the mounts of the Thunder People. I didn't know how the Sioux would take having them mined out. Probably about like they took the gold miners. Which meant we'd better be well armed and have some trade goods and whiskey.

Red Cloud hand't had a drink since '47, when he killed his best friend while they was guzzling white man's whiskey. He didn't recall having done it but he was so ashamed he never touched it again. Red Cloud was one of them Indians you see you realize you are in the presence of a great man, like Washakie. They was bigger and wiser than the rest of us.

A little yardpuller engine coupled up to our cars and moved us off the siding and gently pushed us into a passenger train's caboose until the couplings locked. There was a hiss as the steam brakes was connected.

Salt Lake City. I had had a bad time with the damned Mormons, especially that madman Brigham Young. He was crazy like a goddamned fox and utterly ruthless. Didn't believe a word of their dumb book, he told me, but it was a good way to make a million dollars. He talked of a million dollars like preachers talk of heaven, only with Brigham the million was a sure thing.

Brigham was a scoundrel, sure enough, but I had to give

the man some credit. He'd led his people to the arse end of nowhere and built an empire. He had to know that while the railroad would end the Mormon hold on the Great Basin, it would also assure him of his million dollars.

Cope then plied me with pleasant but sharp questions about where I come from—upstate New York, and how I come to be in the West—I deserted the Union Army, but after Appomattox, so no one much cared—and how I got on with the Indians.

"Well," I says, "that depends. Sometimes we find ourselves tryin' to kill each other, and sometimes we have an amiable meal together. They's good people really."

Cope nodded.

"They're in the way," he says. "America is knitting itself together, we have millions of immigrants coming to our shores, and the Indians are doomed."

True enough. Both Red Cloud and Washakie saw that, but the Sioux was more numerous and fierce than the Shoshones, and I knew it broke Red Cloud's heart knowing how many of his brave warriors was going to die.

"I cannot tell them the truth," Red Cloud said to me once. "They have only their love and bravery to offer the People." Indians is supposed to be so stoic, but when he said that and looked at me there was tears and he let them well and fall, running down his lined cheeks. His eyes were so sad I began to cry, too.

But fate's fate, and them as can't see it is the happier for it. There's only death at the end for all of us, anyway, but some of us try to do our best. Not that we ever know what that is.

"I understand that you know Red Cloud and Gall and Spotted Tail and Sitting Bull and the others," says Cope.

I nodded.

"What will be their reaction?" he says.

"Them I can talk to," I says, "though I may have some odd orders for the fellers I hire. Its them damn Cheyennes worry me."

Cope nodded and sipped brandy.

"Go on," he says.

"They ain't as big a tribe as the Sioux," I says, "but they are one hell of a lot meaner. Red Cloud told me till about 1800 they was farmers, and then some prophet told 'em they had to move out on the Plains and learn to live by the horse and the buffalo, or they'd lose the tribe."

"Lose the tribe?" says Cope.

"Have their ways changed by missionaries and such. You know how tedious those bastards are."

Cope laughed.

"Most important thing to them is they keep their ways," I says. "They are real religious and strong on family."

"Do you know any Cheyennes?" says Cope.

I nodded. That cutthroat Blue Fox I knew real good, and a few others. Bravery is a common thing, actually, more common than cowardice is, but them Cheyennes was pure crazy when they were fighting. I seen one charge a company of cavalry once and run the lieutenant through with his lance and then the Cheyenne fell and there was twenty-three bullet holes in him, about half of which should have killed him outright.

"Will you talk to them?" says Cope.

I nodded. Blue Fox wouldn't kill me, there being honor among scoundrels, and I wouldn't probably have to look for him more than a mile ride away from camp toward dusk. Cheyennes can flat disappear on a blackrock plain with no more cover than pebbles. I half expect, when I am in their country, to step on one when I get up to piss in the night.

The train give a lurch and began to build up speed. The cars clanked, and soon the wheels was clacking over the joints in the rails and we was headed to Salt Lake City.

Cope went on asking his penetrating questions about the country we was headed to and the Indians we would have to contend with and the people I proposed to hire on.

The engineer blew a long lonesome blast on his whistle, and we headed down the sagebrush, with the black mountains up ahead.

I was getting peckish, and no sooner had I recalled my hunger than a maid come in with a big tray with pickled buffalo tongue and cheeses and bread cut in little squares and pickles and a tureen of turtle soup. I fell to, ravenous as a lame wolf on a dead carcass.

"Oh, Kelly," says Cope, standing up and swaying with the car. "The lovely Miss Alys de Bonneterre will go with us. She's one of my assistants. Studied art at the Sorbonne. She'll be sketching geological features and specimens."

I nodded.

She would while the light held, I expected, and I also expected that the dark would be a different matter indeed.

Oh, yes.

I made a note to get some best buffalo robes and more soap than I am wont to carry.

CHAPTER 4

I have seen some ridiculous sights in my time, but perhaps the best was what awaited us in Salt Lake City.

Cope's cars was pulled right up to the main dock, and it was all covered with prominent Mormons, a brass band, bunting, and a long red carpet.

Standing at the end of the carpet was Brigham Young his own self, beaming.

"It seems that Young is terribly grateful to me," says Cope, "since in the Book of Mormon horses are often mentioned, and of course modern horses did not arrive until the Spaniards brought them."

"That skeleton is about the size of a small dog," I says.

"All Brigham cares about is that it is a horse," says Cope, "I have to admire a man who makes do with what's available."

"All the same to you," I says, "I believe I'll just rest up here. Me and Brigham don't get along so good."

"Au contraire," says Cope. "He asked after you and specifically recommended you to me. He had most admiring words for your abilities and honor."

"That crooked son of a bitch likely just wants to hang me," I says, "and he's got good reason."

"Kelly," says Cope, "Brigham is a statesman. He said all is forgiven and demanded I bring you along."

So I drug back to my rooms and got my coat and hat and me and Cope got off the train. The other passengers was having to hike back to the station.

When the door to the parlor car opened the brass band struck up a tune and all of the Mormons cheered except Brigham, who chose to look all prophetic. I followed at a little distance from Cope, warily looking for signs of law.

"Professor Cope!" boomed Brigham. "Salt Lake City welcomes you, a distinguished scholar!"

Huzzahs.

A seagull overhead took a shit, and it hit the brim of Brigham's hat, spattering white blots on the black silk.

Suddenly there were a hell of a lot more of them, and all the bastards had the runs. A sleet of bird shit fell and the band and worthies fled for the safety of the station. We mobbed through the doors, a lot of men mopping at their coats, and even Cope had a turd on one shoulder.

Brigham was right next to me.

"It's a sign from God," I says. "As a fully equipped prophet, would you mind explainin' it to me."

Brigham smiled at me like a weasel does at a chicken.

"I notice," he says, "that you ain't got any on you."

"That must mean something," I says.

"It means I am going to talk to Professor Cope without your damned Gentile insolence," says Brigham. "There's two dozen Sons of Dan here, awaiting the least excuse."

The Sons of Dan was killers Brigham was known to send after apostates and anyone else he disliked. They always cut the throats of their quarry, something to do with Blood Atonement. But they was just killers, that's all.

A statesman. Well, I had killed John Wilkes Booth for one of 'em.*

"He's under my protection," says Cope.

"Better yet, he's under mine," says Brigham. "But since you are payin' this scamp, tell him to hold his tongue. I don't want my faithful disturbed."

Cope nodded. I was going to quit anyway. It was only so much fun to needle Brigham because he didn't believe the hogwash he preached anyway. What he believed in was Brigham Young.

The somewhat smeared faithful was getting restive, and so we trooped out to a long line of carriages and I got in with Cope and Young and a monstrous young Mormon thug who looked at me like he was sizing me up for chops.

"Levi," says Brigham, "don't stare at Mister Kelly. It ain't polite."

A shock run though me of a sudden. I suspected he was one of the sons of that polygamist I'd shot with the buffalo rifle. No wonder he hated me. Him and his probably two hundred brothers. Bein' a Mormon could be a good life and I probably would have joined up but I can't stand sermons.

We trooped off to the biggest hotel, and there was a reception laid on, tables piled with food. One dish caught my eye.

*See *Kelly Blue*

It was green and had little orange shreds of carrots in it. Calves'-foot jelly. It sorta looked like moose puke, but the Mormons tucked into it like it was manna.

Brigham rapped on a lectern for order, and the faithful, reeking slightly of incontinent seagulls, formed up and looked all interested and Brigham gave a flowery speech praising this Gentile genuis for having found incontrovertible proof of the Word of the Book of Mormon. There had been horses in America.

No doubt Brigham would have a revelation in the matter of who ate 'em all, but not today.

"Professor Cope!" boomed Brigham.

"Hear hear," says the faithful. Flies had appeared and was very interested in everybody but me.

Cope made his elegant way to the lectern and he got there and he cleared his throat and a flunk brought him a glass of water. He waited a moment for the rustling to die down, and then he talked.

The world, he said, was uncountable millions of years old, and creatures which were the ancestors of every living thing on earth today had lived back then, and e-volved. Professor Darwin and a feller named Wallace had thought really hard and divined that over enough time a lizard could have feathers and fly. There had been huge beasts, dinosaurs, terrible lizards, stalking round a few million years ago.

The horse he had found was small, but its bones were that of a horse.

No huzzahs. The audience was Mormon, true enough, but before this they had been Baptists and the like, and here Cope was explaining that the Bible wasn't true.

They didn't like it one bit.

Some cleared their throats.

Cope went on, but he'd lost his audience, and I could hear flaps shutting on ears with soft pops. These was people who were not over particular about what they believed, but they damn well had to do it hard.

Cope thanked them for their attention and he quit and walked back to me and Brigham. There was a lot of men muttering and glancing our way, and not even Brigham's stern stare could stop them.

Brigham shrugged and he led us out the back door of the hotel, with Levi the giant close behind, and we got into a carriage and the driver took us to Lion House, the mansion Brigham had built to house him and his forty-odd wives.

Levi went somewhere when Brigham and me and Cope ended up in Brigham's study. It was musty and cluttered and Utah was governed from this room, not to mention other places the Mormons had gone to. They was hardworking and brave and they had taught themselves irrigation and the desert really had bloomed. The railroad meant that Mormon crops would now go east and west, and it also meant that the folks they called Gentiles would come in numbers. Things would never be the same.

"You've been most kind," says Cope, "but I fear I have perhaps shaken the faith of some of your flock."

"Don't worry about it," says Brigham. "They're too stupid to be bothered long. This wasn't for them anyway, you saw all the journalists. By the time the newspapers get done garbling what you said all that they will have right is that there were horses in North America like the Book of Mormon says. This will help my missionaries."

"Well," says Cope, "we need to return and get on with our expedition."

"I see your friend Marsh is also planning one," says Brigham.

The name Marsh got Cope all stiff, and his face flushed. It was right obvious that whoever this Marsh was Cope did not like him one damn bit a-tall.

"Scholarship has room for all," says Cope, trying to be noble, but there was a petulant whine in his voice.

"Room it may have," says Brigham, "but the top of any place is big enough for only one man."

I had been looking around at the photographs and carved furniture and gaudy lamps by Tiffany, and my eye fell on a small table that had something on it covered by a red cloth. It was lumpy, whatever it was underneath.

Brigham walked over to it and he pulled the cloth away and there was a reddish rock with something yellow-white on the top of it.

Cope went to it, his head began to bend forward, he was very excited but chose not to show it more than he could help.

I looked at the thing. It was a claw, a hooked one. It looked like the curved spur of a fighting cock.

It was just about a thousand times larger, was all.

"Where did you get this?" says Cope.

"One of my faithful found it," says Brigham.

"It's new to science," says Cope.

"That may be," says Brigham, throwing the cloth back over it. "But we will see about that, in time."

The two men locked eyes for a moment.

There was a fierce glow between those two strong-willed fellers.

I had seen that glow before. It was the kind that other men die in.

CHAPTER 5

As luck would have it, when we stopped in Laramie the first feller I happened to see was Mulligan. Mulligan went barefoot all the year round, dressed like a poor white's scarecrow, and spoke with such an adenoidal accent it was damn hard to dig words out of the noise.

But as a scout he had no peer. Now, I ain't bad and there's plenty others that ain't bad, too, but damned if he couldn't *smell* Indians at thirty miles, adenoids notwithstanding. He was also a few inches shy of five feet and many a man who bullied the little Irishman regretted it. He fought with fists and bare feet and speed and fury. He could live on rocks and small lizards for months at a time.

"Cope wants to hire you," I says.

"Whynnadoat?" says Mulligan.

27

Cope was looking dubious, but I offered Mulligan a hundred dollars a month and he nodded. Then Mulligan loped off.

"He didn't ask when he was to start," Cope complained.

"When we start, he'll be there," I says. "He's about the best scout there is."

Cope shrugged and went off to the hotel, dodging the tumbleweeds that the wind was rolling along. Red Cloud told me the white men had brought them. He said there were no words to describe them in the old songs.

With the winter coming on the buffalo hunters were getting ready to go out as soon as it had been cold long enough to make prime robes of ratty summer hides. It varied with the weather and the years, and the hunters would start high where it was already winter and work down to the Plains. They was hard men, and the hunter had one thing his men didn't—good eyesight. In the West you had to have good eyes, or you'd end up a skinner covered in blood all the time, till your clothes was stiff as they'd been painted, filthy and lousy, with the buffalo mange, itchy red patches all over your body. A hunter might employ as many as ten skinners.

There was others come on in, too, and it was them I was interested in. Prospectors who had been looking for gold, some of them with good educations. They had ranged all over the Rockies looking for float quartz, and many of them wanted only to find the gold. They'd sell out right away and move on, for it was the looking that they liked. Strange people, perhaps, but we all have our own hearts.

Sir Henry was a Brit, and he well may have been a lord—we had some of them around, too. He was well-spoke and a crack shot with pistol or rifle and he rode one pale mule and the other mule carried the few things he needed to live. He had a big black umbrella about six feet across that you could spot him easy a long ways off, what with the black cloth so wide above his head.

I found Sir Henry at Rosie's whorehouse, consuming a fresh lobster the train had brought, while a wench sat on his lap naked feeding bites of sweet white meat to him. He washed down the last of the lobster with a mug of champagne and the wench went off laughing, telling him to hurry.

"Cope," says Sir Henry. "Pennsylvania. Marsh is Yale. I expect they hate each other's guts. Did you inquire if we might have to fight a small, nasty war?"

"What over?" I says. I knew there were fossil bones all over Wyoming, surely enough for anybody.

"You don't know many college professors, I take it," says Sir Henry.

I shrugged. A couple had come west and paid me to escort them round the country, seemed decent enough fellows to me.

"They have," says Sir Henry, "the morals of Apaches and the honor of Turks. Odd people. They will backstab one another over trifles and claim scholarly disinterest. Cope and Marsh are rich, too. Almost all professors in this country are. The colleges pay little."

"Cope is wealthy," I says. "He's got a couple private railroad cars."

"Marsh has three," says Sir Henry. "I saw 'em in Cheyenne. How much does he propose to pay?"

"A hundred a month," I says.

Sir Henry nodded.

"Tell that cheap bastard I wish to offer my services gratis, out of interest in the work."

I nodded. I had always suspected Sir Henry was not in all

this for the money. Other thing was once Sir Henry had been set on by three drunk brothers who took exception to his monocle and his accent, and Sir Henry had killed all three in seconds, just as soon as the first of the fools reached for his gun.

Sir Henry had very pale blue eyes that never blinked, and he was almost effeminate in his dainty habits and snaky walk. But he was a killer and damn good at it and I expected I might have need of him and not for the Indians.

It took a short trip around the saloons for me to find another five men who between them had a good century of looking carefully at all the land between Mexico and Canada. Bob, Will, Jake, Lou, and Mopey, and I left it to them to round up some teamsters and wagons.

Cope had rented a warehouse and supplies come in daily, crates and crates of food and scientific instruments, tents and bales of blankets and what-all. He told me he'd done a couple other expeditions and more or less knew what to get, but I should read the manifests and see if there were things we might need. So I took the papers back to the hotel and I had a bottle sent up and a seegar and I began to read through them.

Cope was meticulous, right down to needles and thread and a seamstress to repair things. A carpenter and tools and a list of lumber, a good medical kit.

I was used to traveling a thousand miles with a few pounds of jerky and oats for my horse and some coffee if I was feeling like indulging myself.

There was a soft tap at my door and I got up, with some papers in my hand, and went over and opened the door and it was a moment before I looked up.

Alys de Bonneterre was standing there in a silk gown with

a necklace around her long white neck and rings glittering on her fingers. A rich perfume wafted in the door.

"I need to talk to you," she says. She walked past me without waiting for my answer and took a seat on the little sofa, prim as an aunt stopped by for tea.

She asked questions about Wyoming and the trail we were to take, very acute ones, and so I got a sheet of paper from the desk and I drew the mountain ranges on it and the trail that led up the eastern side.

She wanted to know about Washakie and so I told her he was one of the greatest men I had ever known. There was a butte up there called Crowheart Butte. Long ago the Shoshones and Crows had met there and prepared to battle for the hunting grounds, and Washakie had called a council with the leader of the Crows. It was foolish to make too much sorrow, he argued, I will fight your best warrior and who wins, his tribe will win the hunting grounds.

The Crows agreed and Washakie and the Crow warrior fought and Washakie killed the man and then he cut out the warrior's heart and he ate it.

Most ladies would have dithered at this tale, but I suspected Miss de Bonneterre was made of sterner stuff.

She was. She laughed, a rich deep laugh.

"I must meet him," she says.

"He'd like that," I says. "He purely loves beautiful women. He says they are the best thing on the earth."

"He sounds charming," says Alys.

"He's a randy old goat," I said, "and he is charming."

Alys looked at my bottle of brandy and so I offered her some, and having only the one glass we had to share it.

She took a little case from her purse and opened it. It was full of little Spanish cigarettes. I lit one for her.

I'd been right, this hoyden was used to getting what she wanted, and I suspected that right now that was me. Well, Washakie could wait his turn.

Alys asked a few more questions and the last one I was looking down into the snifter while I spoke, something about my worries about the Cheyennes.

When I looked up she had that same little pistol Pignuts had gotten to know so well pointed right between my eyes. Her hand didn't waver, and her face had gone all smooth and her eyes very cold.

Now this was baffling. One minute she's giving off heat and the next she's got her shooter pointed between my lights.

"What the hell are you doing?" I says, getting angry.

She just looked at me for a long time.

"Take off your clothes," she says finally.

"I will not," I says, and she fired the gun once and I heard a lamp bust across the room right behind me.

There was something in her eyes said I'd better, so I peeled down till I was naked as a jaybird and I stood there, turning red. I had been with a lot of women, but this was embarassing.

Alys began to laugh and laugh. She stood up and let the hammer down on the little pistol and before I could lunge for it she said, "Now it's your turn to hold the gun on me."

CHAPTER 6

Alys slipped off in the night, about maybe fifteen minutes before she would have screwed me to death. Some of the furniture was limping if not downright busted, and the bed looked like there'd been a couple bull buffalo fighting in it.

Outside it was snowing, big fat wet flakes that would be piling up high. I have seen blizzards in Wyoming every month of the year. July is no exception. I damn near died in one up to the Wind River, and the day before it hit was hot enough so I wasn't wearing a shirt and by the next morning I was scrabbling for wood to keep a fire going and wishing I had my buffalo overcoat along. It snowed six feet.

And Cope wanted to head off into this dangerous country at a time anything with a grain of sense was in a burrow, sleeping for the next few months.

The clerk was a friend of mine and I gave him money to discreetly replace the busted furniture and wire the chandelier back together. Some of the cut crystal had flown out the window to the muddy alley below. I found a snot-nosed urchin and advanced him a quarter and said a dollar would await him if he found all the pieces. He set to work with a vengeance.

I limped down the street to a restaurant and had a big breakfast and a lot of coffee, and felt some repaired. Then I went back to the hotel and got the manifests Cope had me read and I moseyed on down to the warehouse.

There was people running in and out of it and a couple of the city's law there, and Cope, looking cool and enraged, was standing just inside the door, tapping one elegantly booted foot and chewing an unlit cigar.

"Someone broke in last night and tore up the place," says Cope.

I waited, figuring his speech warn't done.

"It's that bastard Marsh," says Cope.

"Lookin' for what?" I says. "We ain't been out to find nothing yet."

Cope looked at me like I warn't too bright.

"He wants," says Cope, "to steal my *ideas*!" He had a look in his washed-out eyes that I'd seen before, in folks the syphilis had mostly et up.

Oh, joy, I thinks, off to the Great Unknown with a madman I got to figure on.

Cope's flunks were putting things back in crates and checking lists and rushing to and fro.

"Here's your manifests," I says, handing them to him. "Seems you thought of everything."

That was crap. I couldn't think of everything. Cope even

had a bakery wagon and a passenger list for that carrying a
dozen laying hens and a milch cow.

Alys de Bonneterre arrived, looking fresh and lovely,
decked out in men's riding clothes, obviously tailored to her.
Her pants was soft calfskin and her coat Morocco and she had
on a big John B. Stetson hat much like mine, cream-colored
with a band made of, so help me, rattlesnake skin.

I resolved to temper my strong lust with caution. This
wench could be a lot of trouble, and worse yet, she'd be that
only if she decided to.

There was a lot of flap these days about what women could
and could not do, but Alys was going to do as she damned
pleased and to hell with everybody. I had to admire her, and
suspected if the neighbors had a grain of sense they'd burn
her for a witch.

She ignored me, which I expected.

She went to Cope and the Professor spoke angrily for a
moment, glancing once in my direction, but Alys said something that brought him up so short he turned very pale and
then he straightened his shoulders and went on over to the
flunks, who began to work even faster.

Alys looked at me blank-faced and then gave me a slow
wink and then she walked over to a couple of big leather
trunks and she opened them and looked briefly and shut them
up again.

I thought for a moment of the fellers I had hired and recalled that they was all steady enough except Mopey, who had
been bit by the Bible snake and was given when in his cups to
beller about the end of the world and the bad habits of his
friends. Usually he did this and fell over backwards, passed-
out drunk, but once he'd got it in his fool head to lecture

Will and Bob in a whorehouse, Mopey's text a pick handle and some garbled mush from the Old Testament.

The Kraut, I seemed to recall, had interrupted Mopey's sermon with one hammerlike blow to the top of Mopey's head, delicately catching the unconscious Mope with finger and thumb and tossing him in the snake bin out back, where Rosie installed the drunks who had got into bad whiskey. There was a lot of that around, and some of it even had strychnine in it, not enough to kill you but plenty to make you foam and twitch and see things usually weren't there. That had happened to me only once and since I had been mighty careful of my whiskey's provenance.

It was the big black bugs runnin' around just under my skin I remembered best.

Mopey and I had to reach a deep understandin' about him mindin' his own goddamned business. Also that he wasn't to touch a drop of booze on the trip or I'd fire him and he could take his chances ridin' down alone, with the Cheyennes about. I got along fine with Blue Fox and the rest, but Mopey would end up screamin' for three or four days, the Cheyennes was every bit as good as the Apaches in that department.

Cope walked past me without a word and out the door. Alys sauntered over, insolent hips swaying just a little.

"Poor Jonathan," she says. "Othniel knows just about all ways to upset him. Jonathan is brilliant, but rather highstrung."

"So who the hell is Othniel?" I says.

"Surely Jonathan has mentioned the distinguished professor Othniel Marsh?" says Alys.

"The name," I says. "But who is he? Exactly."

"When Mister Darwin opened the box," says Alys, "he changed the way we think about the world. The Bible became nothing more than some good poetry and suspect history. Science is God now, Kelly, and Jonathan and Othniel both seek to be the Prophet. They haven't got a scruple between them. I hope you have been acute enough to hire some very hard men. Othniel and Jonathan would kill for a good specimen, just so long as they didn't have to *do* it."

"There's surely plenty enough old bones up there for both of them," I says.

"*Which* old bones will be the question," says Alys. "Jonathan got the Eohippus, the Dawn Horse. Othniel needs something even more spectacular."

"Like what?" I says.

"The biggest prize would be the bones of a creature that lies between apes and man," says Alys. "After that, anything that the press likes. Bigger. Stranger."

"I thought they was professors," I says. I'd met a few, and they was sort of nice fools expert in things no one gave a damn about.

"They seek to found a whole new science," said Alys. "Now be a good guide and find me a decent place to have lunch."

So I took her to the toniest restaurant in town and we took a discreet table behind some potted palms and aspidistra and Alys demanded a wine list, which the waiter promptly brought. Since the railroad, the hotels vied with one another in the matter of delicacies. Fresh oysters and clams and lobsters, even strawberries, though the tiny ones that grew near the rivers here were sweeter and better than any I have ever tasted anywhere. If it comes from far away, it has to better that which is under your feet.

Alys had two dozen oysters and a bottle of white Bordeaux and I had a lobster, a huge one, nearly three pounds, and some nice Sancerre.

We had coffee.

"I haven't been entirely honest with you," said Alys.

I tried hard not to let my moustaches fall off in surprise.

"Oh," I says. Here it comes, Luther, you can always slink off and see the Pacific Ocean for the first time.

"Jonathan has hired me as the artist," she says, "to do the drudgework of sketching specimens."

"That's what he says," I says.

"I have other things I wish to do," she says.

First she'll tell me what, and then ask how much I want for helping her screw Cope. I didn't like the man, so the price would surely be low.

"Jonathan knows I spent five years in Europe, studying art, and music, and languages, like any well-bred young lady of good family," says Alys.

I attended the coffee in my cup.

"But that was not exactly what I did," says Alys.

I nodded.

"I studied paleontology in France and Germany," she says, "and I corresponded often with Darwin, who wrote back in reply to my first letter that it was not necessary for me to claim to be male. How he found out I don't know."

I looked at her.

"So you want to make them both look like fools," I says.

"Only by doing better scholarship," says Alys. "I would pay you well to help me."

I nodded, my patented *yes. Maybe. Depends*—

"Can you hire someone to follow us and see dispatches of mine get to Cheyenne, to my agent. He'll see they go where they need to."

"Of course," I says.

There wouldn't be any need to hire anyone. Blue Fox

would be around the whole damn time, just out of sight, and I knew that humiliating Cope and Marsh would appeal to him mightily.

'Sides, neither of the professors had gone to Dartmouth.

CHAPTER 7

If I was going to help Alys, who I liked, I couldn't be saunter-ing off to meet up with Blue Fox. There'd have to be someone who could sneak past our guards and not blunder into one of Blue Fox's young bloods. I had hired one, the estimable Mul-ligan. All I had to do was find the demented little bogtrotter. I thought hard, hoping he would read my mind but at the last I rode back to Pignuts' place, to leave inquiries. None of the swells would go near the saloon.

When I come in Pignuts about jumped out of his skin and he began to scream if that damned bitch was with me he'd put two loads of buckshot in her, and he had his sawed-off in hand to make good on his promise.

"She ain't with me," I says.

"I never seen a woman like that," says Pignuts, letting the

hammers down slow on his piece. "She shot me through the other ear when I said I couldn't stand the stink no more and when I dug up her brother's corpse she didn't blink. Made me chop him up and boil off the meat in the kettle. Maggots all through him. I get all the bones clean and she wraps them in linen and rides off. Flips a five-dollar gold piece over her shoulder. It ain't right for a woman to act like that. It just ain't right."

Pignuts had some notions about proper female behavior, and it seemed Alys had busted every one of 'em.

He had a neat hole through each ear, precise one side to another. Alys had studied on the pistolero's trade, too.

"Well," I says, "them rich folks don't have no rules anyway, you know that."

"It just ain't right," says Pignuts. This from a feller chops the teeth out of them as expire in his sal-oon, in hopes of gold.

"I never seen anything like her," Pignuts went on.

"I doubt she'll ever be back," I says.

"AND LOOK WHAT SHE DONE TO MY EARS!" he bellers.

Pignuts was so ugly he was actually improved as the neat holes in his ears drew the eye away from his face, which looked a lot like ferret's been hit with a sledge.

"I'm lookin' for Mulligan," I says.

"He ain't been in," says Pignuts, automatic-like.

"Pignuts," I says. "It's *me*. Kelly. You seen Mulligan?"

Pignuts struggled with his conscience for a moment, which was made up mostly of fear that if he blabbed the feller whose privacy done been invaded would come back and blow Pignuts' head off. It was that sort of place.

"He was in last night," says Pignuts.

"He out in your hoosegow?" I says.

Pignuts struggled hard again.

"Maybe," he says.

Pignuts was so exhausted by this bout of honesty he had to have some of his own whiskey, and the shot stiffened him up and his eyes teared though they was shut and he shuddered and grabbed the bar and then he shit his pants.

"Thanks, Pignuts," I says, stepping back quick-like from the reek. "You done piled up some treasures in Heaven."

I rode my horse round back to the place Pignuts stuck his casualties and pulled the pin out of the hasp on the door and hollered Mulligan's name. Nothing.

I took a deep breath and stuck my head in and saw a couple bodies on the floor, none small enough to be Mulligan's. I backed away and turned around and there was the little bastard, stroking my horse's neck.

Mulligan grinned, showing brown stumpy teeth.

"Yumph," he says.

"You want a drink?" I says.

Mulligan shook his head.

He clasped his hands all prayerful-like and looked up to Heaven.

"Glad to see you done been saved," I says. "Now I got a favor to ask of you."

It weren't much, just sneaking off every few days to hook up with Blue Fox, who might or might not take a notion to tie Mulligan to a tree, stick a few thousand pitchwood splinters in him, and set him alight.

Mulligan shook his head.

"Mumpf havva kilpf Cheyennes," he says.

"How many Cheyennes have you killed?" I says.

"Mumphflook," he says. Mulligan kept his ragged pants up with a piece of clothesline. He had a sack tied to it which held his worldly possessions. He opened the sack and took out a

thread which held a number of dried ears. He counted carefully.

"Elebum," he says.

"Well, you'll just be meeting up with Blue Fox," I says. "You
kill any of his relations?"

"Thirp," says Mulligan.

"I'll see I can work something out with him," I says.

Well, it wouldn't do to set off without having made proper
arrangements, so that left me with riding up the trail in hopes
of meeting up with Blue Fox, and that when he wasn't in a
mood to give me a bad end. I figured fifty-fifty. Dartmouth
hadn't took, or maybe it had.

A warm wind had melted most of the snow, and so I just
set off, figuring that I could at least get a message to Blue Fox,
even if he was off someplace.

There was a well-traveled trail going north out of Laramie,
lots of teamsters in trains carrying goods for the miners, and
little groups of bold settlers who wanted to get in first, even if
the Indians was still powerful and not eager to have new
neighbors.

The trail was worthless to me, of course, but along it there
was any number of places Indian scouts holed up to keep an
eye on things.

One place in particular I thought a good bet. It was three
small mountains stuck up out of the Plains with a good view
from the top for forty miles in any direction. I'd have to go
up at night and hope if there were scouts up there, they was
bored by now and wouldn't be real vigilant. There was a trail
on the back side of them, and if I could get up top without
being spotted and having a rock rolled down on me, I might
could have a palaver instead of a fight.

I got to the range ridin' slow and dark come and I made

a little camp and a big fire and I slipped off on my big bay, ridin' around behind the mountains. I found the trail up and I rode on—my horse could walk soft he needed to—and the mountains wasn't real high. I tied him in a stand of bullpine and went on up toward the crest. There was a little sort of roofless cave up top kept the worst wind off and screened fire from sight below. If there was Indians, they'd be there. It was damn cold.

I got closer and kept well to the shadows, movin' slow, and the wind brought a whiff of cedar burning. Then a pony whuffled and then another. I wetted my finger and knew my scent was blowing away from the horses, and I crept closer.

I peered through a slit in a slab of rock and saw two braves by the little fire. A rabbit was cooking on a stick. Two men, two ponies hobbled near them.

When I suddenly appeared in the firelight across from them they reached for their rifles, but I had a gun on them, and I spoke in Cheyenne.

"Easy, my brothers, I wish only to send a message to Blue Fox. I did not come to kill you."

They relaxed. I knew one of them, Wolf Running, a good warrior with a sweet moon face and a lazy nature.

I could have killed them both, and they knew it, so they motioned for me to come and sit and I did.

I said I wished to talk to Blue Fox, that it was important, and I gave them some tobacco and I got up and left, taking some care on the way back to my horse because all I knew a couple more braves could be coming up the trail to relieve Wolf Running and his friend.

My horse was standing still where I had left him, and I untied his reins and turned him around and I got up and rode back down toward the flats.

The night was moonless and the sky was a deep, deep blue with the stars glittering, they seemed so very close. Up here near the Rocky Mountains the air is so clear the joke was you could see a bird's tongue across a wide valley.

Some rocks cracked above me, the frost had loosened a few, and I ducked against the mountain wall and waited till they had quit flying.

The starlight on the Plains threw everything into strange pale colors, or black shadows. It could be a ghostly place, and the weird rock of formations which the wind had carved could be hellish organs if it blew just right.

I went north around the mountains and hooked back to the main trail and I made another dry camp, not wanting to attract attention to myself.

I built a tiny fire and huddled over it, waiting the light. I chewed a little jerky and wished I had a cup of strong coffee.

I dozed.

I woke up suddenly because there was something cold on my throat and someone chuckling behind me.

"You are quite careless," said Blue Fox.

CHAPTER 8

Blue Fox got all hospitable after having his little joke, though he couldn't resist giving me a shallow cut right over my jugular just to annoy me. My collar rubbed on it and it itched and I resolved to repay the favor. But that would have to wait. For one thing, if I could get Blue Fox in on the joke that Alys was thinking of playing on Cope, he wouldn't spend so much time scalping the foolish on the expedition. Blue Fox was one of them folks has a horror of boredom.

His Dartmouth years had given him a mortal loathing of professors, and I banked on that.

So I explained the deal to him. I needed to get papers out of the camp and down to a feller in Laramie, who would take them from then on.

"The blonde who whipped and shot Pignuts?" he says.

"Then boiled her brother's corpse? A rare woman. What could a good Christian gentleman like me do but place myself at her service?"

This was a little rich, and I give him the eye.

"Far as anyone knows at my dear alma mater, I am carrying the Word of God to my heathen Cheyennes," says this scoundrel. "Tell folks what they want to hear, they'll believe it."

I had noticed that in life.

We had built up the fire, and Blue Fox had provided a rack of antelope and two bottles of claret, the labels only a little bloodstained. So that was what happened to the toff took off from Cheyenne with his apartments on wagons, two flytiers, a dozen gun dogs, and four coachmen. Nobody who knew a damn thing about how this happened was out here. He hadn't been heard from in four months and wouldn't be again.

The rack sizzled over hot coals and we munched cattail roots from a little spring nearby for a salad, and by and by we had antelope a little smoky from the fire. It was delicious. The claret was superb.

"Yer keepin' a good cellar these days," I says.

Blue Fox just grinned with his white teeth, and his merry eyes twinkled. Probably at the memory of how the toff and his servants died. Blue Fox had a wider world from his years at Dartmouth, and he knew the bitter fate his people faced. Smile he might, but there was a sadness back there in his black eyes that was old as death.

"I sorta thought Mulligan might act as the go-between," I says.

"That sawed-off bogtrotter?" says Blue Fox. "He's killed eleven Cheyennes!"

"Fair fight," I says.

"What," says Blue Fox, "has *that* got to do with anything?

He's about the size of a ten-year-old and my warriors sort of shrugged when they saw him. When they saw him. He's about the best of you scouts."

Suddenly there was an eerie howling, one not from this world. But it was, and we both gave a start. It was the wind high overhead, a mad ghostly scream that meant bad weather was coming down from the north.

"Cope proposes to go out now?" says Blue Fox. "The damn bones will be in the same place they've been for yea how many million years."

"He's afeared Marsh will get there first," I says.

"Do you have any idea how *many* fossil boneyards there are in Wyoming?" says Blue Fox. "You couldn't haul a hundredth of them away you had a railroad going up there."

"It don't make a lot of sense to me, either," I says.

"It does to me," says Blue Fox. "I watched Summit Springs and the Dog Soldiers dying. Quite a scrap. I've only seen one other brawl worse."

I waited. Blue Fox had been East, I guessed, when the Hayfield and Wagon Box fights had happened.

"Well?" I says finally.

"A faculty meeting," says Blue Fox.

He opened the second bottle of claret.

We drank.

It was damned late and so we dozed for a while and in the morning we shook hands and Blue Fox rode off, a strange man. He could wear the leather clothes and paint of his people, and then tuck his braids up under his hat and put on cowboy costume and pass easily for a dark-complected white. A lot of the Cheyennes was very light-skinned. One particularly loony feller had showed up claiming that they was Welsh and he talked Welsh at 'em for some time.

The Cheyennes was real patient with him—God knows how he managed to walk right into their camp—and *I'd* have cut the fool's tongue out after about hour or two, but they figured he was just crazy and therefore sacred and they let him stay. Finally, he understood that they didn't have a word of Welsh and he left. I don't know what happened to him after that.

The wind had picked up high overhead again—the air on the ground was real still—and it began to scream. I didn't like it one bit. It meant there would probably be a damn blizzard, and in Wyoming that meant the snow would fall and then the wind would push it round. It could fill coulees and draws that was a hundred feet deep, and if you was unlucky and wandered out on what looked like solid ground you'd sink and smother and likely they'd find your skeleton and your horse's stuck in a cottonwood top come spring. A couple of friends of mine had died that way, found with the birds pecking on them forty feet off the ground.

This damned expedition was lookin' worse by the minute.

Blue Fox would leave us be, but there was still the Sioux and the Sioux was Red Cloud and Spotted Tail and Sitting Bull and they knew damn well what the railroad meant. They also knew what the buffalo hunters meant. That was Sherman and little Phil Sheridan, and they was soldier enough to see that the Indians lived on the buffalo, and if the buffalo was gone, they would have to come into the reservations, to live on hardtack and salt pork left over from the War and get about half-pestered to death by Baptists, which you will admit are very pesky indeed.

No damn wonder the Plains people was ready to fight to the last man.

Oh, yes, I was not happy on that day down in Utah when the railroad pegged itself together. This was some fine country and I had rode through it early on and met some fine men and that was then and the now didn't look at all encouraging.

The wind screaming overhead was about right, and it fit my mood exactly. I liked civilization well enough it stayed in its place, but it ain't an improvement, you ask me.

Time I got to Laramie and was leaving my bay at the stable the wind had reached down to the ground and quartered around to the north and there was stinging little ice shards in it and we was in for a norther. The hotel, with its warm light from the kerosene lamps and the promise of steam heat looked mighty inviting. Why was I going to do this I purely could not say, as I had more than enough money in the bank to live well till spring and then see what the warm weather brought.

But I'd taken the money.

So I walked on down toward the warehouse Cope had rented for the mounds of gear he was taking on the expedition. It was bustling when I left and now there was just one forlorn flunk there, sweeping the floor.

"Where is everybody?" I says.

"Gone," says the flunk. "I'm staying to watch the goods."

"Gone where?" I says.

"Marsh announced a fossil find yesterday," says the flunk, "and he challenged Cope to a debate."

I brightened considerably. I would not, after all, have to spend the winter months in the arse end of nowhere, icicles depending from my nuts. I could stay here in lovely Laramie, warm and well-fed, close to the whorehouse.

"You seen any of my men?" I says.

"Cope paid 'em off," says the flunk. "Real generous-like. So I was lookin' for 'em I'd try Rosie's. They got money for a while, 'fore they's back to bummin' quarters for a drink."

"Mulligan?" I says.

"Ain't seen him."

Mulligan would have flat disappeared to wherever it was he went.

The cut on my throat began to itch terrible, so I left and went up the street to a sawbones, who scrubbed it with carbolic acid and covered it with a bandage. Charged me a dollar.

Life was good. I went to the hotel and into the saloon and I set myself up to the bar and ordered a bottle of brandy and while I waited on that I went to the table with all the delicacies on it and filled a plate with buffalo tongues and anchovies and pickles and cheese and crackers.

Time I got back to the bar and had set my foot up on the rail there was a young hand there, in the sort of expensive English clothes that rich pilgrims wear out here. They was good clothes and the sort Sir Henry wore.

The hand was light-built, gloved, and had a big hat pulled way down, and high-tooled boots cost a cowboy four months' pay.

I poured myself a big snort of brandy and eyed my plate, thinking on what to eat first.

The young hand turned to me, looking out from under the wide white brim of the hat.

"While big men fight great battles for scholarship in the East," says Alys de Bonneterre, "little women get there first."

"Shit," I says.

"Watch your fucking mouth," says Alys. "I'm a lady. And you gave me your word."

"It's going to be damned cold out there," I whined.

"Trust me," she says. "You won't feel it at all."

CHAPTER 9

I'd been in the West only a little over four years, and I had seen much, true, but I hadn't been looking for bones in rocks. I had mostly been learning how to keep my hair and the lay of the land. I had had the best of maps—it was between Jim Bridger's ears, and in my possibles there was the soft square of antelope hide he'd drawn me a map on, the mountain ranges, rivers, and passes. Everything was right that I'd actually seen, right down to the precise number of days it took to ride from one to another.

There was another feller who'd taught me much, and he was Washakie, once my father-in-law, till my wife, Eats-Men-Whole, died of a fever with our child in her belly. I hadn't been the same since, and there was a coldness round my heart.

Alys de Bonneterre had a coldness there, too, and it made

it easier for me. She was using me and that was that and I would not be surprised the day she no longer knew me.

But for now she needed me and so we left Laramie when the blizzard lifted with our mounts and two packhorses, headed north to the lodges of the Shoshones, on the Wind River. I hadn't seen Washakie for a couple years, and it would be good to see him again. And he could tell me where to find the fossils.

Once some Cheyenne scouts come riding hard at us but when they got close and saw me they peeled off without a word and went back to stalking the buffalo hunters. There wasn't many of them this far north, but there is always some bold souls who think death is for other folks willing to go someplace just to be first.

We found six of them. They'd been skinned alive and their hides pegged out like they did the buffalo. Their wagons was burnt and the stock gone, of course, and god-awful as the sight was I couldn't really blame the Cheyennes.

Alys wasn't no more bothered by this than she'd been by digging up her brother and cleaning off his bones. There was something very hard in the woman, as in many women, and it warn't put on.

The ground was hard froze and rocky as hell and so we went on and left the burial services to the wolves and coyotes and ravens. It was the natural way out here, and I had never once expected anything else for myself.

It took eight days hard riding to make Washakie's camp. He was in a bend of the Wind River, where the fierce blows come down out of the mountains scoured the grass clean, and there was cottonwoods thick on the river's edge, so if the grass run out before spring the braves could strip bark and feed the horses that. Good patches of saltweed, too.

About two hours from the camp Alys looked back and gave a start—there was a couple young braves not far behind us grinning like mules eatin' chitlings, and she hadn't heard them come up. I had, but I hadn't looked back either. The boys was only twelve or thirteen, and I didn't want to humiliate them.

Even younger boys took our horses and traps when we come into camp, shouting "Kell—eee Kell—ee" and eager to open the sacks of gifts I had brought. And I had brought a fine little rifle for Washakie, a Holland and Holland single-shot breechloader I had found in a Laramie pawnshop. Washakie liked fine things and pretty women.

The old goat greeted me hurriedly, then turned the charm on Alys, and she fairly glowed. Washakie had such a presence at times I felt there was a light around him.

After about fifteen minutes of honey and needling me with veiled references to my Sioux name—it's Stands-In-The-Fire-And-Argues—got from Spotted Tail, who come on me as a green pup waltzing across the Plains without a care, and ever after had told with glee how I'd argued in the matter of not having my balls cut off and I was so excited I was standing in the fire when I did it, and when my boots began to burn I hopped around and caused no end of mirth. Looking back, I was so pitiful that the Sioux decided not to kill me.* Folly's usually bad but not always.

Washakie pointedly ignored me long enough to make his point—I could drop dead and he would care most graciously for Alys, but when it was apparent that I warn't going to oblige, he greeted me formally and we embraced.

---

*The complete account is in *Kelly Blue.*

I purely loved the man. Have you ever known anyone from whom pure goodness shines?

Formalities over, a mob of kids and women and friends from years before piled into the lodge, just sort of accidentally with the bags of gifts I had brought. There wasn't much, combs and little mirrors and packets of bright German dyes and tobacco and some candy for the little ones.

Washakie invited Alys to a feast, forgetting my miserable and inconvenient existence, and finally in the weariest of tones allowing as how I could come if she really, really wanted to have me around, but for his sake, it was a dull afternoon and maybe they could burn me at the stake or use me for target practice or . . .

"You love Luther," says Alys. "Enough of your bilge."

Being fifteen hundred miles from the nearest fit place for a ship, bilge was a new word to Washakie, and he had Alys explain it to him at great length.

And then we were shown to the lodge we would have while among the Shoshones. It was the standard size, eighteen feet across the base, and already set up with piles of prime robes and waterskins and pitch pine for cooking or making coffee.

Our eyes met and so it warn't long before we were between the robes, at least some of the time, and things was reaching a crescendo when one of the brats had his head stuck under the side of the lodge says to his pal:

"Your parents ever do that, Leaf?"

Alys stopped dead in her tracks so to speak and looked round and saw any number of friendly, grinning faces regarding her. Most women would have screamed and dove for cover, but all she did was smile right back and come at me again. She was damned adaptable, I'll say that for her.

We fell asleep, it had been a cold and tiring ride, and just before I fell off Alys stuck her tongue in my ear and whispered that I would pay and pay for that one.

After we rested we dressed and went on to Washakie's big lodge, where a mighty kettle of buffalo stew was simmering, and women were making flatbread on hot stones. The lodge smelled of good food and sweat and fine feelings. Indians live close to one another, and to watch their families is a joy.

There was a great feast, and the two little mouthy bastards been watching us screw sang a song about us.

I offered to translate this bit of scurrility for Alys, but she said not to bother, she could figure it out. Well, that was easy enough, the little bastards were using hand signals that left nothing out. Our fellow feasters roared.

Old Washakie beamed. Nothing he liked better than making a fool out of me, not that it's hard to do.

Then there was singing, and every time I hear Indians singing the old songs the hair on the back of my neck stands up, because there's thousands of years in it and it speaks to old blood. Man had been around a long damn time, and most of the time like this.

Finally, we went off to sleep, and someone had lit a fire for us and the lodge was warm, smelling of pine pitch burning, clean and sweet. We held each other and for a time there was a great gentleness between us. We were much alike.

I woke in the night and went outside to piss and the stars was low overhead and I finished and Alys came out, too, and squatted with no more care than she'd been raised here.

"They are wonderful," she says, when we were in the robes again. "You really love them don't you."

Yes, I did.

"But you fight them," she says.

"Got no choice," I says. I didn't explain. There was clever men who had enough on me to hang me more or less anytime they cared to, and that was that. I didn't like it, but I knew, too, that America was growing and it would squash the tribes within a few years, with war and with whiskey. The Canadians had done that long ago, with trade goods and trade rum and the sly grace of the British, who was used to subject peoples.

"How did you meet Washakie?" she asks.

"Jim Bridger," I says, "and them two old monsters about killed me. Thing about Jim and Washakie is they got evil senses of humor and they liked nothing better than settin' me up and knockin' me down, for the joy in it."

"I doubt it," says Alys.

Cheap explanations wasn't going to do for this woman.

She run a long finger over my nose and lips and made a line across my forehead and she kissed me real tender-like.

"You know there are books about you back East?" she says.

I nodded. Pulp tracts in which I rescued maidens and delivered long-winded speeches before vanquishing whole mobs of redskins.

"Ain't a word of truth in any of 'em," I says.

"Of course not," says Alys.

"I just kinda like it out here," I says.

"Enjoy it," says Alys. "You can't do that much longer."

CHAPTER 10

We stayed in the camp for a few days, and then Washakie himself decided to guide us to the fossil bones. He looked to be maybe in his forties, but he was nearer seventy, and the year before, I'd heard, the young men had said he was past his prime, fit only to sit in the camp, and Washakie had slipped off alone. He came back a month later with six Blackfeet scalps, traditional enemies of the Shoshones.

Warriors is always brave, but the damned Blackfeet was crazy to boot. One of them explained to me once that they lived out on the Plains where there was no place to hide and so they had to be meaner than their neighbors.

Smallpox hadn't wiped them about out in '37 and '46, they'd have been a hell of a lot more trouble than the Sioux, probably.

It had warmed up a little, the Black Wind from the west had come, warm air from the Pacific, and it was pleasant to ride. There was plenty of game and Washakie tried out the new rifle I had brought him after wrinkling his nose at the little bullets, but the gun shot flat and fast and after a couple shots he carried it across his saddle and when an antelope ran hard away Washakie swung on him and broke his neck at three hundred yards.

We had fresh meat and Alys made up some rice we had, the first that Washakie had ever tasted. He wrinkled his nose. It had no taste at all, he says, white man's food generally didn't. He liked anchovies, though.

We got out on to the wind-carved Plains and Washakie pointed off toward a long wall of rock about half a mile away and we rode over and there was bones sticking out of a yellow-brown layer in the rock.

Alys laughed in delight. She said these was some of them big lizards, actually fairly small big lizards, and had only been about twenty feet long. She looked at them hard—we hand't the time for excavation—and she made some notes, calling the things dip-lo-dicus or something like that. My Latin's rusty. I keep it that way.

Washakie said the bones were often in that yellow-brown layer and if you saw it, probably there was something in it.

I'd traveled through the Big Dry, between the Yellowstone and Missouri Rivers, and seen the head and horns of a critter had a huge helmet six foot across with three horns sticking out and a beak like a turtle. I didn't care to bring it up at the moment, because it was about five hundred miles away and the country thick with Sioux, some of whom I got on with and some I didn't. The huge head warn't going no place and that would have to do.

Then Washakie took us to a spot where there was big whirled snail shells, some of them nine feet across, and Alys took a day to draw them where they was. She said they was ammonites, which sounded more like a biblical tribe to me than a clam or whatever it was. She said they was ancestors of the nautilus, them pretty shells you see cut in half in parlors.

Washakie took us to a bank of rotting stone had horse bones coming out of it, and, Alys said, camels, too. Well, all right, and I asked if there was any goddamned rhinoceroses about and Alys picked up a dinky little bone and said there sure was.

She took some of the horse teeth and camel foot bones and other little specimens and she carefully wrapped them and marked them and entered them in a little book she carried.

Washakie was a patient man, and he seemed to enjoy taking us round. I had been through the country many times, but my eye was always on the ridges and the country about, rocks was rocks and not likely to lift my topknot but there was plenty of Indians who would I got all careless.

I went out one morning to shoot an antelope and I did and I gutted it and cut the best parts out and headed back, and damned if Blue Fox wasn't down there across the fire from Washakie. So I put on the sneak and come up quite behind and roped him from my horse and backed up sudden enough to pull him over and give his neck a burn but not enough to hurt him.

Then I walked my horse forward to let some slack in the rope and Blue Fox lifted the loop over his head and went back to talking to Washakie like nothing had happened. I joined them and Blue Fox gave me one of them dazzling smiles of his would fit a cobra good it had more teeth.

Alys was digging some bird bones out of a clay bank and so I sat down with Washakie and Blue Fox.

"Our necks are even," says Blue Fox. "Want to move up to hair?"

"Oh," I says. "Let's leave it be."

"Fine," says Blue Fox, "for now."

"He brings sad news," says Washakie.

"There is measles in our winter camp," says Blue Fox.

Measles was an irritation to whites, it flat killed Indians. Especially young children. They fevered and busted out all over in suppurating spots.

A thousand Indians died of white man's diseases for every one died fighting, and that's the truth.

"Missionaries brought it," says Blue Fox, "along with their preaching."

I didn't ask what happened to the missionaries; I didn't need to. Whatever they got they deserved.

Alys come over then, and she warmed her hands by the fire and damned if she and Blue Fox didn't strike up a conversation—they knew some of the same folks back East. Well, I supposed Blue Fox was the sort of oddity people wanted to meet, at least if he wasn't in a killing mood.

Seemed that a cousin of Alys's, one David, had been in Blue Fox's class.

"He was fairly stupid," says Blue Fox. "What's he doing now?"

"He got his inheritance," says Alys, "and since he was working in a stockbroker's office, he bought a lot of shares in silver mines in Nevada. He made so much money he's retired."

Blue Fox laughed and laughed at that.

"Well," says Blue Fox, getting up, "I must go. You will be safe from us, Kelly, when you come, and so will Marsh and his people. I explained that men were coming to pick up rocks. Our elders declared you all broken in mind and therefore untouchable."

"That's fair," I says.

Blue Fox swung up on his pony, after bowing to Alys, and he rode off whistling some air, not Cheyenne.

We slept short that night—Washakie wanted to get a move on—and long before dawn we was riding back west, the horses and us breathing plumes of white in the cold air.

That evening we made camp in a barren place, and it was not even a good camp, and I wondered what the hell Washakie was thinking. He sat by the fire drinking hot tea and smoking his pipe—a briar I had given him, and in time Alys got restless and she wandered off.

I thought it safe enough, hell, there wasn't game around and the Indian trails was many miles away.

Alys screamed and Washakie and I was up and running toward the sound and it was plain luck she wasn't far. There was a couple huge wolf-dogs circling her and they was about to move on in when Washakie's rifle boomed and one of them fell flopping. I hit the other, a bad shot far back, and the dog snapped at the place the slug hit.

Alys had her little pistol out and the monster came at her and she stood calm and shot, just a popping and the beast sagged and sank down and died.

"What are these?" she says.

I'd killed a couple others. The toffs who come to hunt sometimes brought wolfhounds and mastiffs and sometimes they crossed with the buffalo wolves, not often, but when they did the pups grew big and mean.

"My God," says Alys. "Those are the largest canids I have

ever seen or heard of." She was breathing a little hard but other than that seemed fine. I looked at the skull of the one she'd killed. There was five holes in the brainpan.

We was standing in a little dish of stony soil, with stacks of rock sticking up here and there, and it looked like ten thousand other places in this wasteland.

Alys suddenly dropped her little pistol. She was looking down at her feet. There was something there, some sort of long funny-shaped rock, but I couldn't make more of it than that.

"Oh my God," she says. She began to move, looking down. She walked slowly around in a tight circle and then she bent down and touched the rocks, brushing a little dirt away.

"Can't you see it?" she says.

"No," I says.

"This is a pelvis," she says, pointing.

Pelvis it might be, if it was about ten feet long. I saw part of what could be a leg bone.

I went to her and she pointed and made gestures and I finally saw what she was so excited about.

One of them huge lizards, seventy feet long or more. She nodded as she walked, muttering under her breath.

I may even have seen it first, and when I did I goggled. It was a skull, one with huge teeth in it, eight feet long.

It was too big.

I went over to it and Alys was so lost in her thoughts she took a few minutes to look over and see what I was standing on.

"My God," she says.

Then she explained. Long ago this had been a sea, and this was the shore, perhaps the mouth of a vanished river. The big dinosaur was a plant-eater, and the skull was a meat-eater, and they had died together or perhaps apart and the river had brought them to this spot and there they were buried by mud and sand and slowly turned to stone.

Washakie wasn't around.

We found him sitting by the fire, a shit-eating grin on his face, mug of tea in hand.

"I thought you might like that, my daughter," he says.

Alys went over and put her arms around him and kissed him on his weathered cheek.

CHAPTER 11

Washakie's people began to stir early, and so I dressed and went out in the sunless cold to see what was causing all the commotion.

"Big party of Sioux," says Washakie. "Long way from their winter camps."

It ended with Washakie and me going alone to see, them. Shoshones and Sioux get along, but warriors is warriors, and having all the young bloods facing each other could set off a fight the leaders didn't want.

Red Cloud himself was leading the party. His warriors was mobbed up behind him, all wearing the red blankets that gave the chief his name. He had had another name, but when a friend of his said that his warriors sitting on a hillside while

Red Cloud parleyed covered it like a red cloud, he took that as a sign.

Indians got their politicians, too.

Washakie and Red Cloud hailed each other, and they got down from their horses and embraced. They was two great men and Red Cloud's party stood down respectfully and so did I. There was plenty of Sioux I knew, but they were too dignified to notice me until the opening ceremonies had concluded.

Finally, Red Cloud deigned to allow that I existed, and he grinned and said how pleased he was to see Stands-in-the-Fire-And-Argues. Make one mistake and it follows you forever. Then again if I hadn't been so downright amusing, Spotted Tail and that bastard lot of thugs he roamed with would have killed me certain, so my dignity was a small price to pay.*

The Sioux had swept down from their winter camp on the Tongue River to kill buffalo hunters. There wasn't many of them working far enough north to threaten the Sioux, but Red Cloud wanted to let them know that he wouldn't stand for it, and so him and his men had swept down through many winter ranges and killed every white man they came on. Several warriors were carrying the big heavy rifles the hunters used: some even had the brass telescope sights on them. You could kill a man at over a mile with one of these, if you could hit him.

A young warrior looked familiar to me was carrying the party's warpole, and it had maybe thirty scalps on it, and if the hunters was bald the Sioux made do and left the ears on. Oh, whites will wring their hands at the barbarity of it all, but what was being done to the tribes was pretty obscene, too. We

*see *Kelly Blue*

weren't going to kill every Plains Indian, but we were going to kill their whole world out from under them.

Turned out Red Cloud had rode over to see if Washakie would like to come along and kill a few buffalo hunters. Red Cloud was a courteous man.

"No," says Washakie, "the Shoshones are few and the whites are near. And I ask you to kill hunters only far away from our hunting grounds, for the soldiers will fall on us like wolves if the hunters are killed here."

"The Sioux are many and we do not fear them," said Red Cloud. "The Shoshones may come to the Tongue if they wish. We will keep them safe."

Washakie launched into a long speech praising the bravery of the Sioux and their victory against the whites that had closed the Bozeman Trail. He praised Red Cloud's wisdom. This went on about an hour, and Washakie was about down to praising the hairs on Red Cloud's ass but the answer was *no* and Red Cloud knew that before he come.

They was both canny politicians and they both knew that they and their people was doomed but Washakie had a hold on his warriors that Red Cloud didn't.

I suddenly recognized the warrior with the warpole. It was Crazy Horse. He had his face painted entirely blue. Usually he wore no paint at all. He was canny enough to know that the simplest dress made him stand out more than the most paint and feathers. Well, there was something going on and I would find out or I wouldn't.

I was motioned over to the two chiefs and Red Cloud looks at me, eyes twinkling, and he says that he hears I have a beautiful woman so crazy she laughs at the sight of rocks.

She laughs at the bones of Thunder Horses, I says. She is a wise woman with her own visions.

"She's crazy," says Washakie. I could have hugged him, for if Red Cloud was convinced of that, Alys at least would be exempt from all attacks. Indians ain't civilized like us whites, and them as is insane are honored and cared for. We, more civilized, put them in chains and cages and treat them as though they was plain evil.

"Kelly," says Red Cloud, "what do you wish from us?"

"I got some crazy whites want to collect old stone bones," I says. "They're harmless."

"They will not kill more than they can eat?" Indians had real strong feelings about wasting the game the earth provided.

"They will not," I says. I would have to explain to Cope that there was to be no shooting just for the sport of it. You kill it, you eat it.

I put my hand on my heart and gave my word. I had to keep it now, and if some idiot shot anything just for the hell of it, I had best kill them right then. We was going to be watched and our every move would reach Red Cloud, and if he chose to send his warriors, there wouldn't be anything left of us but rotting corpses and burned wagons. The fellers I had hired would do it, but I had my doubts about Cope and his flunks.

"Take your filthy hands off me!" yelled a woman, behind us.

Alys. God damn it.

I turned around slowly. Four of Red Cloud's men had surrounded her and one had the reins of her horse and the others was dashing in and tickling her. Kitchy-koo. And Alys is in the center of these ugly bastards, laying around with her quirt.

God, I prayed, please don't let her start shooting.

Then Alys let loose with a stream of cussing that flowed like

a marvelous and burning river, describing the obscene acts
their parents had committed giving them life, their horrible
odors, their crossed eyes, and numerous other insults and the
fact that all was said in perfect Sioux first made the warriors
goggle a little and then they roared with laughter and the one
with the reins gave them back to her.

Red Cloud and Washakie was about doubled over, arms
around each other's shoulders, tears running down their
cheeks.

I was pissed off, you bet. I strode over to Alys, still atop her
horse, and I reached up and grabbed her coat collar and
jerked her off and dumped her on her butt on the ground. I
let her fume about ten seconds and then I jerked her to her
feet and I raised my hand, and whispered, "Take out your gun
and shoot around my feet," and she did that right quick with
no questions.

So there I was dancing while she popped away, and we was
the toast of the day. Warriors was laughing and falling off their
horses, hollering to me that my balls was the size of mouse
beans, let a woman treat me like that.

Alys was a clever girl. After making me dance the pilgrim's
jig she tossed her delicate little pistol over her shoulder and
she fell to her knees and picked up a rock and began to ex-
claim loud nonsense in a tongue never heard on earth, and
point to this and that wonder in the stone. She placed the
stone on her pistol and she ran around like a pecking hen,
cackling and holding two up to the sky and yelling.

The effect was wondrous.

The warriors mostly put their hands over their mouths.
Then they all backed away and bunched up a couple hundred
yards off.

Alys went to Washakie and Red Cloud. Those two old

scoundrels was harder stuff. They wasn't laughing but they was looking at her and shaking a little from held-back mirth.

Alys shut up then, and she put her head close to Washakie's and Red Cloud's and what she said made these two whoop with laughter and look over at me.

I stood on my dignity, such as it was.

Red Cloud went off to his men and he swung up on his horse and they left, a stream of brave men riding the lands they knew, keeping safe their women and children and old folks.

Alys had an arm around Washakie's waist and his around her shoulders and they grinned at me like old friends got you dead to rights and there's nothing worse than that. Your friends know you, you see.

"Pretty good, huh," says Alys. She looked like a little girl found with a busted cookie jar and crumbs all over the floor and so she'd brazen it out with beauty.

"Didn't know you spoke Sioux," I says. It somehow didn't surprise me.

"A little," says Alys.

"You don't mind," I says, "what did you say to my esteemed chums, Red Cloud and that old bastard you are hugging there?"

"Why," says Alys, "I said you were a great warrior."

Right. But there was a disclaimer here somewheres.

"I said you were a great hunter," says Alys.

I nodded. Yes, yes, yes . . .

"And I said we were fucking last night and your arse rolled into the fire and it was a great ride and I plan to do the same tonight."

I closed my eyes. I couldn't remember when I'd been so happy.

Stands-In-The-Fire-And-Argues.

Now I'd be Burning Ass and the songs would follow me all the rest of my days.

"I think I am going to beat you now," I says.

"No, Kelly," says Washakie. "She's tougher than you and a lot smarter. Quit while you can."

I walked off to my horse.

CHAPTER 12

I warn't all that put out with Alys, because I have noticed in life that if folks are laughing at you they generally don't take the time to kill you. The Sioux had an opinion of me, and they was welcome to it. Small price to pay for my hair. Red Cloud and the other chiefs had some control over their young hotspurs, but not all that much.

But I didn't want Alys wandering off on her own anymore; she could have easy ended with her throat cut this morning. She was a damn bonehead, what she was.

So I sulked. I give off visible black fumes and I didn't respond to her jests.

I was flat amazed. She folded up just like that, finally busting into tears and begging me to forgive her and promising never to do that again and . . .

I put on my most patient and long-suffering look and I says dealing with Indians is a complicated business and I would much appreciate it she didn't muddy the damn waters again.

She promised. Blubber blubber blubber.

"Oh, quit," I says finally. "Nice act."

"It's not . . . bawlllllll . . . an act!" she whimpers.

If I live to forty I will never understand women.

Spotted Tail had told me long ago that women was lawless and a man was a fool to ever figure that he knew what they *wanted.*

So here is Alys de Bonneterre, tough enough to boil her brother's rotting corpse down, tough enough to shoot Pignuts's ears, all gone to syrup and regrets.

Something in me didn't believe a word of it, but there it was.

It did provide me an opportunity, though, since I did not care to spend the rest of the winter freezing my arse off while Washakie offered up more fossil bones. Time enough in the late spring, when the chances of being froze to death was only fifty-fifty instead of one hundred percent, which they was now.

"Time we went back to Laramie," I says, all puffed up with manly force.

"Of course, Luther," she says.

"I ain't getting out of that damn hotel till the grass greens up," I says.

"Of course, Luther. I am going to eat good and drink a lot and rest up. Of course, Luther."

All this submissiveness was making me real nervous, for I knew damn well it warn't Alys.

But she kept it up and so we packed our traps and wished all good things to Washakie and headed back south toward Laramie and the railroad. The weather was clear and not cold, the wind from the west was damp, I expected there was a hellacious blizzard tearing up the Plains farther east.

It had been cold enough so that pelts was prime, buffalo to weasels, and trappers and wolfers and hide hunters would be out now until the end of March, getting as many skins as they could.

I kept us close to the foothills and away from the main trail 'cause the Indians might attack anyone coming up from the south and I didn't care to get caught in the middle. Oh, it sounds heartless, and most folks would say I was obliged to help my feller whites out, but the truth was it warn't my fight. They was not supposed to be up here by the terms of the treaty, and what happened usually was miners and hunters went anyway and a lot of them got killed and scalped and then the Army got sucked in after 'em and there we were.

The soldiers mostly hated fighting the Indians, not because they didn't like fighting, but because they felt the Indians was in the right and the whites was in the wrong. The Army always got the shit end of the stick.

One night we camped in a cave high on a ridge and we could see out over the Plains to the east. I had noticed there was a good-sized party of robe hunters off maybe five miles, maybe fifteen or twenty men.

The Indians attacked in the dead of night, which they don't usually do, and Alys and I watched. We couldn't see anything but flashes from the rifles from the hunters—the Indians was using bows and arrows so the flames from the barrels of their guns wouldn't give them away. The hunters was in a circle firing out, and then suddenly there was a part of the circle gone black and the other flames quickly went out and it was over, except for some screaming, the ones slow and stupid enough not to shoot themselves.

We headed on, to get away from the noise. The starlight was enough to ride by and we had no quarrel with anyone. Scouts from the party down below had cut our tracks and they knew who we was. I avoided them coulees the Indians like to hide in, cuts in the earth six or eight feet deep, just enough for a horse, out in safe-lookin' country. The Indians would come up out of nowhere. Like I've said, what folks mostly die of out here is attacks of the careless.

Alys was plenty game and she was a good horsewoman and so I pressed us hard and we rode all the next day, too, stopping to rest our horses till their wind was back and going on. A horse can go about forever if he has enough breaks at right times, and so we cut almost two days off the time it had taken to go north.

Finally, Laramie was spread out below—damn place even had streetlamps now, and the windows of most of the buildings had a warm yellow glow to them.

We come in a bit after eleven at night and the clerk at the hotel had our horses taken back to the stables and we went on up to my rooms—I'd rented them far in advance, for rail travel was uncertain and if the passes was closed to the west, then a lot of passengers could pile up before the passes opened again. Laramie was a great place to be a hotelkeeper. There was no fixed rates for rooms.

I ordered up hot water and Alys sent a maid off to her digs for clean things, and I let her soak good and long while I sat sipping brandy and smoking a seegar, reading the papers that had piled up. The news was grim everywhere and I thought happy stories don't sell no newspapers, but somewheres someone must be doing all right.

"Do you know which Indians were attacking the hunters?" Alys called from behind the screen round the bathtub.

"Cheyennes," I says. "Too far south for Sioux."

"It was awful to watch," she says.

That stumped me, since all we could see was the lights going out around the circle.

"It's worse when you imagine," says Alys.

"Uh-huh," I says, "if you think so."

She got out of the tub and I could hear her move while she toweled herself and then she just walked around the screen with nothing on but the towel wrapped 'round her head. She was a beauty, sure enough, and she knew it.

"Don't be as long as I was," she says.

A good look at her and that seemed fine to me.

We had a good romp and then we was both hungry. The dining room was closed but the desk got us some sandwiches and a hot tureen of soup, oyster stew this time, and oranges from California, they was being shipped from there now.

We slept and she snuggled close and her breath was warm and sweet.

I sleep light and the knock on the door came damn early and I had the pistol I keep under the pillow in hand like that—I cultivated being ready, it was a real good idea, but it was just a knock and when I went to the door there was a waiter with one of them little carts all covered with breakfast. I found some small silver for him and I took the cart and I was about to close the door when he says:

"Your train leaves in two hours."

Wrong room, I thinks, but I wanted to go back to sleep, not to argue, so I just nodded and shut the door.

When I turned around Alys was pulling on her clothes and had that look women get when there's a lot to do and not much time.

"Your train leaves in two hours," I says.

"You're coming with me," she says.

"Hell I am," I says. "I am staying right here in this nice room I paid for, handy to good grub and Rosie's whorehouse and a nice long rest."

I was annoyed.

Alys just got up and walked over to me and hauled off and slapped me hard enough to move my head a ways.

"Rosie's?" she says, damn near spitting. "You have the goddamn nerve to mention *Rosie's* to me."

I nodded and she wound up to belt me again but I caught her wrist.

"You are touched," I says, "if you think I am getting on a damn train. I don't like the East, and I ain't going."

"Aren't I better than any whore at Rosie's?" she says, lower lip quivering.

Goddamned women, I thought savagely, they always play dirty and *cry*.

CHAPTER

13

Alys had her own private car, of course, and we got in and the damned wench handed me a wedding ring—fit, too—with a remark that people in the West minded their own damn business and folks in the East minded everybody's.

"Did goddamn Darwin have words about women evolving for no better reason than to drive men crazy?" I snarled.

Alys just made a purring noise, like a big soft cat.

"You're a lucky man, Kelly," she says, "and too damned dumb to see it. How about this?"

She hands me a paper, which is, so help me God, a marriage license, right down to the Wyoming Territory Seal and a fair forgery of my signature.

"Very nice," I says. "Now did this actually happen when I was taken drunk, or does my memory still work? Is your family at the other end of this track?" I says. There was a possibility for devilment somewheres in this. I have got in more trouble from my damn dick than any other foul and treacherous friend and no, buddy, I do not want to hear your story neither.

"All dead," she says, "but for Uncle Digby. Believe me, you will understand one another perfectly."

That was scant comfort.

I dug a bottle out of the liquor cabinet and poured a dram of whiskey and sat by a window looking out at all the horse turds in the streets. The train blew and the couplings clanked and we begun to move out on to the main lines.

Alys had real good taste, I will say that for her. The car was in blue and pale cream and there was paintings on the walls, a couple by George Stubbs, and no man painted horseflesh as well as he. Rich folks I had known well enough to be in their houses seemed to think several layers of rubbish on every flat surface was high fashion. Well, I supposed it was.

I was trying to stay surly but really I was just as glad to be going. I have many talents, but one I lack is luck at cards. There may be more unsuccessful gamblers than me, but they all shot themselves some time ago. Boredom over the winter would likely cost me all I had in the bank.

Several worthy tinhorn gamblers would starve to death in Laramie, I thinks. It cheered me some.

No doubt Alys had her reasons for all of this, and in time I would learn them. This could be worse, I thinks.

Train travel then was a slow business compared to later, the engines was able to go at most forty miles before stopping for water for the boilers, and from Laramie I figured eight, maybe even ten days to get to the East Coast. If that was where we was going. Alys hadn't seen fit to tell me where the journey ended yet. And I was damned if I was going to ask her.

There in her own domain she got back to her customary haughtiness, it was in her blood for sure. There was three servants, all women, and she was both kind and firm with them. One round-faced old Irishwoman, one of them servant ladies knows everything about the family, Alys treated with real deference, though, if it warn't in front of the other two.

Mrs. McGinniss. She reminded me of a couple of great-aunts of mine.

We come into Cheyenne in the evening, right after an excellent Irish stew and trifle for supper, and from here on we would be out on the Plains clear the hell to Omaha. Travel was safe, I had heard, and the Indians had been beat back both by soldiers and the railroad workers, almost to a man veterans of the War, and able to drop a pick and shoulder a rifle just like that. The Indians had killed more men than accidents had on the Union Pacific tracks while they was a-buildin' it, though as usual disease killed the most. The Central Pacific run east from California, and largely built by Chinese. They drank tea and the water had been boiled, while your Paddy fool would drink out of the nearest ditch. Cholera come soon after.

We layed over a couple hours in Cheyenne, and then the train pulled out—the night was pitchy black. Mrs. McGinniss pulled the curtains in the parlor of the car and bade us good night. Alys had a big bedroom the other side of a bath, even had hot and cold water in taps.

We retired. Cool she might be around the servants, but she was just as hot in her own parlor car as she had been in the buffalo robes in Washakie's camp. She had ice on the surface, but it weren't thick, and that over molten stuff, like the rivers of red-hot stone that flow under volcanoes.

She was her own, for sure.

I drifted off, lulled by the train's wheels clacking soft over the cracks between the ends of the rails, and the swaying. Felt safe there, rolling along over the Plains.

At least it did until glass shattered and rifle fire in the night sent bullets through the holes where the windows had been. I woke up right smart then and had my Navy Colts to hand and the train was slowed down a lot and seemed to be getting slower.

Indians. They was out there yelling like mad, and they must have done something to the tracks. I could hear firing coming from the cars up ahead. We was the next to last car on the train.

Mrs. McGinniss, in a thick white nightdress, was flat on her face in the parlor, crying out to the Virgin to save us all.

Most of the ructions was up ahead, I supposed the Indians was trying to kill the train crew so the train couldn't go anywhere. Alys had run around blowing out the lamps, just a few small ones, and we was in the dark and the wind was blowing cold through the two broken windows on the north side of the train.

Suddenly a warrior appeared in the window, trying to dive through, and I shot him at a range of eight feet and the big slug shoved him out and he made no sound as he fell. I was down then below the sill of the window and I knew I stuck my head up I'd likely be killed.

From the whoops and the fire I guessed there was a hundred or so warriors out there. I had no idea what the train had by way of defense. But there was a steady stream of fire pointed out and I hoped there was some soldiers in uniform or out and that they had plenty of ammunition.

Alys threw me some clothes as I lay there, and I struggled into them, guns close to hand, and pulled on my boots, so if the fight moved outside I would have a chance.

Mrs. McGinniss was praying mighty hard. She seemed well occupied so I left her be, she was down low enough so she was about as safe as she could be, under the circumstances.

A hand grabbed the sill above me and then the other and I fired through the wall of the car and the fingers stiffened and slipped off, and I scooted flat away from where I had been and several slugs holed the wallpaper.

Then something thumped on the roof, a warrior was up there and must have slipped and fallen, and since the roof was thin it bulged and I shot at it and heard a yelp. I fired again and either missed or killed him.

Then it suddenly got real quiet and the firing up front fell off.

The Indians had left, or they'd overwhelmed the men up there.

Then a conductor busted through the door, minus his hat, a repeating rifle in his hand. He was young and had a bad scratch on the side of his head and an epaulet of bright red blood.

He seen Mrs. McGinniss and he bent down to make sure that she was all right and then an arrow appeared in the top of his head and buried itself in him up to the fletchings and he just crouched there quivering, already dead.

There was maybe half a second all this took, and then a shotgun boomed, sending loads back down the narrow hall. I heard the breech being opened and I looked over and there was Alys thumbing two more brass shells into the scattergun and she snapped the breech to and she pointed it back down the hall and she waited.

One bubbling groan.

The train started moving again and I heard cheers up in the cars in front of us and I started to move back to where the Indian Alys had shot was. It was jerky going, what with me swiveling my head to see if there was any others coming through the windows behind me.

"I'll watch the windows," says Alys. And I got up to a crouch and ran into the hall.

The warrior was dead. One load had ripped into his chest and the other into his face. He still clutched his short bow in his right hand.

The other two servant women was dead, brained with a war club. There wasn't anything behind us but the caboose and I looked out the window in the door. It wasn't there.

Somehow the warriors had got that coupling undone.

There was fire coming from the caboose, but there was a lot of Indians surrounding it.

The Indians was easy to see, because the roof of the caboose was on fire.

The men in it didn't have a chance, they'd have to run.

Alys's shotgun fired again and I ran back to see what there was.

CHAPTER 14

We stopped in the next town, and things was so confused I can't remember where it was exactly. There'd been quite a few wounded in the cars ahead, and they was carried off to hospital and the dead—eleven, including the two servants in Alys's car—was hauled off by an undertaker. A lieutenant came through, inspecting, and he said he was sorry, the attack had come from nowhere.

It had come from the Cheyennes, actually, but there was no way, 'less you stood soldiers every quarter mile from Omaha to Cheyenne that you could keep the Indians from attacking they had a mind to.

Alys got Mrs. McGinniss topped up good with laudanum, and the old lady finally went to sleep. She'd wore bare spots in the carpet she prayed so damn hard.

The train got moving again pretty quick and some carpenters the railroad hired quick boarded up the holes where the glass used to be in Alys's car and they was let off at Oglala to catch a train back.

Some railroad muckety-muck, all oil and smiles and hand-wringing, oozed through offering sympathies and by the bye making the point that it warn't the railroad's fault. He was worried that if passengers felt there was a high possiblity they could be killed and scalped, they'd likely not buy tickets.

Since one of the dead servants had been the cook, we was forced to go up to the dining car, a fairly long walk up carpeted aisles to an elegantly appointed coach, with white linens and vases was stuck to the tabletops had flowers in them. Of course having your own table was out of the question, and you had to take such seats as you could find. We waited a bit till the worst feeders gobbled and left and then we went to a half booth had one gent in it, a survivor of the fight back West. He had a huge bandage round his head, like a turban.

We settled down and looked at the menu a bit and then I happened to glance up at our tablemate and I about had my gun out 'fore I could help it.

Blue Fox, of course, in a suit with vest, a fob, and watch. I saw he was a member of the Elks.

"Good evening," says the son of a bitch.

"You buy a ticket or happen to find one?" I says.

"Miss de Bonneterre," says Blue Fox, "allow me to introduce myself. I am William Drouillette."

Them half-breed Frenchy Indians was all over the damn place, so for all I knew he could be William Drouillette. Had his braids all tucked up under the bandage. I could see his point—Indians was not well thought of on the train at the moment.

Alys looked at him cool for a moment.

"Are you now," she says, finally.

"He will help us on the expedition," I says, in a low voice. I hoped she'd not set off a riot in the dining car.

"Delighted," says Blue Fox. "I've heard so many good things about you."

"Indeed," says Alys.

I noticed a long fresh cut on the back of his hand.

"You need couriers to carry papers back to an agent," says Blue Fox, "and I am at your service."

Alys warmed to him after that, and we had a terrible meal and when we left Blue Fox come along with us. Least I could do was offer him a drink, seeing as we would be working together, so to speak, come the next spring.

Mrs. McGinniss was out cold and snoring like a beached walrus, far gone in opium dreams. Alys finally went into her room and rolled her on her side so the booms wouldn't drown out all conversation, and Blue Fox and me and Alys sat by the porcelain stove, snifters in hand, us gents with seegars and Alys with one of her Spanish cigarettes.

"Cope, eh?" says Blue Fox. "Hear the man speak at college. Clever, and he knows it."

"This Dartmouth man," I says to Alys, "is also Blue Fox of the Northern Cheyennes, and utterly reliable long as he feels like it."

Blue Fox peeled off his turban and his braids flopped down: they was a good yard long.

The Cheyenne Alys had filled with buckshot had been hauled off, of course, and we both was mighty curious what hand Blue Fox had in our entertaining evening. Alys asked.

"Done against my advice," says Blue Fox. "Better to keep

after the soldiers and the buffalo hunters. Strike the regular rail service and you're striking at money, and money is what America worships most."

"How much does he know?" says Alys to me.

"You're hoping to make Marsh and Cope look like fools," says Blue Fox, "and strike a blow for the rights of women. You want equality, come join us Cheyennes. Oh, we go off and scalp and kill and have a high old time, but us warriors is about the most pussy-whipped fellers on earth."

Alys threw back her head and roared.

She had a real laugh, not one of them feminine titters.

I thought of a curious fact, that women who was kidnapped by the Plains tribes almost always chose to stay with them, even if they could return to white civilization. They got a lot more respect with the Indians than they would in the East, for sure. Too, there was always the suspicion that they would have been raped and worse yet, enjoyed it. You know how them Christians is about sex, they just can't get enough of bothering other folks about it.

"I believe you saw Red Cloud recently," says Blue Fox.

I nodded. The son of a bitch knew we had, and I was fairly sure he knew down to the last grunt our palaver together.

"Well," he says, "just make sure that you eat what you kill."

With that he got up and wished us good evening, and wrapped his head up in the bandage again. And he was off, walking up the moving train to wherever he was riding.

"What an interesting man," says Alys.

"Oh, he is that," I says, "and don't never trust him. I ain't sure what he's up to, and he'd keep close counsel. We've tried to kill each other on a few occasions, and I expect we will again."

Suddenly we was both exhausted, all the fear that had run us the night before drained out of us and we was just plain damned tired. So we went to bed.

Over the next few days Blue Fox was a frequent guest, and him and Alys spend a lot of time chattering about Darwin and some feller name of Wallace who was in on the evolution business at the same time but was less well-known.

Blue Fox said there was a small museum at Dartmouth devoted to natural history, and that Professor Othniel Marsh was there once, visiting. He asked to see the museum's collections, and the bursar said of course, but he would have to be accompanied by not one but two guards. Seemed that Marsh was notoriously light-fingered around specimens Yale didn't have.

Marsh still managed to steal three small fossils, which was discovered in his rooms while he was out giving a speech.

The bursar left three little notes in their place.

Marsh never said a word and neither did anyone else, and in time he was sent off on the train, handkerchiefs fluttering, and no unseemly accusations from the college.

"But about two weeks later a very skilled burglar broke in to the museum and removed the specimens, and the burglar was never caught. One of the fellows from the college was at Yale and contrived to find the three specimens. He lodged a complaint with the president, but that worthy simply said that no *Yale* man would think of stealing—which wasn't the same as saying no Yale man would—and so the fellow from Dartmouth hired a burglar, who filched them and they were returned."

Alys snorted.

"This essay in scholarship is a marvelous tale," says Blue

Fox. "One wonders how grown men find time to so indulge themselves."

Alys had a few stories of her own. I didn't much mind that these idiots wanted to steal rocks from each other, but there was something in this that didn't bode well for the summer.

The fellers I had hired was a tough bunch, and if a price high enough was put on it, they'd cut a throat or two to get the specimen. And I expected Marsh would have men equally eager for all that fun and profit. The West attracted men like that, and most of 'em come to early ends, not, I think, that they cared all that much.

The train rolled across the wintered fields of fat and prosperous Illinois toward Chicago, and the thousand miles of track that led on to New York.

We pulled into the main station about five in the afternoon and got out on the platform, which was filled with relatives and everyone anxious to find their travelers.

One tall man in coachman's rough costume was looking for someone, and when we passed him he raised a hand.

"I am here for William Drouillette," he says. "Did you see him on the train?"

"No," says Alys, bold as ever. "But then we have a private car."

While we waited for the cab I ordered up, the crowd thinned.

The coachman was the last to turn away.

I hadn't seen Blue Fox on the platform.

CHAPTER

15

"The Grand Union Hotel," Alys says to the cabby. We put our two small bags in the coach with us and the feller took off right smart, headed south. Even in cities I look up at the sky, a habit of wantin' to know where I am.

"That bastard killed Drouillette and took his sleeping room," says Alys. "He must have been with those Indians."

I sighed.

"You want to get your papers back to Laramie," I says, "it can be done with Blue Fox's help or not at all."

Alys swiveled round to face me.

"Kill him," she says. She was the sort of girl cuts right to a good tight solution first thing.

"He's gone," I says, "and that's that. No telling where. He could show up at a tea in New York, all I know."

"Why would he bother to attack the train and get on and kill some passenger?"

Alys might get to the end of Blue Fox, but I thought maybe not. The truth of the matter is the man was mad and *enjoyed* jumping from one world to another. And a madness like that grows and shapes to something terrifying, some elemental force of evil been around for a while, and scared people into making up gods by the thousands to be some shield against it. I got no better explanation. There ain't one.

I have a great respect for warriors, whether they wear paint and feathers or Army blue, but hard as many men had tried to kill me, there weren't no malice in it at all. We just happened to be the ones got to try conclusions on behalf of others.

But Blue Fox was different, and he flat scared me. For one thing, you got no real way of figuring what a crazy man will do.

Alys kept a suite of rooms at the Grand Union—I'd passed by it, but it was far too grand for the likes of me. The doormen all was retired infantry sergeants, I'd lay gold on.

We was hustled up to the rooms without no sly glances, and I wondered if I was the first to come there with her, and then I thought not. Like me, she did what she pleased and be damned to the public, whoever they are.

We got cleaned up and I would go in the morning and get some more clothes.

We went downstairs for supper and then walked on the promenade for a while. The stink of coal smoke was every-where and had been since Laramie. Chicago was bustling, fac-tories turning out goods and the slaughterhouses running 'round the clock. Now that the railroad went clear to the San Francisco Bay it would get even busier, heart of America, out in the corn.

We went back up after ordering some whiskey and brandy

and seegars and soda and such, and was into our second drink when there was a firm rap on the door like police give the world round. I knew of no warrants out on me for the moment, except a couple in Utah and one in Arizona—a clear case of mistaken identity, since I had never been there.

I opened up and there was a constable and another man in black, quiet and leathery, a Pinkerton for sure.

They was pleasant, asked if we had seen Mr. Drouillette on the train. I said we had dined with him and shared a drink or two in the private car.

"Could you describe the feller?" says the Pinkerton.

I says he was dark enough to be Indian and black-haired, and dressed well right down to a waistcoat, watch, and Elks fob.

"Dark you say, sir?"

He looked at the constable.

So I gave a detailed description of Blue Fox, right down to the cut on the back of his right hand.

"You're Kelly," says the Pink, "and I will tell you that though we have Mr. Drouillette as probably dead, he was blond and tall and two conductors who had been on the train from Salt Lake are also missing. They would have known what the real Mr. Drouillette looked like. So I am afraid your dark-complected friend is a triple murderer."

I'd guess Blue Fox's victims was over a hundred, what little I had seen, but I warn't going to elaborate.

"The railroad regrets any inconvenience," says the Pink, "and will raise hell in Washington." The Pinkerton man looked at Alys and blushed—he'd forgot there was a lady present. He spluttered apologies, and the two of them left.

"That man is a perfect monster," says Alys,

I nodded, no disagreement there.

I wasn't going to say nothing at the moment, but I would be right happy to kill Blue Fox I could find the bastard, so long as I killed him far away from the lands of the Cheyenne. If he was there when we headed out from Laramie in the spring, I couldn't touch him, and mad though he was he knew that.

He would have shed the late Mr. Drouillette's duds by now and look like someone else, and be out there headed somewheres but I knew in my gut I'd run on to him someplace out East, New York or Boston or one of those hellholes.

I was in a black funk and thinking so loud Alys heard my thoughts, for she came behind the chair I was slouched in and she leaned down and put her arms around me and whispered that I just had to do it.

"You know," I says, growling, "I could have stayed in Laramie being drunk a lot and . . ."

"If you mention that whorehouse," Alys purred, "I will use a shotgun on you . . . sweet Luther."

Right then I resolved first opportunity to cut and run, go to the West Coast and bide a while, until the Cheyenne madman and the lunatic scientists and this luscious wench had killed each other off. I would be nice and safe, and I purely hate getting dragged into fights I ain't planned on. And I plan damn few, and favor a single shot from a buffalo rifle. You want a brave feller stalking down the dusty street to fight with other pistoleros, go look up Hickok.

"Poor Luther," Alys murmured. "He wants to run and hide and let all of this go away, but I won't let him. You black Irish son of a bitch, you're as transparent as glass, and I will break you up like a cheap windowpane you run out on me."

"How could you think that of me?" I sputters, trying to sound convincing.

"People who get reputations as glowing as yours is are all the same, Luther, my sweet, unprincipled fellers come out looking best," says Alys.

"And how," I says, "do you figure that about me?"

Alys run her fingernail down my cheek, digging it in just enough to hurt a little.

"Women," she purred, "have to be ever so much more clever than men. You are so big and strong and powerful, which is never, my dear, a substitute for brains."

I felt something cold in my ear, and I knew that it was her little pistol. She laid the barrel lovingly in my earhole and explained the life of Luther from henceforth, and how short and painful that life would be if I gave in to my baser instincts, as I had all of my life, and . . . *disappointed* her.

That was a real unkind cut. My mother never laid a switch on me, or a hand, and all she had to do was fix me with her merciless black eyes and say, mildly, that I had *disappointed* her. My father could have beat me to death and it wouldn't have hurt so bad.

Alys nudged me to get up and she walked me back to the bed and pushed me over on it and started pulling off my boots and we coupled desperately for a long time and finally fell exhausted.

Doing the woolly deed with this wench was the most strenuous exercise I could remember. Oh, I had worked hard at other things, but this left me drained everywhere.

Alys laughed and she got up and walked out to get another drink, naked, with her hair down and falling to her round butt. She lit a Spanish cigarette and she sat down on a brocaded chair and put one heel on the seat, wanton as a happy whore, and she smoked and laughed and looked at me with those enormous blue eyes.

I had to laugh, too.

I come out to her and took a chair and we drank; I had a seegar and some whiskey and the air felt cool and good.

Alys lifted up the tabletop and brought out some cards and a cribbage board and we played for points.

Time to time she'd ask a sly question about other women, but I just said their faces was just a blur and I couldn't quite recall and by morning my mind would no doubt be an utter blank.

"Good answer," purred Alys.

Clever dog, Kelly, I thinks.

We finished the game and retired to the bed again and this time we was slow and gentle with each other, and we was both near to sleep. A long trip and a long day.

Just before I dropped off to sleep she run her finger down my cheek, on the line her nail had scratched earlier.

"Was I right, Luther?" she purred.

"Right about what?" I mumbles.

"All your mother had to do with you was say she was ... *disappointed*?"

"No," I says. "She beat me with a frying pan."

Alys laughed softly and told me to shut up.

CHAPTER 16

My mother had a saying that she applied time to time when she was fetching me up. "What's the use in being Irish if you can't be *thick!*" she'd say. When I had to light out at fourteen for far places, something about the bishop's daughter, and I joined the Union Army in time, barely, to end the War, I didn't leave no forwarding address. She found me anyway. One day, when I was hunting for a fort way out in Minnesota, there was a letter from her. *Dear Son, what's the use . . . your loving mother, p.s. things always look darkest just before they go pitch-black.*

Alys went along with me to buy duds and I ended up out-fitted like a damned stockbroker, down to white tie and tails. I could read her plans for Mrs. Kelly's son Luther right down to the fine print, and thoughts of living out my days in Mongolia kept bubbling up unbidden. I resolved to keep an eye peeled for an opportunity to cut and run.

Not that I didn't like being with her. I liked it too much and I had lost once and didn't care to have that torn feeling in my chest again.*

It took three stores 'fore she had me properly fitted out for slaughter, and she had the parcels wrapped up and the cabby piled the boxes in the trunk and those things needed to be tailored was to be sent on soon as they were done. She crossed the palm of the shop owner and he vowed to keep his wage slaves at it night and day, and no mistake.

We went back to the hotel and I was looking forward to a good dinner, a long romp, and sleep, but all I got was one drink and, time to pack my things and then it was back down to the trains, where Alys had borrowed some great friend's private car and we was on our way to the East.

The car was all done in various purples and reds and yellows and reminded me of buffalo innards.

Not long after the Commodore would have express trains that would do the Chicago–New York run in twenty-four hours, but it still took two days for us to get there then. We come clanking and swaying into the big city and my guts clutched. I can be happy when I'm about half-lost in the middle of nowhere and two weeks hard riding to the pale edge of white settlemen, but cities made me sweat and jump worse than being dry-camped and a war party looking for me.

I had a few, and was tamped down enough with the booze to bear up, or so I thought, but Alys had been giving me flat looks for the last couple hours before we come into New York,

*See *Kelly Blue*

and finally she says, well, we'll just go on to Boston, it's quieter.

She had enough prominence so we was coupled up to another train within half an hour. I gratefully passed out.

I woke up again because the train started bucketing around like it was about to hop the tracks. We'd run plumb into a nor'easter and sleet was slamming against the windows and sounding against the metal hide of the parlor car. The winds got so bad the train slowed down to a crawl and stopped someplace for a few hours. I repaired myself with a lot of black coffee and food and Alys perked up a little.

Her father had been a drunk and he'd died in convulsions, she told me, right in front of her, when she was eight. They was in the library of a Sunday afternoon and the old man drank about half of a whiskey and soda and got a startled look on his face and he fell over backwards and jerked a while and was gone. Her mother had died when Alys was born.

I could see the sad, bewildered little girl in her face, under the mature beauty. But when she talked of her Uncle Digby she brightened considerable.

Uncle Digby, it seemed, was to meet us in Boston, if the nor'easter ever died down enough for us to get there.

"I so hoped you would be awake to meet him," she says dryly.

"Right," I says. Orders is orders and besides I had done revealed a basic lack of backbone, which flaw in my character I felt she ought to know about.

We didn't get to Boston till afternoon on the following day. The storm tides was so high we passed not a few boats up on land, and bashed by breakers on the way in, and the sleet was still slamming in when we come into the station.

A conductor brought us a note from Uncle Digby, apologizing for not being there. He was to home, and his coachman would see us there.

The coachman was a young Irisher who hollered, "Miss Alys!"

We was drove right away off to Uncle Digby's, the coachman remarking that he'd go back and get our things. In time we pulled in to a porte cochere stuck on a huge pile, in the style of the time, sort of like a wedding cake all garnished with pills.

Digby dashed out and hugged Alys for a while, and when he looked at me he gave a cheerful wink. He wasn't all that much older than we was—I figured him to be in his early thirties—so he must have been her mother's much younger brother.

The weather was filthy enough to get under the roof of the porte cochere and so he hustled us into the house, where some French servants hollered and kissed Alys and even smiled at me some. That was some relief, I was half-expecting dour Irish ticking off the mortal sins of the household.

Alys went off to "freshen up," accompanied by the servants, and Digby took my elbow and steered me off to his library and study, a place full of books floor to ceiling but not a lot else except a snooker table under a big Tiffany lamp.

He went to the sideboard and demanded me to name my poison and I admitted I had been pretty well poisoned recently, and so he made up some cocktail of liqueurs and a raw egg for me. I drunk it down and in about fifteen minutes the whips and jangles had gone and I felt relaxed.

"I expected the wench to find the odd dinosaur," says Digby. "But as for potting the famous Yellowstone Kelly, well it surely surprised me."

She hadn't just arrived with me in tow, thank God.

"When my sister died her last words to me were to watch out for her daughter," says Digby, "which I did till she was five or so, and then all I could do was stand back and pray a little. At ten she announced that her finishing school was unspeakably boring and she demanded relief. So I sent her to a real school in Switzerland. Didn't see her for a good ten years, and when she came back she was Alys entire."

Digby walked with a limp and he held his left arm a little oddly, and there was a white streak in his black hair, the sort a ball leaves when it cuts the skin deep. I suspected he'd been an officer in the War, and the marks was from that, but unlike most men he didn't have mementos hanging on his wall. The library was damned spare.

Digby plied me with questions as we played snooker, neither one of us giving much of a damn who won. Finally, he stood up just as he was about to take a shot and said if I found the game as boring as he did, perhaps we could find something else to do.

I laughed and we put our cues up and he led me along the banks of books, pulling out those he thought might interest me. I loved to read, and there was classics now in paperback books; the Union Army had whole freight trains of them brought up to the lines and a soldier could buy one for a nickel. But the paper was cheap and yellowed quick and the bindings broke easy and often the wind would take the pages you hadn't read yet.

These books was bound in Morrocco leather and stamped with gilt, all of a piece.

I had made my choices in life, and it occurred to me that what was racked up on the walls here was the only thing I felt bad about leaving behind.

Digby even had the full quarto Audubon *Birds of America* on a walnut stand made special for them.

Alys finally come back all glowing from her bath and she

just marched over to the sideboard and poured herself some brandy and she lit one of her Spanish cigarettes and she walked around the library on Digby's arm, a real procession. Time to time they'd put their heads together and laugh.

After once such bout of hilarity Digby looked slyly back at me and he winked again.

He excused himself for a moment and went off and Alys took my arm and we walked around the library, her arm in mine.

Digby had been a soldier all right, and wounded at the battles of Chattanooga, the Wilderness, Petersburg, and at last the day before Lee and Grant met at Appomattox Courthouse. He'd been a cavalryman.

He had a boxful of medals, said Alys, and letters from Lincoln. They were stored someplace.

Old soldiers in trouble either stopped by or wrote him, and Digby helped them with money.

He never talked about the War.

But three years ago he had been prevailed upon to speak at the dedication of a cemetery, down in Virginia, and he had gone and there was a huge crowd there and a big platform filled with dignitaries.

The cemetery was new, and the graves didn't even have crosses on them yet.

Some pompous orator spoke for an hour by way of introducing Digby, and then Digby rose to speak.

He waited till the cheers died down, and then he walked down the steps of the platform and over to the thousands of graves and he made his speech to them, with his back to the platform and dignitaries.

There was a little wind and it swept his words over the soldiers sleeping there.

He spoke for a few minutes to them, and then he walked

away, and no one had heard what it was that he said but the dead.

So he was never asked to speak again, said Alys.

I nodded.

Yes, of course, good man.

CHAPTER 17

We was near the stomping grounds of Othniel Marsh, and so a few days after we got there we all belted up and headed off to hear him lecture some scientific society or other. Like them things at that time, the audience was all men but for Alys, who kept her eyes demurely down.

You know the types, pustle-gutted rich folks with a mild itch for the new. Or lean and hungry Yankees all with a buzzard's eye for profit. Them last has always reminded me of critters that can't kill their own meat, but is practiced at waiting till something else does.

Marsh heaved himself up after a long introduction which I can't remember, frequently broken by clapping. A flunk carried in some giant easel-sort-of-tripods and then levered up huge pen-and-ink drawings of strange creatures, and all of the illustrations had a man down in the right-hand corner, for the scale.

I supposed that whales might be the same size as some of the monsters Marsh had drawn up, but not by much.

They was the god damnedest beasts. One meat-eater had a head way too big for the enormous body, and a grand piano could have made a nice snack for the son of a bitch. A much bigger one was a plant-eater, with a long skinny neck and a big fat body and a tail twenty-five feet long. The rest was smaller, but not a one looked a bit friendly. They'd either lift up a washtub-size foot and squash you, or snap you up on the run without breaking stride.

I resolved not to think so bad of them damn pale river-bottom grizzly bears no more. Had one gnaw on me once a little, but I had to admit I had lived.

Marsh was one of them sorts salts his every speech with a lot of Latin tags, so everyone knows how learned he is.

It was a great time for science, he ended, adding that it was a hell of a good time for the audience to pony up.

Mercifully, we didn't stay for the reception.

I had a mild interest in all this, because I was to take Cope and Alys and about seventy others up the Wyoming trails come spring, but the babble about hip joints and jaw hinges and teeth passed by me. The beasts had been dead, thank God, for sixty million years.

We went out of the hall and smack into a bunch of Christers, marching around with signs mostly with the words misspelt, all bellering that heresy was being committed right there inside. Their ringleader was a pale and slack-jawed preacher who held a Bible in one knobby fist and who bellered passages from it, which didn't seem to have any connection to anything. I was sure his flock thought him a genius.

I had noticed Digby getting a bit pale during the lecture, but his expression didn't change. Alys had noticed, too, and she told the coachman to drive to a hospital and when we got there she summoned some surgeon and Digby went off with the man.

"He has a wound which won't heal," says Alys, "but McMasters is very good. Digby almost died six months ago, but McMasters got the wound cleaned out—he used maggots—and if that damned Digby wouldn't wait until I could smell the rot, he might even get healed."

She went off after them and I sat and smoked. She was gone maybe fifteen minutes and when she come back she said Digby wanted me to come in and talk.

He was lying on a table and there was three burly men in clean white smocks there, the orderlies hold a man down when he's being cut on. Digby was mostly undressed, and, I could see the wound, a double one, where a ball had gone through his thigh leaving a hole so big it wouldn't close.

Some of the flesh at the edges was black. Gangrene.

"I have to do a radical surgery," says McMasters, "or you'll be dead within the year."

Digby nodded.

"You should take the ether," says McMasters.

Digby shook his head. No.

I suddenly knew why. The speech given to the graves. Digby felt he had caused all them deaths somehow, or part of them, and the more he hurt the better he felt. Well, people don't make a lot of sense at times, 'cept maybe to themselves.

Do or let the bastard die, I thinks, and I walked over and grabbed Digby by his shirt and jerked him up and with my face about six inches from his I said all them men he'd led in all them graves would say he was a damned fool and this was no god damned way to remember brave men.

Our eyes was locked hard for maybe a minute, and then I saw a spark in his, a little twinkle of good humor.

"Thanks, Kelly," he says, "and I'll take the ether."

McMasters had it ready, and I could see the surgeon was in haste, so the wound must be right at the spot where maybe he could save him tonight but not tomorrow.

I went out and saw with Alys and it warn't long before McMasters come out nodding, saying he'd got all the proud flesh and cut some good away, too, to make both holes like mouths that he could sew closed. Soon as Digby come up from the ether he wanted him out of here, there was infections in the air and he'd be safer at home.

"Some of the staff," says McMasters, "still think that slapping a loaf of bread on a bad wound to assure a good flow of pus is helpful. Men like them killed ten times as many soldiers as Lee and Grant together."

Pretty quick the orderlies come out, with two of them carrying Digby and he was stuck in the carriage and we went back to his house. The orderlies had rode along on the back and they whisked him upstairs to his bed and left him to us. The ether had worn off and the pain was getting bad, but Digby's smile had a cheroot in it and he didn't let on to the pain, but for the beads of sweat forming on his forehead and trickling down.

I looked at the bandage on his thigh, it was loose, as they should be, and I thought a poultice of the blue-green mold grows on bread would help. The Indians use that, they soak a moss in a paste of flour and water and let it set cool a day or two. It halts putrefaction cold.

Alys listened to me and she nodded and damned if the cook didn't have a good stock of moldy bread, for a man come to get the kitchen slops as hog feed regular and he'd not been by because of the nor'easter.

So we scraped off the mold and got a fair amount and I made a paste and we went back and I daubed Digby's wounds good and put fresh lint packs on them. The paste should be applied every four hours or so.

I got up that night every four hours and changed the dressing and damned if the last time, at four in the morning, if Digby warn't sleepin' peaceful-like.

McMasters showed up at eight sharp the next morning, and here it comes, I thought, he'll pitch a fit over my interfering and there will be hell to pay. Not that I warn't prepared to pay it, I had grown uncommon fond of Digby.

Folks will surprise you though, and damned if McMasters didn't nod when I explained what I'd done. Then he watched while I put more of the paste on, and bandaged Digby back up, while Digby made jokes about how damned ugly the nurses was 'round here.

Digby was lookin' a hell of a lot better and he had a good appetite and the doc and me left him wolfing down a breakfast and we went to the library, where McMasters pulled a notebook out and began to ask me a lot of questions about not only the tree mold or bread mold—grows both places—but about any other medical lore I had got from the Indians.

He knew about decocting red willow bark for headaches but not much else. Oh, I hadn't a lot, but he mostly was interested in the trailing groundvine the Indians call heal-all, and I did promise to send him some next summer, when it would be growing.

Then he did the god damndest thing.

He asked me if I knew a really good medicine person he might come and study with?

Most whites thought Indians was dirty gut-eatin' scum best all killed off, except for a few of them ladies get the vapors over cattle bein' dehorned and the like, and to have this feller want to come West to see about what the Indians knew about their world was purely amazing.

I says take a trip up to the Wind River and see Washakie, who'd be happy to help. I knew plenty of others, but they was Sioux and Crow, and none of them was real fond of whites right at the moment.

Man's inhumanity to man was well-known to both of us, so we didn't remark on it, and McMasters said brightly he'd see me in the summer and appreciate an introduction to Washakie.

Digby healed up real quick, and McMasters looked at the fresh red scars and he beamed. He'd been working on the wound for five long years and here it was, cured.

Digby still had a limp but not so bad, and he moved vigorous-like, getting better every day.

Alys announced we was going to have to go to New York, and I threw up my hands.

Cope and Marsh was going to debate.

CHAPTER 18

This here debate between Cope and Marsh was, mercifully, not till after the holdiays, and so Christmas and the new year came and there was a lot of real happiness, because Digby was healed up at last. I couldn't imagine five years with a wound turned gangrenous every once in a while. Digby had sand, all right.

There was galas and balls listed in the newspapers, but Alys and Digby wasn't the sort to spend their time on such nonsense, and I was grateful I didn't have to go to some such and have to do the polite to folks so damned dumb all they could think of to do was admire one another. For their costumes.

I whined some about having to go to New York but Alys

was firm as could be, just shaking her head and pressing her lips tight together when I tried to negotiate a way I could go back to Laramie.

"And Rosie's?" she says sweetly. "You know, Luther, I am an excellent judge of character and I know I can trust you just so long as I can *see* you."

Then she asks Digby if he'll challenge me to a duel if I should betray her honor.

"Stogies and whiskey at ten paces," says Digby. "First man to down his drink and light up wins."

"Then," says Alys evenly, "I guess I'll have to watch out for myself."

"Kelly," says Digby, "you ever want me to shoot you as a simple act of mercy, I would oblige."

I laughed.

"Keep it in mind," says Digby. "You may need it."

Alys run that fingernail down my cheek.

"Yes," she says. "He may."

We took the train down the day before the debate, just a suite, since Alys had sent the private car she'd borrowed back to Chicago and though the one she owned had been repaired, the railroad had lost it someplace and thought they'd find it but they didn't know exactly when.

The railroads was booming, growing so fast whole trains got lost.

Digby had given me a brace of fine British pocket pistols, all silver-chased and only .30 caliber, but each held five bullets and they could do some hurt at close range. He even added a couple small chamois holsters, which fit inside the waistband of my trousers.

With those on board and the knife I kept in my boot I

KELLY AND THE THREE-TOED HORSE

might not be happy going to New York, but felt I could give a good account of myself.

That old New York, back in January of 1870, was dangerous. There were tens of thousands of people living any way that they could, hiding in cellars and abandoned buildings, and hordes of orphans who would swarm around unwary visitors and strip them bare and even kill them. The police was underpaid and there wasn't many of them and they mostly just guarded the rich neighborhoods and the factories and left the immigrants and the poor to fend for themselves.

The city stank, too, of horse shit and vile smoke from the factories and coal from the houses and great piles of garbage on empty lots in the poor sections. Huge rats scurried around in broad daylight, big brown bastards I hadn't seen before. Digby allowed as how they'd come from the China trade and killed off the smaller gray ones I knew.

"Evolution," he says, "is not a pretty business."

We stayed at the Hartford House, Digby in his rooms and me and Alys in a suite. The desk clerk eyed me and Alys down his long nose whilst we was registering.

Then the bastard demanded a wedding certificate.

He got the words out but barely, for Digby reached all the way across the marble counter and grabbed the man by the throat and lifted him over, explaining in a whisper that he did not care to see his beloved niece insulted, and if amends weren't made, someone was going to die right now.

Then Digby dumped the clerk on his arse and began to slam his walking stick on the counter, bellering for the manager. Which worthy soon appeared.

He offered to fire the clerk, Digby said no, just install some manners in him.

After that you'd of thought we was the last rich relations on the face of the earth. Nothing too good.

The debate was to be held at three in the afternoon, at a hall a short distance away.

We was shown to some uncomfortable chairs, so we wouldn't snooze whilst the great men debated, and it was a time when ladies wore hats with half an orchard and a bunch of dead birds all piled up like some natural disaster. Plenty of egret plumes, too.

So many people showed up there wasn't chairs enough for all of them and so Digby and I offered ours to some ladies all wore-out from carrying their hats and we walked to the back where there was bunches of men near the walls.

Some of them was in the cheap suits of the workers, and I give a start when I seen a tall dark feller in a turban, he looked a little like Blue Fox had in the bandage, is all, but this feller's was dark blue silk and had a deep green jewel the size of a plum on the front, all sparkled round with diamonds and a shimmering cloak of silk, too. A couple big, tough-looking A-rabs was to each side of him, and they was all motionless as statues.

Cope and Marsh was far off and they was introduced and their claques cheered or booed, depending. I have always admired disinterested scholarship.

Cope got to go first and he had a magic-lantern slide show which no one could see, and when he realized that he just talked louder about the little horse he'd bought off Pignuts' bartop. Pignuts warn't mentioned.

Then all of a sudden one of the workmen pulled out a pistol and he charged the dais, yelling something in Eye-talian I could not make out, and when he got near he leveled his pistol and Cope and Marsh was wild on the wing. I noticed

both of them took cover behind their assistants and the little
Eye-talian was a terrible shot and he soon went down in a mob
of bluecoats and their truncheons rose and fell, long enough
to kill him outright.

A couple beefy cops lifted the Eye-talian up and dragged
him out, bleeding, head lolling, and then Cope and Marsh
edged back up to the stage and they recommenced.

Each remarked "My learned colleague . . ." before lacing
into the other, and even them words dripped with loathing.
These two flat hated each other.

Looked to be an interesting summer, I thought.

It got fairly boring listening to them two argue about something was hard for me to understand, so I let my eyes wander.

I was about half-dozing, really, standing there, and it took
a moment for me to recognize the feller way off to my left, I
suspect because he warn't hiding his braids. It was Blue Fox,
all nicely trucked out, with a soft black hat on his head. He
wore a herring-bone tweed suit and had his long hands atop
a gold-headed walking stick.

Digby followed my gaze.

I started toward Blue Fox, with about half a mind to just
up and shoot the bastard right there and say I was a man-
hunter and where the hell was my reward. Seemed a good
enough idea.

I edged a little and tried to keep out of sight and I wasn't
no more than twenty feet from him, a hand on one of my
pistols, when he turned and went right through some red-
velvet curtains led someplace. It took me some time to go after
him and I found some stairs going up and down, and since
the street was lower, I went down and out a side door. It had
been snowing and I could see the tracks of a man and, betting
it was him, I trotted along looking up now and again to the

street. It was busy with traffic but no one on foot, and it had started to snow so bad you could see maybe a hundred feet.

I saw him, over past the cabs and carriages rumbling along.

I dodged through and saw him again, slipping into an alleyway between a couple tall buildings, and when I got to it I looked around careful, but there was no one there, and going down it I found it went off at a right angle and come out on another street.

New York had a sort of express cab that run on wooden rails, and when I got out to the main way one was coming toward me at a good clip. It passed and was maybe eighty feet away when I spotted Blue Fox clinging to the back.

He held on with one hand and waved the other and the snow swallowed him up, the cab was the fastest thing around and there was no way I could catch him.

So I went back to the hall, to find the lecture over and the journalists shouting questions.

Digby and Alys was in the foyer and we went right out to our hansom. I was wet through from the heavy snow.

Alys shrugged and so did Digby. She must have told him who Blue Fox was.

When we got back to the hotel I sent a note to the Pinkerton office, saying the man who had killed William Drouillette had been at the lecture.

But Blue Fox was gone, for sure, and nothing come of that.

CHAPTER

19

I finally got enough of the East and so I put my hoof down and told Alys she could kill me she wanted to but I was damn well going home. To such as it was.

Digby was sailing to England for some business and we saw him off, and he promised to look us up in Wyoming come the summer.

I expected some bloodbath, but Alys said, fine, let's just go and so we packed up—me leaving all the expensive duds she'd bought me in Digby's house.

"You looked so handsome in them," she says, pouting.

"I ain't going to show up in Wyoming in them duds," I says. "Friends I got it would be a death sentence for me."

Would of, too. Get grand on the boys and they'll eat you for breakfast. I done a little chawing in my time, too.

115

"Matter of fact," I says, "if there was a way I could arrive ordinary-like instead of in that damn wheeled mansion of yours it could be healthier." The boys would have growed bored there not having much to do but cadge drinks and lose at cards, and they got especially savage at such times.

"No," says Alys, "I am not going coach."

She had a point. Her car was comfortable. The railroad had finally found it and it was right here in Boston awaiting us.

So we loaded up and Alys had several reddish-leather trunks with her supplies—inks and papers and reference books and such—and a cook, a skivvy, and Mrs. McGinniss got on board. Mrs. McGinniss spent a good deal of time praying to all the saints for deliverance from the merciless savages, and I couldn't blame her. It had been a terrifying time during the attack. I remembered the sound the arrow made as it went more'n two foot into the conductor, from the top of his head down. A wet, slipping sound, like bootheels on ice.

And that crafty bastard Blue Fox, slipping onto the train, out of the warpaint and into the dude's duds like that. He moved easy between the white and Indian worlds.

Too damn easy. I wished to Christ I'd been able to bore him through a few times with my little pocket guns. I'd feel easier about the expedition, sure enough.

I warn't in no hurry to get home, long as I knew I was at least headed there, and Alys was all sunny at the prospect of a couple months in a knocked-up railroad town hadn't been there ten years before, and all them cultural amenities Laramie was so justly famous for.

We was stuck for an entire day at a bridge had washed out, and things was so jammed up behind us took that long for the railroad to dig us out and send us by another route.

We finally got to Chicago and I was feeling all generous so

I says, well, we could stay here a few days I guess. New York and Boston had great pretensions, but Chicago was rough as a cob and there was a few rich fools tryin' to gild the city, but it was still a crude frontier town grown up too fast, and most folks in it was interested in making money and nothing else. The Irish was there in mobs and they was getting a grip on the city's politics, and your Irisher is a born liar and cheat, so they took to office like ducks to water.

Good thing we stayed, for one of them blue northers come howling down across Nebraska and Kansas and it carried a big load of snow, so heavy that trains was stalled all along the tracks, the plows couldn't get to them, and lots of people froze to death when the fuel run out, even though they burned the wood furniture in the cars. Behind the snow come the cold and it was forty below.

Time they got that all sorted out three weeks had gone past. The newspapers reported that all sorts of greenhorns thought they could make a fortune shooting buffalo, and was caught out in the storm. Almost all of them soon froze to death, but three didn't, though their arms and legs had to be amputated, and they was sent back to their relatives to be carried around like sacks the rest of their days.

Then it got warm and the snow went mostly and off we went, on the end of a long passenger train had three big pullers on the front, the railroads was desperate to get people moving.

Alys flat asked me about the possibility of being attacked by the Cheyennes and I told her Indians wasn't so dumb as to do that this time of year—the worst blizzards is near the spring. They'd stay warm in their lodges and wait for good grass. Their horses would be tucked-up and weak from the winter.

We passed little stations had coffins stacked high on the platforms, settlers who'd died and was being sent back East for burial. The two winters before had been mild and then along come the deadly one, and these folks had no idea there was storms on earth so bad you couldn't make it from the barn to the house without a rope to guide you. They had built flimsy and they had to heat with buffalo chips, and they couldn't outrace the cold reaching in through the walls.

Whole families was found holding hands around tables, where they'd died praying for deliverance that hadn't come.

Time we got to Laramie the sun was out and there was just a little blustery wind and Alys's car was put off on a siding. It was late March by now and the thaw could come anytime, and then the rivers would choke with ice and jam and flood. And the carcasses of buffalo shot and skinned would begin to rot and there would be flies in clouds everywhere.

Oh, it was real romantic, let me tell you.

I allowed as how I'd saunter up to the saloons and see the boys, and Alys said, fine, but you saunter as far as Rosie's, you will wish the Sioux had caught you first.

I nodded. I'd got back into my rough clothes and old beaded coat and I jammed my worn John B. Stetson on my head and I went up the street, glad that the mud was still frozen. When it thawed you'd sink to your knees and there was many a good pair of boots under the streets hadn't been buried there a-purpose.

Bob and Will and Jake and Lou was at the first place I went. They was happy to see me as only broke fellers can be when they encounter a prosperous friend, and I bought a few bottles for them and settled the tabs they'd run up, taking their promises of repayment but not expecting anything.

Sir Henry was in the next place, looking prosperous as he

always did. He was good at cards, hell, good at anything he done, and I could see from the chips in front of him the afternoon had been profitable.

I had a drink at the bar and Sir Henry cashed in and he come on over, smiling a little, and we shook and I inquired about the health of all.

"Pignuts is dead," he says. "Somebody cut his throat and scalped him and took off in the snow and no one felt like goin' after him."

"Blue Fox," I says, and I mentioned our encounters.

"I will kill him on sight," says Sir Henry.

"Fine by me," I says. Would be, too, if Sir Henry's sight was a piece away from the expedition. I thought of offering him a reward, but didn't. Sir Henry was here because he liked it, and killing come real natural to him.

I saw one of the men Sir Henry had been playin' cards with turn and commence gettin' up and he had a gun in his hand, and I was about to warn Sir Henry but he'd seen it in the bar mirror. He wore his guns backwards and he cross-drawed so fast I hardly saw it and he killed the man, four shots to the heart, before the fool could get his iron up.

The other two men at the table goggled and kept their hands well away from their coats.

A big puddle of blood run out from the dead man. The barkeep pushed a mop bucket around the end of the bar and the wheels went skreek skreek across the rough planks. The barkeep grabbed the dead gent by the boots and drug him out the door and left him on the boardwalk porch. Then he come back in and mopped 'fore the blood got all sticky. He was right practiced at it.

Sir Henry had tucked his guns back away and gone back to sipping whiskey and chatting pleasant. Soon a constable come in and he talked to the barkeep, slapped Sir Henry on the back, and went out.

Inquests wasn't long on formality in them days.

Suddenly there was some hollering out in the street, and Sir Henry and me and some others went out the doors see what the commotion was.

There was a horse, pretty exhausted, shambling down the street, and the body of a man on it, bent over the saddle backwards so far his spine was broke. His legs and arms flopped with the horse's walk.

"That's Mopey's horse," says Sir Henry.

Sir Henry caught the horse and I cut the rawhide thongs that held Mope on and slid him down to the mud. He'd been castrated and his face skinned, but not scalped.

"Mope was just goin' twenty miles up," says Sir Henry, "get a coat he left at Lost Soldier Station."

Lost Soldier warn't no more than a roadhouse and a couple cabins, a day's travel away by wagon.

"Won't be anybody alive up there," says Sir Henry.

Just Blue Fox, I thinks, by way of welcoming me back.

CHAPTER 20

A squadron of troopers left the next morning for Lost Soldier, and I went along, telling Alys that I expected I should. Blue Fox had killed everyone there for the pleasure of it, and to warn me that he was around. I couldn't trust the bastard, and it would be best I just killed him and hope the Cheyennes was as tired of his antics as I was.

He wouldn't be there, of course.

Alys wanted to come along, but I said no, what we was going to find would be past unpleasant and I would be back by night-fall tomorrow.

The lieutenant leading the squadron was green as grass, out of West Point less than a year. When I asked if I could go along he looked so grateful I thought he'd cry. He was a boy still, though he was older than I was, I was sure. This country puts age on you quick.

The trail was dry, the wind had scoured off the snow and it was fairly well laid, only a couple places were flooded and we went round those easily. We rode hard, needing to get there well before nightfall, to bury the dead and make arrangements to live through the night.

I had seen plenty of what we found there, but for one thing.

There was one living man. He'd been blinded, castrated, and his wound fired, hamstrung, and then his hands was nailed palms up to the floor with long heavy spikes. He was just moaning a little when we found him, and the lieutenant gave him whiskey and the man sobbed out that there had been eleven people at the station, and they'd been picked off one by one, he was the last and he'd been clubbed from behind, and when he woke up the knife was cutting off his balls and then the iron was slammed to his groin, red-hot. He had fainted and come to nailed to the floor.

Rats had chewed his fingers.

"Never . . . saw . . . nobody . . ." he says. His eyes had been gouged out first thing. "Nobody . . . shoot me . . . Mother of God shoot me . . ." he moaned.

"Go out and check your troopers," I says to the looie, and he went and I put one of my little pistols in the man's earhole and pulled the trigger. Wasn't no more than a pop, but he was dead as he slumped to the floor. Poor son of a bitch, he'd been two days like that, at least.

I went outside and the lieutenant was swallowing hard and I motioned for him to come along and we walked away from the sergeant he'd been talking to.

"He'd have died of infection," I says. "I give you some advice. That sergeant of yours, listen to him, things here ain't like you was taught to West Point."

"One man?" says the boy.

I nodded. I didn't tell him about Blue Fox, he was scared enough as it was.

Hell, *I* was scared. Blue Fox had gone 'round some corner and met the Devil and they liked each other.

The troopers buried them all in a common grave, the ground was hard and stony even when it wasn't froze, and then they piled up rocks good and thick. Blue Fox had let the pigs out of their pen, so none of the ten dead when we come had a face or hands left. Two was women, their intestines pulled out in a long loop, fore they had their throats cut.

One of the troopers gave a holler and we went to him. He'd been back in the little truck garden the stationmaster kept, and there was this scarecrow there, except it was real well dressed. In the herringbone tweed I had seen Blue Fox in New York.

"Animals," says the young lieutenant. "Vermin. No human would do these things."

Some, I says, like Blue Fox, but I'd seen worse butchery that whites had done, even soldiers. Not many soldiers, but some. And if we was so civilized, I says, how come there was twenty thousand starving orphans in New York?

The lieutenant wanted to set up a heavy guard and feed bonfires all night and I told him go ahead, but Blue Fox is long gone and we won't see nor hear anything but the wolves and coyotes howling.

"He's right, sorr," says the sergeant.

The lieutenant went off a ways to puke and me and the sergeant looked at each other.

"Let him stand guard," I says. "He ain't going to sleep anyways."

"It was me, we'd head back now," says the sergeant. "Blue Fox come and gone, but there's nothing to be done here now."

I nodded. I got on my horse and rode over to the retching lieutenant and I told him he could stay he wanted but I was going back now. It would be a couple hours after dark when I got there, but staying the night in the station held no appeal. And I rode on.

The troopers caught up before I'd gone five miles, and we made time, pausing only to let our horses' wind recover for a half hour and then riding hard again.

I left my horse at the stable and walked to Alys's car. I pulled off my boots and I hollered her name and after a time Mrs. McGinniss come out of her quarters and said that Miss de Bonneterre had gone up to town.

This was right interesting, since there warn't no place a lady could go in alone, all there was was saloons and dance-hall girls and . . .

"That connivin' wench," I says, knowing just exactly where the hell she'd gone. "Mrs. McGinniss, you pray for Miss de Bonneterre's lovely arse, because if she's where I think she is, I am going to welt it up real good."

"She needs that, sorr," says Mrs. McGinniss. "She's willful as the Devil and stubborn as a mule."

I made my way to Rosie's and stalked in and brushed through the beaded curtains that covered the entrance to Rosie's private quarters, to find Alys and Rosie having a snort and laughing like hell. They each had a Spanish cigarette lit.

The both looked up when I crashed in. Alys looked startled for about half a second, and then she thought she'd brazen it out.

"What a nice surprise, Luther," she says. Her eyes wavered just a little. I think my face was black with blood.

"Luther," says Rosie, "you behave."

Alys weighed possibilities a moment and then she come off the chair like a greyhound gating and scooted through another set of beaded curtains and headed for the back of the house.

I leaped after her, and was in full stride when I stumbled, and I looked down to see it was Rosie's leg, just sort of out there, accidental-like, before I crashed into the doorjamb hard enough to knock the curtains down.

I seen stars and I fell back hard and I lay there a moment before bellering with rage and struggling up to my feet, but the monstrous Kraut was there by then and he grabbed hold of my collar and held me up like I was a kid. I squirmed and flailed but it did no good.

"Luther," says Rosie, "you must behave. Miss de Bonneterre and I was just having a discussion of a pro-fessional nature."

I blew off with a string of compliments I usually save for my horse when he steps on my foot.

"Wolf is not going to be patient forever," says Rosie. "Now why don't you just sit down and have a nice drink."

Wolf twisted me round so I could look into his pale yellow eyes for a moment. He nodded once.

"Seems a good idea to me," I says. "I'll tan her ass later."

Wolf shook his head once.

No.

"Right," I says. "I am all calm now."

Wolf pulls up a chair for me and drops me in it like I was a bag of laundry and he padded off. Rosie was pouring me a nice drink. I had my pocket guns but I doubted they'd do more than piss Wolf off and besides if I did kill him I would hang, as Rosie was a good deal more respected in Wyoming than President Ulysses S. Grant.

For excellent reason, too.

"Drink your drink, Luther," says Rosie.

I did.

"You can come out now," Rosie warbles.

Alys slid back in through the busted doorway. She kept a wary eye on me.

"Don't fear," says Rosie. "Wolf and Luther had a nice talk, and Luther is the very picture of calm and decency."

I started to say something smart but Rosie put a finger to her lips and I shut up.

She and Alys went back to the discussion they'd been having.

What did I like, *exactly*, that Rosie and her girls provided.

Rosie launched in to a straight-faced lie, about trapezes and batteries and feather dusters and what-all, and I swelled and was going to cry foul, but Rosie kicked me under the table.

Alys was rapt, and time to time she'd give me a sly glance.

I had a drink or five and sat there listening to this fabulous tale, and if Rosie'd not had such a poker face even Alys would have caught on.

Finally, we took our leave.

"Come back anytime," says Rosie, to Alys.

I was about to roar the hell she would when I was lifted up by a giant, Teutonic arm and spun around.

Wolf shook his head.

No.

CHAPTER 21

Mud and slush turned to dust and wind, which is a Wyoming spring, and the god damnedest assortment of fools arrived. They had the notion that since there was a railroad to Wyoming, it was a resort. Oh, there were plenty of stinking hot springs here and there, and at the time they was thought to cure just about anything from consumption to imbecility. Never mind the local gentry might slow-cure your lumbago head down over a small, very hot fire.

It had been a killing winter for the buffalo hunters and great stacks of flint hides was all along the railroad clear through Nebraska and Kansas, and the flies was coming up, a little slow because the nights was still cold, though there was plenty during sunny days. Alys hated the little bastards and she got in a frenzy, every morning there'd be windrows of them on the sills and drifts on the floors and she'd shriek for Mrs. McGinniss and the other two servants to clean them up.

"Hell," I says. "This ain't nothing. Wait two weeks and the whole town will be six inches deep in the bastards."

Cope hadn't arrived yet and wouldn't for two more weeks, and I figured Alys would be needing a long rest in a place with padded walls by then. For a girl who boiled her own brother down she sure hated bugs. We all got our weaknesses.

Cheyenne got most of the crowds and the fools hired other fools claimed to be guides and off they went, south if the guides had any wits at all, there was a little miserable country between Cheyenne and Denver and enough of bad weather and alkali water to make the dudes think about how nice it was back to home. But others went north, and the small pack trains of dudes and their guides—all one notch up on the fool stick from them as was payin' them—were just the sort of prey Blue Fox would eat and leave only the pips. There was also a band of bored Sioux roaming around like a pack of wolves off their heads to the north.

Maybe the Indians will get tired of having to ride out and all the way up to the mountains to cut new warpoles, I thinks, and maybe scalps can pall just like too much butterscotch fudge.

Alys cranked up the screams each day as the flies piled up higher and higher, finally reduced to blubbering DO SOME-THING!

"Well," I says, "Boston got them sea breezes and not so many flies, you know."

She flung her cup and saucer at me, and I looked at the tea staining my shirt.

Just then I looks out the window and there was a sight, ladies and gentlemen, that even I, hardened by years of idiots coming West, found hard to credit.

There was these three big boxcars, much taller than the usual and painted purple with gold stars and some sort of emblem. I could have managed that, but there was this elephant coming down a ramp.

The elephant had been painted. It was pinto. It had a big headdress on and ostrich plumes waving from the top.

"Gawd," I says, goggling a little, "lay the track and the circus comes."

Alys looks where I was staring.

"It's not the circus," she says. "It's Masoud."

"Of course it's Masoud," I says.

"Remember the tall man in the silk turban at the debate in New York?" says Alys.

I nodded. Him with the giant A-rabs to each side.

"He's unbelievably rich and terribly bored," says Alys. "And I'll bet he's here to collect fossils."

Another elephant was coming down the ramp. Painted pinto. Headdress and a mahout in a rag of a loincloth waving a hooked stick at the beast.

There was a little hill not far away, and there was about forty A-rabs putting up a huge blue tent. Camels. A flock of sheep.

Mrs. McGinniss got up, there was a knock at the door. She opened it. There was a lawyer there. I can spot 'em easy. They stand crooked.

"He wanted to speak to you, Mr. Kelly," says Mrs. McGinniss.

I went to the door, one hand on my pocket gun. Some folks like to shoot gophers for sport, but I . . . never mind.

"Lucious Hooper," says the shyster, "I represent Prince Masoud al-Diloof."

"How nice for you," I says, searching for the outline of a gun on the bastard. I could claim he was a-drawing down on me.

The lawyer cocks one of his two glass eyes on me.

"Prince Masoud wishes to engage your services," says the lawyer.

"I'm engaged," I says.

"He will double your pay," says the lawyer.

"Not enough," I says.

"Triple," says the lawyer.

A shot rang out and the lawyer's hat flew off his head and he retreated out the door and took cover behind a stack of boxes on the platform.

I turns and looks at Alys, who had her little pistol in hand, wisps of blue smoke wafting up from the bore.

"He was getting close to your price," she says.

A clever girl, that Alys.

"Masoud is so rich," said Alys, "that he'll buy you if he has to buy Rosie's and deed it over to you."

"Really?" I says, looking interested.

Alys smiled at me cheerily. She walked over to me, her lips puckered for a kiss. I bent down to taste those lovely lips and a bang and a flame missed my balls by not much. I hopped around with my hands on my crotch for a while, bellering that she'd lost her damned mind and what the hell . . .

Alys lunged a dainty linen napkin into a pitcher of water and she wrang it out and offered it to me.

"Cold water is good for burns," she says, "and I will thank you to act a gentelman. Deal's a deal and all that."

"I was just funnin'," I whined.

"Ho ho ho," says Alys. "Now, you miserable bastard, you better remember this. Masoud may be rich, but I am merciless. I know you, Kelly. You are not backing out or sneaking off. *Don't disappoint me.*"

The lawyer was hollering from behind his boxes, and I

noted for purely scholarly reasons that we was up to ten times what I was bein' paid. I thought of hollering throw in Rosie's and I'm your man but Alys gave me one of them looks says *you'd . . . better . . .* not and she walked back to the door and shot at the lawyer till he scampered off.

"Won't do no good," I says. "He'll just come back. And if you kill that one, there'll be another. They's kinda like cockroaches."

Just then there was a god-awful eruption of noise, trumpets and cymbals and drums sounded like they was about twelve feet across and an elephant much bigger than the first two passed by. There was a howdah on its back the size of a steamboat cabin and a gold throne which Prince Masoud was holding down. He looked straight ahead, the world was *down there* to him and always would be.

The three elephants squelched through the mud and went over to the huge tent, and then the damnedest thing happened. Masoud's flunkies all lay flat a moment, and then some made steps out of theirselves, five people high on hands and knees, and the Prince regally walked down the naked backs of his subjects and put his booted foot on a gold carpet and he sauntered into his tent and the flaps closed.

"You know," I says to Alys. "Wind comes out and up about dusk and that damned tent is going to be headed for Mexico."

"Fine," says Alys, "but you're not."

My nuts itched a little, but the cold water helped. She didn't really try to hurt me, not that accidentally made much difference.

Watch yer Irish mouth, I thinks, yer balls depends on it sticking shut.

I went off to put on a pair of trousers didn't have powder burns at the crotch and I inspected my privates for damage.

Just a little red. Well, she did have an interest in their continued good health.

"Kelly," Alys says from the doorway, "there's an envoy here. You had better speak to him."

"Why not you?" I says. "It's your house."

"I'm a woman," says Alys, "and he wouldn't deign to hear me. Women in their world are beneath notice and can't speak unless spoken to."

"Damn," I says. "Tell me more."

"Get your Irish ass out there before I give up and just kill you," says Alys. "The gunsmoke gave me a headache and I MAY JUST KILL YOU FOR THE PEACE!"

So I moseys out to the door and I can see a gent standing in it, or most of him anyway, he was so tall that the jamb cut him off at the shoulders. Big necklace of assorted gems and a green sash.

The feller steps back when I come to the door and I crane my neck and look up at his nose hairs.

"Prince Masoud commands you to dine with him," rumbles the feller in perfect English.

Those two huge A-rabs been on either side of Prince Masoud at the debate in New York was now on either side of his butler, here.

"Please tell the prince thanks," I says, "but I can't."

There was a ringing of steel and two scimitars was lightly touching respective spots, jugular and lower lip.

"Delighted," I says.

"Come alone," says the giant butler, "at eight sharp."

CHAPTER 22

It looked to be a long night ahead, so I took a nap and I woke up some when Alys slipped into bed with me. Then I sank back down and was resting pleasant when a jolt of electricity run through me, I knew what it was because a piece of ball lightning had bounced right into me on a mountain in Montana once and it felt like that.

I done rose about four foot straight off the bed and saw Alys down there looking at a couple of wires with a puzzled frown on her face.

"What the hell?" I roared when I come down.

"Maybe I hooked it up wrong," she says. "I ordered this Patent Electrical Stimulator some time ago and it just got here."

"Jaysus Christ, woman, why are you trying to kill me?"

"Oh, Luther," says the wench, "I just wanted to please you. Rosie mentioned these the other day."

"I will ride north alone," I says. "I will carry a red flag so I am not missed. The Indians will sweep down to kill me. AND IT WOULD BE A HELL OF A LOT SAFER THAN I AM HERE."

"Well," says Alys, "why don't you look at the directions?" and she offers me a couple sheets of paper.

Liddell's Patent Electrical Stimulator for the Relief of Neuralgic Complaints.

I gathered up the wires and such and the battery and I threw them out in to the mud.

She looked so melting and lovely I had a go right then and it was a while 'fore we wound down.

Electrical Stimulator indeed.

"Alys," I says, her breath sweet on my neck, "will you quit. I got it. No Rosie's. I got it."

"Go and look over toward Masoud's tent," she says.

I did. There was a big yellow one set up now, right next to his blue one.

"The yellow tent is a place Luther Kelly does not go," says Alys.

"What's in it?" I says innocently. Masoud's concubines, for sure.

"Your death," says lovely Alys, "is in that yellow tent. Masoud is well-mannered. He will offer you your choice of pleasures. Girls or boys."

"Waste not, want not," I says.

She didn't rise to the bait and so I went off to take a bathe and shave and put on my best duds, which was what I always wore.

Eight o'clock was nigh when I went out the door into the

dark and found Masoud's flunks and a big white horse saddled with a golden saddle looked like a hurdle. I stepped on the back of the flunk in the mud to mount and another led the horse along and we went over the golden carpet to the front door of the huge tent. I got down and a flunk motioned me to a chair and he pulled off my boots and I went on in in my socks.

The tent smelled of incense, curry, and unwarshed feet.

Masoud was on a reclining sofa-looking sort of thing, sipping from a golden goblet. The giant butler took me over, patting me a bit on the way for arms, but I'd left my guns on the dresser.

The butler fell on his face and crawled forward when he got close to Masoud and I was damned if I was going to follow suit till I felt a pair of sharp steel tips digging a little into the back of my neck and though they was men of few words I knew it was them guards, who seemed always to have just the right gestures to get the message over.

I wriggled over toward Masoud, glancing back once to see my chums with the scimitars, and there they was, standing loose, their big curved swords point down and their hands atop the hilts.

The butler announced me in some lingo I didn't know and then he wriggled off.

"Please take the other couch," says Masoud. "But take care not to let your head rise higher than mine. A stupid custom, but my people have seen so for a thousand years. I apologize. Nothing would please me more than to come and ride as a cowboy, but I cannot."

The accent was British and when I slid on to the couch I saw Masoud's eyes, black and twinkling. He was holding a sheaf of magazines or catalogs.

"Are you hungry?" says Masoud. "Or thirsty? You drink whiskey, I believe?"

A hand appeared with a gold cup and half a bottle in it and I took it.

"Thanks," I says. "I ain't especially hungry." Having my balls damn near shot off and then waking up electrocuted had damped my appetite.

"Apologies for my assistants," says Masoud. "In my country my every wish is instantly taken for granted. I know you are obligated to Professor Cope, even more so to Miss de Bonneterre. If you would explain to my chamberlain that you have taken an oath to your God, promising to guide Cope, that will be enough so they will understand."

Masoud snapped his fingers and the giant chamberlain crawled over and he listened while I laid it all off on God, nodded, and backed away.

"This catalog," says Masoud, "fascinates me."

It was from Abercrombie & Fitch.

Masoud had already marked a bunch of stuff, elegant, expensive, and perfectly useless, but he was eager for my suggestions and we settled on their Patent Highly Revolving Automatic Duck Plucker, the illustration showing a fat fool in hunting togs gaily turning a crank whilst lots of floppy little rubber fingers ripped the feathers off a canvasback.

Never head West without one.

I also modestly recommended their Pneumatic India-Rubber Raft as just the thing for crossing rivers dry-shod. Masoud ordered ten of them. Then he clapped his hands and a flunk crawled in and took the marked catalog off to the telegraph office and the delight of Abercrombie & Fitch.

The important business done, we ate, and it was delicious,

I enjoy hot spicy foods and this was some of the best. We had some sweetmeats and little cups of strong black coffee.

He asked me to recommend a guide or two for him, and I says he could do worse than Buffalo Bill, who was down in Denver whoring through the winter as was his custom. He couldn't do much worse, but I thought that overdressed son of a bitch would truly enjoy Masoud's notions of roughing it in the wilderness, especially with a tent full of houris along.

I was much gratified when the chamberlain was summoned and ordered to fetch Cody, and I positively grinned when he went out the front door with the two thugs close behind. Nothing I like better than doing a favor for a friend, especially one like Buffalo Bill, since the stupid son of a bitch had about got me killed on several occasions, worrying about his public whilst I was left to worry about the goddamned Sioux closing in.

Don't get me going on that bog Irish bastard.

It was a fine evening with thoughts of Cody either being beheaded for insolence or fucked to death.

Masoud still hadn't offered me the pleasures of the yellow tent, and though I wasn't inclined to partake—my balls still burned a little from Alys's near miss—I was curious to see what Masoud had by way of ladies in there.

Finally, Masoud allows as how if I would perhaps like to look over the ladies in the yellow tent and see if anything suited my fancy, he would be delighted and honored and so forth and so on.

I allowed as how I would be delighted and honored and so forth and so on merely to see the lovelies and so forth and so on.

Masoud highly recommended a lovely Circassian girl, blond and blue-eyed, who had just arrived.

"Circassian?" I says.

Part of Turkey, says Masoud, and famous for the beauty of their women, a tribute of girls was sent along each year.

If she'd just arrived, I says, didn't he want first dibs?

Oh, no, says Masoud, the guest is to be so honored.

Perhaps, I says, and no insult meant if I felt the time was not right.

Fine, says Masoud, and let us away.

He got up and we strode over to a tented passageway and a pair of giant black guards by the far door fell flat on their faces and we went past through a thick hanging cloak of fine silk sheets.

I damn near dropped my jaw. There was about thirty of the loveliest women I had ever seen, wearing jewels and little bustiers and transparent silk pants loose and blooming but tight at the ankles and waist.

"Beautiful," I says to Masoud.

I wasn't supposed to be in the yellow tent at all, but, hell, how I could be rude and refuse after such a generous evening.

"The lovely Circassian is in that little pavilion," says Masoud, pointing to a small silk tent over against the wall.

Years and years dodging death on the Plains had give me a sixth sense, and now it was flat screaming at me.

"Oh, I thank you," I says to the Prince, "but I mustn't, for my heart is given to lovely Alys."

"You live, Kelly," she says, holding the curtains open. She was dressed like the houris in the main part behind me.

"Many thanks, Masoud," I says, heading right in.

CHAPTER

23

Alys and me spent the night in the tent, a fine Arabian night, and we slipped away under the new moon before the sun come up.

Turned out Masoud came to Rosie's, but that he got to do alone, something about how the place was one of our temples and the whores was temple servants. Well, that's true enough.

Masoud would sit in the room in back with Rosie and Alys and they'd chaff him and he'd laugh. The poor son of a bitch had to come to Wyoming find a place to be just another feller. I didn't envy him his god-king's job. Had more rules than a prison.

Him and Rosie and Alys had decided to set ol' Luther up, and if Masoud and Rosie was funnin', Alys was surely not and it was only my quick wits saved my arse.

Highly Revolving Duck Plucker indeed. If my wits hadn't kicked in Alys would have hooked the damned thing up to a steam engine and skinned me with it.

The chamberlain arrived back three days later from Denver with Cody in tow, all flowing blond hair and big white teeth, and them ridiculous thigh-high cavalry boots that fill up with scorpions so nice.

I had a drink with Bill and we talked old times, which we surely remembered much differently. You had to like him, all that drivel about honor and the Code of the West, Cody actually believed and practiced. His word was good as his bond, any friend in need was welcome to the ruffled silk shirt off his back, and he was very brave, I suspected because he knew he was destined for Great Things and no bullet would touch him.

Masoud and Company left the next morning, three elephants in the lead and fifty wagons and the whole damned mess was made perfect when I spotted two Krupp cannon bouncing along behind with some out-of-work Pickelhaubes on the limbers to man them. Even had a tiger in a cage— everybody needs a house cat, I guess.

Cope had been heard from, and was to arrive in two days, and it was about right that he hadn't been heard from for months and now everything had to be ready to go almost the moment he got there.

Would have been tempting to tell Cope to follow the piles of elephant dung and see if Masoud would share the fossils he was bound to find—then you'd have had to work harder *not* to find them. They was that numerous and that common.

I wished to hell I could be perched someplace to see the faces of the Cheyennes when the damned elephants lumbered over the horizon, but then Blue Fox would explain it all away.

I still had to find a way to kill the son of a bitch and nothing was occurring.

Cope's flunks come out of the woodwork and there was frantic activity down to the warehouse and by the time the Great Man got to Laramie we was about set to go. I figured the weather could get nasty, which in Wyoming is like saying the sky might be blue. I don't know why it has the worst weather I even saw, but it does. I saw four sheep flying over-head once, a good thirty feet up, dead but carried on like some milkweed puffs.

Cope was in a terrible swivet when he come, because when he got to Cheyenne he learned that Marsh had left a couple days before and so the race was on, in the name of disinter-ested scholarship.

"Not a word about what Washakie showed us," says Alys. She then took me by the arm and we walked up the street to a shabby little jewelry store, mostly cheap clocks, run by a little white-haired man in pince-nez.

When we come in the little man curtained the windows and hung a sign in the door saying he'd be back later, and we went in the back and there was a small printing shop, with a couple type fonts and a German press.

The feller's name was Adler and he was the one that the papers Alys wanted me to spirit out of the camp was to go to. He'd see them on, to where they was awaited back East.

It suddenly occurred to me that I didn't need to include Blue Fox in the equation, for Cope would want messengers sent back real regular and since they was likely to be my boys—who could get through—a word and some gold and Adler would get Alys's stuff and no difficulty. I had to meet with them later anyhows to talk the expedition over and wasn't a one of them couldn't be corrupted by money except maybe Sir Henry, and Sir Henry I needed close by for killing as the occasions come up.

He was as crazy as Blue Fox, but he didn't have as much evil in him. I often wondered what it was that made Sir Henry so.

Cope ordered departure before everything was ready, and he somehow got the Army to guarantee escorts of troopers for any group of more than four wagons sent up to wherever Cope happened to be.

We left before dawn in a pissing-cold wind had little lumps of snow in it, all strung out a good mile long. I had had a word with my boys and all was set, since Alys in her wealth offered a bonus of a hundred dollars per delivery, they was more than happy to oblige.

Wagon travel is a slow business, especially on the bad trails cut by buffalo and horses but never intended for wheeled transport, and we went up at twenty miles or less per day. Once it took two whole days to cross a coulee with a sandy bottom, the horses made it over but the wagons sank to the axles and the teamsters had to put a couple dozen oxen in the traces to pull one wagon out.

The fossils Washakie had graciously shown Alys was well up north, and Bob and Will and Jake and Lou rode out daily looking for that funny-colored rock meant an old beach.

A week out they found one, and Cope looked it over— there was visible bones in it—and then he set some hardrock miners to work. Alys would sketch as they dug, so there was a record of what was where all the way along.

The bones was dinosaurs, not at all big, and Cope stuck names on 'em like Humpleforplesaurus, often decreeing a new species on a single bone in his hand, he was that sure of himself.

The Humpleforplesauruses give out in a week or so, but my boys had found other places, one of them on the crest of a long ridge. Cope was down somewheres below when Alys and I rode up there, and she got real excited, telling me that there was this huge beast there, something that lived in the ocean. She waved her hands and I began to see what she was talking about, the goddamned thing had a body the size of a big Turkey carpet and a long neck and funny head with a wide mouth and a long tail.

Alys did something then that I didn't figure out for a while, and if I had known what it would lead to I would have stopped her, but all she did was carefully move a rock with a bone in it from one end of the skeleton to another. The rock held the bones was pretty broke up and no one could tell the switch. She didn't tell me why she done it, and I didn't ask.

Cope come along the next day, and Alys was already doing very detailed sketches of the beast in the rock. Cope got a little red and excited and he started with the head and he moved slowly down over what it was he could see until he come to the rock she's moved—hell, it was maybe the size of two hands clasped—and then he let out a whoop and give off a dance, holding the rock and hollering like he'd done struck gold.

He dragged Alys back down to the tent and he stood over her describing the creature, and she deftly sketched in a fat stubby body and a big head with a mouth a yard wide, and a long tail shoving plants into the creature's maw.

It took the rest of the day to get the drawing done to Cope's satisfaction, and he worked late in his tent by lamplight, writing a paper on his amazing find.

Bob was the youngest of the fellers I had hired and he lacked a few items of use in the scout's trade, so the boys let him go first. His boots was about gone and he needed a much better pistol than the stove-up old Colt he carried, and a better saddle. We was like that back then.

Bob stopped after he had been given the dispatch case by Cope and Alys handed him an envelope and he tucked it inside his shirt and he nodded and was off in the dark. Mulligan was out there, beyond the firelight, and I barely saw the little man before him and Bob vanished into the black.

We'd seen no sign of Cheyenne or Sioux, which was not the same as them not being there, and sure enough Bob and Mulligan was back late on the evening of the next day, and Bob told Cope he done give the case to Cope's secretary at the hotel.

After Mr. Adler perused the contents.

The miners mined and the diggers dug and other flunks cased up the Flopposaurus in plaster and the heavy specimens was loaded in the spare wagons and a train was made up to take them down to the railhead.

Cope forgot hisself and tried to give an order to Sir Henry, to go along as a guard, but I saw it going on and I stepped in and got things smoothed out. Sir Henry was just amused, really, but Jake had a short temper and he wouldn't do much more than blow Cope's fool head off the man talked down to him, so I had a real earnest discussion with Cope and he promised not to do that again.

The wagon train headed south with the Flopposaurus, and we went on north.

Things was peaceful, and the weather was mild.

I seen an Indian just at dark on a distant ridge.

Way he moved I thought it was Blue Fox, and then he just

disappeared like the ground swallered him up and I knew it was him.

I rode out after dark whistling and soon Mulligan was there, all wild hair, whiskers, and stink, and I offered a flask of whiskey and said we had some work to do.

CHAPTER

24

My Indian chums, when we wasn't bent on killing each other, was a jolly bunch, and many of them had told me that the Wild West was something the whites brought. Oh, the tribes would scrap now and again, but the casualties was light. The warriors would put on best paint and feathers, and go hop up and down a while and holler insults, but it was damned rare for anyone to get killed till the whites come. The only thing that would provoke a big and very real fight was two bands and one buffalo ground, in the fall when making meat meant living through the winter.

So Washakie ate the Crow's heart that one time, but there was more pitched battles, always over food.

What the Indians did was really more fun than not, and that was counting coup—more honor than killing an enemy was touching him with a coup stick—and stealing horses from each other. I think the women was behind it, clapping their men on the back and inviting them to go prove themselves, so the women didn't have to listen to the pompous, boring bastards recite their exploits over and over. Just like the whites, come to think of it. Most Plains tribes the men was really allowed in camp only in the winter, plenty of time to make some babies and then they was booted out right smart in the spring.

What this done was make Indians the cleverest sneaks in all the world. They could come into camp and steal a horse you had in a pit under your bedroll, and when I first come here I found nothing but a cut rope more times than I cared to admit, first light in the morning and a long damn walk to another horse. The Crows was the best, or worst, depending on where you stand, and one explained to me once they liked the whites because they brought so many fine horses for Crows to steal right into Crow country. Crows would sometimes take everything, right down to boots and smallclothes, and many a man had to walk out stark naked, his outfit in some lodge up the river.

They was absolute masters of the country and they was both bold and subtle, and could lie for days chewing on a little piece of leather, not drinking and not eating and pissing down a stem of grass so it was noiseless, for that one chance to steal or maybe kill they had a reason.

All them tales of atrocities and murder committed by Indians was true, most of the time anyway, but what people don't know is that the whites done it first, and worse, and the Indians was just trying to protect their families and way of life. Hell, when Lewis and Clark come through they had a dustup only with some Blackfeet and those bastards will fight *anybody* for the fun of it.

I was a fair common scout by now, and I had good teachers,
Jim Bridger and Washakie and Kit Carson and old Liver-Eatin'
Jack, the monster the Crows call Bear-With-Man's-Face.

The sight of Jack would have cheered me considerable, but
I'd heard he'd retired and was liking Canada a lot, out on the
Atlantic, far from the troubles he'd known over thirty years
here.

I'd been in and out of Indian camps and them none the
wiser till day, but I only had to fail once to be dead and each
time was a dicey proposition for Mrs. Kelly's son Luther.

What needed to be done now was the killing of Blue Fox,
and he was damned good and further he was smart, in that
insane way the mad are, and had to know I would be coming
after him soon as I could. He was beyond dangerous. I could
treat with any Indian but him, and we both knew it.

Mulligan was eccentric and hated camp, bedding down
near enough but hid from everyone.

I whistled the signal we'd used for years, po-weet po-weet,
and it warn't long before the little man was by me, hadn't
seen or heard him come, of course.

Blue Fox, I says, we got to kill him.

Mulligan nodded. Well, talk was cheap and the task would
likely cost dear, but as long as he was out there things could
go about as bad as they could with no warning.

"I done et with Bad Knee," Mulligan says, talking of a Cheyenne we both knew and liked. "And he says the Cheyennes is
scared of Blue Fox. They can't kill him, because Bear Man
had a vision and Blue Fox is sacred. Mebbe you understand
that, I don't."

I was gettin' good at filterin' words out of Mulligan's sloppy
squalls and grunts, and it surprised me to find him so well-
spoke.

"No use goin' after him," I says. "But what would bring him near?"

Mulligan shook his head. He didn't know neither.

Problem with a crazy man, you don't know what they'll do. Their thoughts run clear to them but no one else.

I could send a message I wanted a parley, but if I killed Blue Fox no Cheyenne would parley with me again.

I snapped my fingers.

"I know," I says. "Newspapers."

I have to explain that anyone who could read on the Plains was starved for print. A single newspaper would be passed hand to hand and tenderly cared for and finally it would crumble to dust, after many had read all the stories they really didn't have an interest in.

Blue Fox warn't the only Cheyenne could read English, I was fair sure, but far as I knew he was the only one graduated Dartmouth, and once you get hooked on print, well, you got to have it. He'd have books in his lodge but newspapers was something else and I bet he'd bite we baited a trap with 'em.

"We gonna peg out a newsboy like a damn goat for a mountain lion?" says Mulligan.

"No," I says. "That'd drive him off, he'd smell the stink fifty miles away. We just need to start orderin' up newspapers and pitchin' them into the camp dump. And wait."

Along with the empty tin cans and offal and such.

"How about Sir Henry low and you high?" I says.

You are hunting a man you got to have two fellers, one up high and one down low. Sir Henry was fast as a snake and Mulligan was deadly with his old Sharps. And they both knew Blue Fox.

All that remained was to start pitching newspapers out on the pile of crap maybe a quarter mile from the camp. The flies was coming on bad even up here, though the main slaughter of buffalo was south and east.

"I'll let you know," I says, swinging up.

Mulligan grinned. When newspapers started appearing at the dump he'd know.

I rode on back to camp and looked up Sir Henry, who was in Cope's tent playing whist with Science, and beating him bad.

I said my piece and Sir Henry just nodded, never taking his eyes off the cards, and Cope said fine, he did trust me with such petty arrangements, like keeping us all alive.

The camp had a few newspapers, and I ordered the teamsters to haul up bales of the damn things on their next trip back. I took the dozen or so I could find and sent a camp boy out to the dump with them, ordering him to weigh them down with a rock, so they wouldn't blow off.

Alys was in her artist's tent, her eyes squinched, sketching yet another drawing for Cope. She did that about twelve hours a day. Where she found time for her own work I did not know, really, she must have cut it in to the bulk run as she went along.

She set down her pen and peeled off her ink-stained chamois gloves and she stretched and then she reached up and pulled me down and kissed me. I slipped into her tent most nights, unless I had to range far out and see what was moving in the country, and now that we was far away from Rosie's and Masoud seemed to have took a wrong turn and headed east toward the Sand Hills she was a lot less short about my bad habits, of which I got a few.

There was no one else in the tent so she put her lips near my ear and told me what she was sending down to Adler, and where Cope was going with his things, and that she was having ever so much fun. Then the wench stuck her tongue in my ear and then whispered a description in detail that would have give Mrs. McGinniss the apoplexy in the matter of what lay before me tonight.

She had some whiskey for me and brandy for her and we sat and chatted about everything but what was going to Mr. Adler, and it was good just to set a while.

Then we went off to the more exclusive cook tent, where Cope and his High Flunks and Alys and me was allowed while lesser folk made do with a chuckwagon outside, and had a fine meal of antelope stew and a watercress salad–some fine feller had run though the country scatterin' watercress seeds, which will ward off the scurvy, which killed more pioneers than Indians did. I don't know who he was, but he was one fine feller.

I had a stogie with Cope, who expanded on the work we was doing and how he was ever so much better than that lying bastard Marsh and so forth and me and Alys listened polite.

I heard a rifle boom and knew it to be Mulligan's old Sharps and I come off the chair and went out and saddled up and rode off toward the noise.

The dump was that way.

It took maybe two minutes for me to get there, and I seen that Blue Fox had taken the bait, all right.

Mulligan was there, down on one knee, and the boy I had sent off with the newspapers was on his knees and elbows on the ground.

Blue Fox had stabbed his eyes, stuck his knife up under the boy's tongue and cut it away, and then rammed the blade up the kid's arse and twisted, and gouts of blood was pumping out the hole in his trousers.

The poor kid was making bubbling noises of misery.

Mulligan reached over and cut his throat quick and the blood shot out three feet and the kid was dead in a minute.

There was nothin' else to do. Would have took him days to die of infection, and no way he could have lived.

"I winged him," says Mulligan. "Not by much."

I went to the dump. The newspapers was gone, and there was a few drops of blood on a rock nearby and horse tracks going off to the north.

"We'll go," I says. "Now."

CHAPTER 25

It was Mulligan and me and Lou set out after Blue Fox. I talked a little to Sir Henry, pointing out that Blue Fox, knowing I was after him, would maybe circle round and try to kill Alys. He had that in him. Sir Henry nodded once and looked at me with his heavy-lidded pale blue eyes.

We come into the tent Alys was in and I told her what had happened and that I was going after Blue Fox and she *must* this once do as I said and go nowhere without Sir Henry, and no place he said it warn't a good idea to see. It would only be for a few days, I finished, surely she could swaller hard and put up with my orders that long. I saw a little gleam in her eye but it went away quick enough when I described what had been done to the boy in under fifteen seconds, likely.

"Why doesn't *he* go?" she says finally, fear for me in her eyes.

"Sir Henry is a better shot than me, and you won't distract him," I says, "and you can talk about punting on the Thames and like that. This I got to do. Blue Fox was always crazy, but he's past any thread to mankind anymore."

That was true enough, and as I thought of it he'd tipped over sometime in the last few months, maybe even on the trip back East.

I had no time for more farewells and I looked at Sir Henry and he winked once, the only time I ever saw him blink and only one eye at that.

Lou was waiting; he was a gangly young Texan who'd rode up from Bandera after his folks died of the cholera and he had in the last three years got a good reputation for being brave and not foolish. He'd been caught out once and surrounded by Sioux and soon as it was dark he slipped into the river and swum till he found a dead bloated buffalo and he used that for a raft till he was a long ways away from the Sioux. Hid his head beneath a flap of hide the buffalo had sloughed off and he bore the stink and when he come to shore he'd lost one boot and so he had to toss the other and walk a hundred miles barefoot. I heard he had so many cactus spines in his feet the sawbones had him plunge his hooves into near-boiling water and then the abcesses opened up and Lou just lay there for a few days until everything festered good and the spines began to pop out. The quack would come with tweezers and a needle twice a day and Lou never complained, not once, just sat there chawing on a plug of tobacco and looking blank as a bedsheet.

When he was healed he went right back out, and he come on the Sioux when they wasn't expecting him and stole his horse back without killing none of them, so he was respected by them Sioux anyway, who called him Takes-Horse-Back.

Lou was about six-six and Mulligan was a good two foot shorter and me in the middle we looked like a rafter line with hats.

We was each riding one horse and leading another and I had a pair of the A-rab/Thoroughbreds I favor for covering country in a mighty big hurry. Blue Fox would likely head east, where the rest of the Cheyennes was, though he could go north to the Sioux. But east seemed likeliest and we banked on that, and at first light if we stayed hard after him, I could maybe cut south and ride like hell and get up ahead of him and wait.

Mulligan's gift for tracking was damn near uncanny, and he found a spot where Blue Fox had rested a bit and damned if there warn't a bloody handprint on a rock. So Mulligan had done better than wound him a little.

He'd come down to the rolling Plains and he'd need water if he lost blood. There was water east and some north, but it was a ways off.

I switched my saddle to my other mount and nodded to Lou and Mulligan and I headed south four miles or so and then cut east, keeping mostly to the buffalo trails. They are good engineers, them buffalo, and if they make a trail a horse likes it fine.

Toward dawn I cut the tracks of Masoud and his bunch, easy to see, since an elephant leaves a real emphatic trail. I come on a grizzly uneasily sniffing a huge pile of elephant shit, trying to figure out what the hell animal left this mass. The bear was so engrossed he didn't bother to notice me and I went by and on, figuring I'd go another hour and then find a good lie and wait. I had a Sharps .45-120 and telescopic sight hung under my left leg and I could hit a man at a mile and kill him.

I found what I was looking for, a hill with a stony summit for cover, even had a few little scrubby cedars sticking out of the rocks, and a good view of five or six trails headed east.

I hid my horses in a handy spot, there was a sort of barn of stone with a spring at the upper end, just sheer walls and no roof. I put nose bags on them with some grain a moment and when they'd eaten it I let them drink and then I saddled the one back up, if I had to fly after Blue Fox every moment could count much.

I waited. He could be laid up back a ways and Mulligan and Lou could flush him, send him my way, or he could just be moving slow and cautious, even backtracking to throw pursuit off.

Minutes crawled by. The sun was at my back, and I had good light and a clear view, as far as I could see, and I knew Blue Fox would maybe not even cross in front of me.

Or maybe he would.

After about ten hours which was probably only one I about half heard something, the wind was from the north, it sounded like . . . a big drum.

Then there was movement far off, maybe ten miles away, and I put my spyglass on it and there was those goddamned elephants, headed right down toward me, and I could see that damned fool Cody out front on his prancing white horse, like he was leading a goddamned parade.

I looked back and there was Blue Fox, riding hard, on the farthest trail I could see. I cursed and run to my horse, he was too far away for a sure shot, running like he was.

I come down off that hill, hoping my spare mount would

up and follow, and I headed straight for where I had seen
Blue Fox head, allowing for time to connect.

When I finally got there and up on a hill I could see him
headed north, right toward Cody and them damn elephants,
and off to my left about two miles away was Lou and Mulligan,
and they was following close on his tracks.

Mrs. Kelly's son Luther was using words she would have
been very *disappointed* to hear me utter.

I came up on a ridgetop at the same time Mulligan did and
I stood up in my stirrups and motioned the way Blue Fox had
gone and Mulligan peeled off north like that, a line that would
cut Blue Fox's. Mulligan wasn't no bigger than a jockey anyway, and his horse hardly noticed the little man on him. I am
big and mine was going a little soft, not bad, mind you, but I
could play him out in five miles and when I looked back the
other one wasn't there.

I let my horse have his head and he plunged down the hill
and up the other side, running flat out like he knew what was
wanted, and when I crested the next long rise I could see Blue
Fox maybe a mile ahead, tucked down over his pony's neck
and making all speed.

Time I got up to the top of the next rise Blue Fox had
slowed and he was going up the side of one of them chimneys
stick up here and there out of the Plains in Wyoming, and
what he was headed for was his very own castle. We could wait
him out, but he could slip away in the dark, or we could
charge, and he'd get some of us.

I recognized the chimney. I'd been hung up there once and
there was even a little spring up there, plenty for a man and a
horse, and a sort of slit in the rock to hide his mount in.

Mulligan saw it, too, and Blue Fox would be there before

we could do a damned thing. Lou was north and I seen him slow and turn toward us.

They spread out to cover the rock Blue Fox was setting on, and I unlimbered the buffalo rifle and put the telescope cross-hairs just above the rim and waited on him showing his face. Trouble was the slug was so slow and the distance so great he could pull his head out of the way when he saw the smoke from the barrel.

I could slip up there at night, and likely get my throat cut.

Mulligan would be a better bet, but the feller atop had all the advantages.

Well, there we was. I heard the rest of Masoud's music now, drums, flutes, and tubas and cymbals, oh, hell they was horns of some sort.

Then I remembered them cannon and Prussians I saw tagging along behind Masoud's unlikely force.

I rode on over to Lou and told him I would be going to get some help and he nodded and spat and never took his eye off the sights of his Sharps. Mulligan was in the grass some-place, your guess as good as mine.

My horse was a little tired but would come back I didn't work him too hard, and we wasn't a long ways up the trail when the other one come running up to us, neighing pleasure at our reunion.

I could see that ass Cody up ahead, and he waved his hat.

I moseyed on up to Bill.

"I got to have a word with Masoud," I says.

Cody wheeled round and led me to the biggest elephant.

CHAPTER 26

I stood on the small porch provided by the top flunk on the human pyramid Masoud used to get on and off his freshly painted pinto elephant. The brute stood calmly, farting like half a hurricane, while I explained that I sure could use his Krupp cannon and Pickelhaubes to blast that bastard Blue Fox off the top of his turret.

Masoud nodded and clapped his hands and the giant chamberlain come on up, stomping hard on the backs of the flunks, which I thought was about how things had been wherever they come from for about the last five thousand years. I tried to step light, but the chamberlain was in a snit and the flunks paid. He probably had one skinned alive back home if he woke up feeling crotchety.

The Krauts was sitting like lumps around their beloved cannon, and most everything in the pack train was dusty, but them cannon was tenderly covered with linen. It was getting on hot, but the Germans had their tunics buttoned up right to the throat. I went up to the oldest and ugliest, a feller so scarred he looked like he'd chased a fart through a keg of nails, and I asks if he speaks English.

Ja.

Well, then, would he mind awfully blasting the top of yon rock a while. There was a . . . FROG! . . . up there.

"Ein Frog?" he says, and licked his chops.

Nothing he'd like better than blowing a goddamned Frenchy to bits of a Sunday morning. It was Sunday, that vagrant thought flashed through my mind.

The big ugly bastard barked and screamed orders and the horses pulled the cannon off to a vantage and in minutes they was uncovered, unlimbered, and setting there gleaming meanly. They was steel cannon, and I had never seen one before, other than the breech with the Krupp stamp on it I had peeked at in Laramie. The shells looked like bullets, only about a thousand times the size.

All the while as I talked and arranged this either Lou's or Mulligan's buffalo gun boomed, keeping Blue Fox's head down whilst I arranged to take his goddamned head right off.

Them Krauts was thorough, carefully taking sights and doing delicate adjustments on the cannon, and then Scarface barked and and the gunners stood to attention and he jerked the lanyards and the shells burst just below the lip of the rock and a big cloud of dust and minced stone shot up.

The Krauts fiddled a little and fired again and this time the shells missed, going on over and landing off toward poor Lou, who I hoped they missed.

Fiddle fiddle.

They really had the range now and they sent a half-dozen shells spang on top of the rock and I seen a reddish tint to a dust cloud and thought that perhaps Blue Fox was maybe blown to bits and it made me feel all warm and happy inside.

Then the big scarred Kraut bowed to me and waved grandly at the dust cloud on top of the rock and they began to clean their popguns, tenderly removing the breechblocks so they could swab out the bores.

I rode on over toward the rock and I could see Mulligan and Lou, who was minus his hat, and they waved to me and then Lou shook his fist in the direction of the gunners.

Well, at least they'd missed.

Time we got up to the top most of the dust had settled and it was an amazing sight. I passed a horse hoof on the way up and that was all we found of the nag. The top of the rock was all chewed and blasted and barren and there was piles of rubble everywhere. Nothing could have lived through that, I was sure.

We looked around real careful, all standing up there sort of congratulating ourselves, and then we all laughed and shook hands.

I'd have felt better we found a little bitty piece of Blue Fox, but if he'd been hit direct there wouldn't be nothing left much and it would have been sticky and therefore all covered in dust and hard to spot.

So we goes back down to our horses and mounts up and waves gaily at Masoud and Company. Buffalo Bill come riding over.

"Wonderful marksmanship!" he bellers. "Them Krauts is a credit to Krauts!"

Bill made me wonder he was going to run for office. Well, he was just the sort of pompous gasbag would fit right in back in Washington.

Bill had been beaming but then of a sudden he got all embarrassed-lookin' and he leaned over and whispered.

"Say, Luther," he says. "Them foss-siles? I . . . heh heh . . . well, got a little drunk and seems I . . ."

A little drunk for Bill was a solid month and why the hell he never woke up in Shanghai with a bad case of the horrors and no idea how he got there I purely don't know.

"And you been leading Masoud and his mob around and no damn idea where you was?" I says.

"Things," says Bill, "are a little blurry, you know how it is."

I laughed. I roared. Cody looked at me angry for a minute and then he looked so miserable I felt sorry for him.

Thing about Bill is he *looks* so damn good, the long-haired ninnie. The costume, the steely eye, the bullshit—poor Masoud had been guided by a feller was blacked out and runnin' on forty-rod. Damn wonder he hadn't blundered into the Sioux, who took a real dim view of Cody, what with his buffalo killing. The buffalo was bread, clothes, homes, farms, and families to the Indians, and they damn well knew what would happen to them when the buffalo was gone.

"The foss-siles," I says, "is due west, and you'll have to find your own patch. Cope's hopping around there and so is that Marsh feller."

Bill brightened considerable.

"West!" he says.

And he rode off. I waved to Masoud up there on his pinto elephant and then me and Mulligan and Lou made tracks back toward Cope's camp.

It was a damned relief to have Blue Fox blasted into mince-meat, and I could rest a little easier.

Our spare horses had got lonely and caught up with us and we haltered them and put ropes on them and on the way we come along some antelope, and they was staring at a piece of cloth flapping from a tree limb, like they will, and so we each shot one, counting down so our guns fired all at once. We gutted the antelope and hung them on the spare horses and we went on, with some fine camp meat. I was going to try and supply the cooks without shooting a single buffalo, since Red Cloud had warned me I had to eat what I killed.

We come to the camp late, a little after dark, since we had rode hell-for-leather on the way out and come back at a brisk trot. We hung the antelope up on the meat pole and went our ways.

Alys was glad to see me. She worried about me, that girl, if I was going to be killed she proposed to do it. She'd had some water heated and I sat in her folding bathtub soaking off the dust and sipping whiskey.

I was bone tired and fell asleep and she woke me and I got dry and got into the robes and fell asleep. I had bad dreams all night and in them Blue Fox was killing Alys in many different ways and all I could do was watch, since I couldn't move, you know how it is with them dreams, things fly around you but you're helpless.

Once I must have screamed because Alys lit a lamp and she shook me till I was woke up and then she held me and stroked my forehead but I woke up again anyway, so often I finally gave up and got dressed and went out. There was high thin clouds made the sliver of moon all wispy and strange and suddenly the coyotes started singing their hunting song so I knew it would be dawn in less than an hour, it was the time when the creatures of the night are headed home to sleep through the sun and the creatures of the day are hoping they'll be missed.

I hadn't seen Sir Henry at all, but now I was dressed he drifted out of the shadows, all dressed in black with his pale face smeared with soot, and he nodded once to me and we shook hands, his thin black-leather gloves was cold and smooth. He always wore them 'cept when he was playin' cards. The moonlight picked up faint lines on the butts of his revolvers, too many to count quick but I knew they was the tally of the men Sir Henry had killed. Rumor was that enough money and he'd kill anybody, lying in wait with his Creedmore, one of them Sharps guns has a barrel that is accidentally perfectly true. They can't make them that way but sometimes it happens. His had an ivory stock, all hollowed out for lightness, and rubbed down to brown with a stain. The barrel was four foot long, a single-shot, but with one of them you don't need but the one shot anyway.

Alys come out and said Cope was through here and we were to go on the next day, up about twenty miles to where Jake had found a mess of old bones.

I had one of them surges of feeling, that I had had enough of this farce, wandering the open and digging up things been asleep for millions of years, so some crooks was professors could get all famous.

"Let's just up and quit and go," I says. "You don't need this. I hate it."

"You need some rest, Luther," says Alys, not responding.

You are tired, little boy, come take your nap.

I kicked at a rock and strode away, enraged, but of course she was right, and that made it hurt more.

CHAPTER

27

Jake was up at the next place, guarding it till Cope could haul up his wagon train. We hadn't seen anyone else, save poor old Masoud, following Cody's blind staggers in wide circles. I rode out to range the country and see if there was signs of Indians, I didn't expect any trouble from them, which is not the same as not getting some. Chiefs like Red Cloud could keep a rein on the young warriors if they was near, but like any other boys the farther they was from Papa, the more rotten they behaved.

And Red Cloud knew 'em and he'd use that fact for his own purposes. He was a deep man, and the only Indian ever to win a war with the whites and quit while he was ahead, not that it did him any good in the end. He lived way too long and saw too much sorrow, and felt it was his fault the hearts of his people were broken.

I'd been told twenty miles, but you never know in this country, and when I asked and got told it was maybe a six-hour ride I thought Jake and his rocks was closer. So I headed that way, high up on the rises to the west and I was on one of them when I heard a big gun boom and it was where Jake was supposed to be so I jabbed my horse into a gallop and went to help him.

When the gunfire got close I did a quiet sneak up behind some rocks to take a look-see and figure what to do.

What I saw was enough to make me stomp on my hat except I had need of it, and no spare.

Jake was pinned down behind some boulders had fallen off this cliff, and there was three galoots potting at him and one of them was sneaking around so he could shoot Jake in the back.

He was going to be there pretty quick so I took my rifle out and I screwed the little rods in to hold the barrel up front and then I took a bead on the bastard and checked the wind and fired a round which come close enough to his right foot so he danced some. He moved back toward the other fellers right quick, and I suddenly recognized him—he was ol' Whinny Bucks, a half-breed Cherokee and what-all who was a scout mostly hung around Cheyenne. So I knew these was Marsh's boys.

It was happening like I was afraid it would.

Disinterested science had got down to the fine art of bushwhacking, and I was damned I was going to fight a war with fellers I'd known, over these fat rich bastards and their goddamned bones.

Money's the root of all evil, 'tis said, and it blooms funny, too. Cope and Marsh and their goddamned crooked-pinky teas and bought journalists.

I hung a hankie on the end of my rifle and waved it, it was sort of white, and I rode down toward the three men been potting away at Jake. Jake had been firing back good and so there wasn't any blood shed, but Jake had that evil, terrible temper and I thought it might take more work to cool him off than the three fools started this mess.

Turned out I knew 'em all. There was Whinny, and Blackie O'Fallon, and Bill Bolt.

When they seen me they let their guns down and waited and I rode up and got off and lit into them.

"What in the pluperfect fucking hell are you boys doin'?" I says.

"That's our dee-posit," says Blackie, looking uncomfortable.

"Assholes," I says. "Shit fer brains. Wyoming's got about ten million tons of this crap and you got to start killin' for it?"

Whinny looked pained.

"We was just tryin' to run him off," he says.

"Jake don't run," I says. "And it's a miracle he don't kill you all, you know what a head of steam he builds up."

The three looked past me and their guns come up and I whirls around and there's Jake, stalking our way with the black look of a man needs some blood and right now.

"Just hold it, Jake," I says. "We don't want to start killin' each other."

Jake stopped, I supposed because he wanted a clear line of fire and I was in the way. Whinny and Blackie and Bill sorta crowded in to what cover I provided.

I was about to point them off toward a place I knew had some bones, just to keep the peace, and then there's this holler and I look over and that fat bastard Othniel Marsh is bouncing down a hill toward us, with a couple of his assistants in tow.

Marsh rode like a turd hit with a club, his hat was gone, and his face was red as a beet.

"I claim all this in the name of science!" Marsh wheezes when he gets up to us.

Whinny and Blackie and Bill looked real uncomfortable.

"It's already claimed," I says.

"You ignorant Irish nobody," says Marsh. "Who are you to tell *me* this."

I had half a mind just to step back and let Jake work off his mad, but this could get out of hand real fast.

"There's another place," I says, soothing-like, "off that way, just as good."

I pointed.

"I'll take that one, too," says Marsh.

The three in front of me looked past me then and their eyes got wide and I turned and there was Jake, carrying his scattergun, a bastard thing that was an eight-gauge cut down and with duckbills on the front of the barrels so the shot spread about thirty feet in a flat line.

"Put them guns down," says Jake. "or I'll kill you all."

Jake was known to be a man of his word, so Whinny and Blackie and Bill shed their armaments right quick.

"You must defend my property!" Marsh screamed, standing up in his stirrups.

"Kelly," says Jake, "explain to that fat sack of shit that it is time for him to go. Now."

Marsh was so furious he was deaf.

His assistants was well back and looking like leaving.

Marsh's horse began to get shifty, and I could see his ears go back, which give me an idea. I pulled out my Colt and shot a couple times in the air, just for the noise.

Marsh's horse was right grateful for the excuse, and he

wound up and let loose and that fat sack of shit flew off like that and he went whumpf on the ground and lay there goggling up at the clouds.

"Get his horse, Whinny," I says. Free of his burden, the horse had decided to stand there all nice and see what happened.

Marsh breathed deep and rolled over to an elbow.

"If you have to kill them," he wheezed at Blackie and Whinny and Bill, "it may be for the best."

That was enough. I walked over and kicked his fat ass hard as I could and I kept on kicking while he squealed and rolled and then he got up. He was frantic.

"Do something!" he screamed at his fellers.

They was all lookin' at the ground.

"Marsh," I says, "you get on your horse and get out of here. If there's any more of this bushwhacking nonsense, I'll kill you myself."

Marsh's life had been kissing asses till he could shit on heads, and he had no real stomach for a fight. He went to his horse all meek and got on and rode away, all disheveled and slumped in the saddle.

"You boys," I says, "probably are in need of work. I'll see what I can do."

Jake saunters up, with that damn bastard shotgun pointed up and the hammers down.

"We's sorry," says Blackie to Jake. "We's rode together and now we done this. We warn't really trying to shoot you."

"Done and done," says Jake, for as hot as his temper was it cooled down pretty quick—and he must have been thinking he could have killed them all and he would be feeling right bad about it just about now.

He shook hands with all of them.

"Fight a war over a bunch of rocks," says Whinny, "that's about right."

Somebody view-hallooed to the southeast of us, and I turned and there was Cope trotting up with his flunks ranged out behind him.

We all stood while the Great Professor went past and down to the old beach stuck in mud that was a hundred million years old and gone to stone. He walked around nodding.

"Capital!" he kept shouting. He even did a little jig.

When he was more or less calm finally I rode over to him and said I'd like to hire these three fellers, well-known to me and we could use them the farther north we went, more the danger from Indians.

"Yes, whatever," says Cope, never taking his eyes off the rocks.

I rode back and told the three they was hired, and they nodded and waited for me to tell them what to do.

"Go north and keep an eye on the main trail for three days," I says.

They could slip off and get their traps and such, and I didn't know how much trouble that would be for them.

It was getting to be good war weather, with the grass up some and the trails drying.

The weather come from the south or west, I thought, and war, well it will come from the east or north.

My sixth sense was itching like a half-healed wound.

CHAPTER 28

Things was sort of peaceful for a few days and the digging went on and this time it was yet another New to Science lizard dead so long I wondered if it mattered. Cope was so damn pleased with the find that he actually was almost pleasant. It must have been a strain for him, for he surely warn't much practiced at it, and so I thought, well, hell, this might not be so bad after all.

Whilst I had been gone, though, running down Blue Fox, the order I put in for newspapers was filled and so we had about a wagonload of out-of-date ones and I thought nothing of it till I heard Cope start screaming in his tent one evening.

Some of the papers was new.

He was screaming at Alys.

She come out of the tent pale-faced and angry, but her lips was in a shadowy grin.

We went clear out to the edge of camp, and she filled me in.

It seemed that Cope had come a cropper, over that single bone Alys had moved. He had described a creature that floated in a sea, sweeping vegetables into its mouth with its tail, but his description of it was dead wrong, for Alys had slipped a neck bone into the works and he'd bitten, swallered, and was hooked deep down in the gut.

The newspapers was full of Cope's blunder, and Marsh had got in on it, too, Cope's most hated rival, and the papers was more or less calling him a damned fool over it all. I couldn't really follow the arguments, but then I didn't much care.

Cope ripped into Alys's tent and he drug out all the sketches that she'd made of the skeleton of the Beast That Bit Cope on the Arse, and he pored over them hard. They was all detailed and he swore and swore as he looked at them and kept badgering her about was she sure she had got it right?

Alys snapped back that she was good at what she did, and the drawings was dead on accurate.

"Someone moved that bone," says Cope. "Some foul treacherous bastard! It could only be Marsh!"

The newspapers was so full of the story they actually sent some scribblers all the way up the trail from Laramie to interview Cope.

The scribblers was them supercilious youngsters come of money and went to good schools and were doing a little journalism till dear old Dad croaked and left them the brokerage or sweatshops or whatever. A bunch of perfumed weasels, you ask me, but nobody did.

I also suspected that some of them was paid by Marsh, since

they was dedicated slippers of specimens into pockets, or maybe they was just good capitalists bred in the bone.

Cope gritted his teeth and put up with them because disinterested science wasn't worth a fart in a bottle 'less the press hollered it from the rooftops.

Alys got some mail, among them a letter from her Uncle Digby saying he would be along about September, that the press of business was hard, and that his wound was all healed up. McMasters, the sawbones, would be coming too and would Kelly know an Indian quack he could pester?

Cope his own self was stuck on the debacle of the Flopposaurus and he'd try to put his mind off it but it just plain did not work. He'd made a fool of himself the world over in the small select world of disinterested scientists, who was plenty interested in their careers and them at the expense of anyone else's. They acted like a bunch of society women clawing and scratching for the best grade of guests come to their godawful balls.

Cope went over and over Alys's drawings and then one day he had them crated along with some other stuff and sent down the line to be shipped back. I hoped this would ease his mind.

Blackie and Whinny and Bill was ranging far and wide, and they brought back bits of what they'd found, including a shark's tooth nine inches on a side and triangular as the teeth of sharks are.

Cope was mighty interested in that, and he said such a shark would be a hundred feet long. I got a chill thinking about it. Wyoming was full of tough customers today, but they was nothing compared to what had been. We lacked critters that could bite a grizzly in half.

Cope had to go off and see where this shark tooth come from, and I sent the three new boys with him as guards, since they'd found the beast. Also I wanted a day or two without Cope screaming about the goddamned Flopposaurus.

Alys and me took the time Cope was gone to go out riding together, far from the camp and the stink and the rest of everybody, and we saw an amazing sight coming up the trail from the railhead.

It was a wagon all painted red with gold symbols, crosses and the like, and a statue of the Virgin in a little alcove on each side. There was some little cages built into it and a blond woman at the reins went to a couple of nags and a little feller in cheap black suitings up at the horse's head leading it along.

He was singing in Eyetalian, operas I guess.

They was down below us and of a sudden the man halted the horses and he run to the back of the wagon and fished out a shotgun and he crept forward and flushed a couple of prairie chickens and he took two shots and the chickens just sailed right on without losing a feather.

There was a long aria from him after that, but it weren't from no opera.

Then he opens one of the little cages and he takes out this hawk and with it setting on his wrist he runs toward where the prairie chickens landed and they flush up again and he lets the hawk loose and it flies up and dives on one of the chickens and that was that.

We could see the hawk land on the bird and the little Eyetalian rush up and clap a blindfold on it and pull it off the prairie chicken. He lifted up the bird and put the hawk back on his fist and he bounded back toward the wagon. The blond woman had hove to and was letting the nags loose to graze.

"Jaysus" I says, "this is as silly as that damned Chinaman."

"What?" says Alys.

So I told her a few years before I was riding up near the

Utah border and I come upon a Chinaman pulling one of them carts and he had this huge gong in the thing, hanging from a trestle.

So I went down to see what was up and he stopped and he had enough English to tell me he'd made it this far and when the Indians come close he'd beat the gong and scare their horses.

He give the gong a nice thump and my horse looked a moment at the noise and went back to eating.

"It ain't foolproof," I says. "You got a gun?"

"No need gun," says the Chinaman. "Got gong."

I never give advice when it ain't wanted so I just shrugged and rode off and thought no more of it till about six months later I was in a Ute camp and I seen this pigtail on the warpole of mine host.

The Indian looked at me looking at the pigtail and he says: "Horse deaf."

And that was that and everybody had a good laugh except the Chinaman who was with us only in spirit.

"Lots of folks come here thinkin' that the West is just what's in the penny dreadfuls," I says to Alys. "But there's plenty of parts where you get killed you ain't real cautious, and sometimes even if you are."

So we wanders on down to where the Eye-talian is and him and his wife was setting a table. Then the lady went off a little ways and plucked and drew that bird in about ten seconds.

When they finally saw us at a range of about fifty feet they both smiles wide and welcomes us and I was pleased to find about half the wagon was taken up with kegs of Eye-talian brandy, they call it grappa.

Alys had Eye-talian, of course, and she and them chatted gaily while I wondered what's being said.

I had more grappa and didn't give a damn anyway.

They fed us a wonderful meal whipped up out of nowheres and we smiled a lot at each other and then I looked over toward some weather and saw it was going to rain damn hard soon, so I tugs on Alys's arm and says we better go, and further they'd better get to high ground, as the place they was setting in might be about ten feet underwater and soon.

The man and his wife nodded and folded up camp and was going up a sidehill trail in fifteen minutes—they was good with their wagon and stock, even if they was probably going to end as hair on a warpole.

Sure enough, they had just got to the crest of a little hill when a mass of water come rumbling down the wash, and we had a dirty boiling river between us. We waved and headed back to Cope's camp.

"He is an editor for an Italian magazine," says Alys, "devoted to hunting and especially falconry. He is here, he said, to get some golden eagle chicks and train them. Stefano and Libretta," says Alys.

"Golden eagles?" I says.

CHAPTER

29

Cope had maybe caused his name to be a joke back East, but there was one place he was highly regarded, and that was Salt Lake City, especially after he described the full-sized horses even though he said they was zebras. The cartoonists had had a lot of fun drawing tiny monkeys riding the little three-toed horse he'd bought off the late Pignuts, and joshing the Mormons. 'Fore they was Mormons most of the Saints was members of one or another of them dismal churches where they spend most of their time persecuting each other or themselves or something. It always has amazed me how the ones who scream loudest how they love Jesus is the ones ought to add except for everything the man was, or did, or taught, or thought, or said.

But when the zebras come along I imagined there was great

happiness in Deseret. Was, too, and being Mormons they thought hard about what to do nice for the good Professor Cope and that was send six missionaries to see about convertin' him.

Mormon missionaries was the sort of folks could bore a coat of paint off a wall, and they showed up in their long glooms and dark clothes and began stalking Cope, who said, well, no, and then anyone else they could pin down for a while, until the fine day they stumbled over Mulligan.

Now Mulligan wasn't in the camp, as I've said, he preferred to sleep in a burrow with the rest of the badgers and how they come on him I can't explain, but Mulligan must have wanted to set them up, there ain't no other explanantion for it.

Him and them two Eye-talians was wandering about with a wagonload of grappa and assorted mean birds.

Had the defunct Chinaman and his gong been along, it would have been perfect.

Anyhows, the Mormons announced that Mulligan had done seen the light and was soon to be baptized, as soon as it rained and there was water enough to dunk him in. I was right interested, since it would be the first recorded instance of Mulligan taking a bath, however brief, and the rest of the boys was interested, too.

Name like Mulligan the little bastard had to be a filthy Papist, and I am here to tell you he was, especially the filthy part.

Situation like this I would not trust Mulligan at all, but the missionaries was so starved for a convert they overlooked many of Mulligan's more dubious qualities, such as no one could understand what he was saying, exactly.

For the rest of us, either we done read too many books to be much interested in one as silly as the Book of Mormon—

it's cribbed a lot from a bad novel published in 1819, written by some professor, wouldn't you know—or we was surely going to hell at the end and preferred it that way 'cause our friends would be there, too.

Finally, the day come when Mulligan was to be baptized—the Mormons had got tired of waiting on rain and so they dug a pit in a seep that filled enough with water so Mulligan could be dunked all the way, if there was a standby to the baptizer ready to poke down any parts that stuck up.

There not being much entertainment in deepest Wyoming, there was a good deal of interest in the proceedings, and one of the missionaries announced he would do it, him being a Bishop, which meant he run a pack of Mormon farmers around some miserable patch of alkali Brigham had pro-nounced heaven only in need of a little hard work, none of which he himself would care to do.

I had friends among the Mormons, but they was poor folk from Europe—Scandinavia, mostly, who had been peasants there for maybe a hundred generations, never owning a bit of land. They come from there to America and Utah, and if the free land cost some time listening to Brigham's bullshit, well, they still had the land.

Like I said, Mulligan had hit it off with Stefano and Libretta and even helped them snatch some eaglets, which is not easy to do, since goldens nest in cliffs and they favor straight down as an angle.

Them two big birds—prey birds grow real fast—had been stuffed with prairie chickens and gophers and they'd fletched out good but was still in the highly experimental stages of the flying trade. They'd leap into the air and flap but they was so fat they'd just land splot on the gound and Libretta would coax them onto a T-stick and put them back on the top of the wagon, which was mostly bird shit white these days—the red was visible only where the wagon got scraped.

Come the day Mulligan's soul was to be saved we all gathered at the river, so to speak, and the convert was ushered along and he had been provided a nightshirt some sister had sewn out of worn bedsheets and it was even mostly white where Mulligan hadn't touched it. The little bastard's mad face shoved up out of the top of the folds, and he looked like a crazy man trying to figure out how to untie the straitjacket.

Stefano and Libretta had parked their wagon right next to the sump where Mulligan was to be reborn and them two fledgeling eagles was perched on their crossbar, and I thought their eyes looked rather like Mulligan's.

Stefano had dug out some organ grinder's monkey Eyetalian military uniform, heavy on the chartreuse and puce and feathers, and he even had a sword long enough to spit a sheep for roasting in a chased-leather scabbard.

The brethren gathered and rewarded us with hymns all sung off-key and heavy on the monotones.

Libretta fell to her knees screaming in fair English that Mulligan's immortal soul was soon to be charcoal and he would fry for all eternity, abandoning the Mother Church like that.

"The Whore of Babylon is the Catholic Church!" says the bishop, eyes righteously flaming.

Libretta made an obscene gesture easy to read the world around, indicating that his wives were happily home screwing about anybody came along. Which they probably were.

The bishop screamed curses of biblical nature.

Stefano asked me, "Is insult, no?"

"Is insult, yes," I replies, faithful translations being the heart of diplomacy.

Stefano drew his sword and held it both hands over his head and he screamed some war cry and lit out after the bishop, who was unarmed since he was to get wet and, well, rust, you know.

The sword of the faithful was a well-kept piece and the edge gleamed clean and the bishop soon was covering ground at a pretty good clip with Stefano close behind, waiting for the chance to smite the Ungodly.

The bishop's fellers were staring that direction in horror, and I seen Mulligan get handed something by Libretta, which was a couple fans made out of prairie chicken feathers. Mulligan waves these at the backsides of a couple of the missionaries, and in a trice, so to speak, I knew.

They must have starved them eaglets because both birds looked and their dim brains said FOOD! and they launched off the top of the wagon and stuck them big yellow talons into, count them, four gristly rump roasts, Mulligan having meant it that way, and there was a duet of screams and the two missionaries so honored lit out after the bishop and Stefano only some slower as it is hard to run with huge talons in your ass and big birds flapping their wings.

We was all highly amused and mostly collapsed on the ground with the wonder of it all and the other three who had been standing around gape-mouthed looked over at the wagon and they lit out, too.

Libretta was shouldering the shotgun that Stefano couldn't hit anything with, but she had a lock on them missionaries and she swung and didn't rush and the gun boomed and one give a yelp and put on more speed and the next one howled and I suspected the charges was rock salt from the way their tried to run and scratch at the same time.

The last missionary was a real young man, almost a boy,

and so Libretta's mother's heart softened and she put the gun back down after taking a bead on his ass.

Mulligan was giving off adenoidal hoots of joy and pointing at the retreating Saints.

Jake showed up sudden at my elbow, and I looks over and he's holding a bar of soap, that yellow kind that'll take the spots off a hound.

"We was thinking," he says, "be a shame to waste all this."

Bob and Will and Whinny and Blackie and Lou stood there real grim-faced, a sense of right gleaming in their eyes.

"Of course," I says, unbuckling my gun belt and giving it to Alys.

Poor Mulligan was so rapt with the view of the running Saints we was right up on him before he turned around, and I am here to tell you I have never seen a look of horror on a man's face like that, not even if they were dying.

We grabbed him before he had a chance to light out or get armed, and strong as the little bastard was he was no match for six of us. We bore him to the font and ripped off his sheet and gave him the first bath Mulligan was ever known to have taken.

We scrubbed the little bastard and used up all the soap and left him spluttering on the bank with his eyes burning.

"He's sayin' something," says Jake, looking at me.

I listened close.

"You know what he's saying?" says Blackie.

"Yup," I says. "He's saying he'll pick us off one by one."

"Still worth it," says Jake.

"We'll see about that," I says.

CHAPTER

30

It got to be summer overnight as happens in Wyoming and a hot wind blew and the dust rose and the land dried and water become a problem to us. There was springs all over but they didn't yield all that much and with all the stock and people and thirst there wasn't water enough to warsh specimens and Cope was annoyed.

He demanded that we find a nice deposit next to a river, which was a tall order, and the water Wyoming has got mostly flows north toward Montana Territory and either the Yellowstone or Missouri. I knew where there was plenty of fossils in the Big Dry, that huge triangle between the two big rivers, but there was Sioux and Blackfeet there, too, and I could go through it alone but they would not take kindly to a mob.

I did not want to go north farther than I had to and I had

fine feelings for Washakie and didn't want him or his people disturbed by Cope, who was arrogant and plain mean. The flap over his bad call on the bones of the Flopposaurus et at him, and the fact that Marsh was there at all et at him, and so did the dust, the bugs, and the lack of conveniences.

He complained constantly and he was so damn rude to some of the people working for him that about twenty up and quit and got a little train together and headed back down to Laramie. They was to be paid off there, but I learned Cope had sent a letter to the bankers along with the group denying them their pay. There's no worse reputation for a man to have than cheating employees out here.

Cody had rode over from where Masoud was camped and told me the prince was going back—half of his people were sick and one of the elephants had died. If he was smart, I says, he'd wait till the lot croaks and change his name and habits, but Cody said DUTY CALLS HIM and I wondered why I was talking to this fool. It was because I liked Masoud and wished him well and he was an unhappy man.

Every one of these expeditions has a time when folks are fed up and want to go home and that's when you find out who's fit to ride with. Alys stayed even-tempered and my boys did and the wagon men did, but Cope's flunks was whining all the time and one of them lost his mind one night and started screaming and then he fell to his hands and knees and barked like a dog and then he convulsed and was dead.

He'd been stealing laudanum from the medical kit and took too much and when we run out, well, he died.

Cope got everyone together and speechified, saying he was here till the snow flew, which made some folks turn pale. His flunks was city folks and this was the high desert and first it was huge and menacing and then monotonous and boring.

Quite a few buffalo was close by, since it was a little cooler high up than down lower, and we shot a fat cow once in a while for camp meat. I just made damn sure the boys knew that we was being watched and that God Help Us if we shot more buffalo than we used.

Red Cloud is plainspoken and he means every damn word he says.

I explained to Cope that we had a ways to travel if he really wanted that much water and fossils, too, but I'd not recommend it. Rumors showed up that there was gold in the Black Hills and the Sioux loved the Black Hills, having stole them from the Pawnees, Sauk, and Foxes, and some other lesser tribes less than a hundred years before, when the Cree run the Sioux out of the Great Lakes country.

Indians was real adaptable and could go from trapping and fishing and eating the occasional moose to getting damn near everything they needed from the buffalo. They was very intelligent and in a few years the Sioux had gone from canoes to horses and they was very good horsemen, indeed.

Gold in the Black Hills.

I'd been in them, and they was beautiful, just rising up out of the Plains, and all covered in firs and pines and cedars. The children loved it up there, way above the heat and dust of the Plains, and it was healthy, too, the water was good.

We found sign time to time, places where scouts had been for a while, but none of them stayed long and there was no horse stealing nor killing.

But every time I looked north I got uncomfortable, like I get when there's a storm over the western horizon but I can't see it yet. The air changes, all I can say.

Marsh had staked out most of the deposits to the west and so it was the north or nothing, and so I said it warn't a real good idea and another year would be better. For one thing, there was fossils all over the place where we'd been, and water, too, and it would be closer to the railroad, so easier to ship specimens east.

Cope said he'd think it over.

Then things began to go all to hell, and from a quarter no one expected.

Lou had been up north swinging wide to count pony tracks and see if there was any movement of big camps and he come riding like hell into camp and he says there is another expedition maybe fifty miles up the trail, not Marsh, not anybody we knew, and where the hell they'd come from had to be from the west, because there wasn't a way through the tribes to the east and northeast and the passes was few this end of the Rockies.

Cope threw a screaming fit like he always did these days and he yelled at me to find out who these people might be, and damn quick. I was curious, too, and so I took Mulligan, who so far had refrained from exacting vengeance, just to make us sweat a while longer, and we rode north hell-for-leather to find out who it was.

Turned out they was a German expedition that was in California and they had got off the train in Salt Lake and gone up to Montana and around the Bighorns and down easy as you please. They was after fossils, too, and they had maybe twenty wagons, and no guide, but they had maps and could read them.

Herr Professor Gottmund had heard of Cope, of course, and Marsh, of course, and he looked forward to making their acquaintance. It had taken the better part of three months for them to make that long hook round the Yellowstone and Pitchstone Plateaus and head down our way.

They offered us dinner, but we said no and made ready to head back down.

Well, then, would we take some delicacies for Herr Professor Cope? Jah?

And the cook comes out with maybe a hundred smoked buffalo tongues on strings.

Oh, God.

"Did you buy these?" I said, hoping to hell they had.

"No, they had shot a lot of buffalo, but there were a lot of buffalo, hein?"

Mulligan pulled at my sleeve and we went off and we stopped a mile south and he said he seen three scouts on the northern horizon and that warn't a good sign. One was keeping watch, more was marking tracks for the war party, which would travel in small groups and meet up the day before the attack.

I goddamned the idiot Germans and hoped they was all killed and scalped. Mulligan seconded my sentiments.

We had to pull back nearer the railroad and if possible get some troops to escort us. The one damn thing I promised Red Cloud wouldn't happen had, and though he knew I kept my word his warriors didn't know one band of whites from another and they would want blood for this.

It was late the next morning before we come on Cope, and he listened and then he shrugged.

"I pay you to see to these things, Kelly," he says. "So see to them."

The teamsters had been in the country long enough so when I explained what trouble we had coming, they loaded up and made ready to leave that night. It was hot enough now so it was better on the oxen to travel at night anyway.

Cope ranted and screamed a while but when it got real

clear he and his assistants was staying on alone—and I'd hog-tie Alys I had to to get her out of here—he give in with real bad grace and flat forbade me to warn Marsh off to our west.

I sent Jake with a message anyway, of course. If the Sioux and Cheyennes killed Marsh, Cope would be a happy man but myself I was hoping that both of them would get slow-skinned over hot coals. I had about had it with disinterested science.

Cope tried to insist that the specimens all be loaded and the teamsters to a man said next year would do.

Sir Henry stayed glued to Alys. He was silent as death and steady as a stone and he meant to get her back safely and he would, I was sure of that.

We left a lot of stores and the tents. Cope bitched about that, too, but I pointed out that living was the first thing and famous came later, if you wished to enjoy it.

My boys drifted out all blackened in the face and their horses had their feet wrapped in leather, to muffle the clank of iron on stone.

The Indians was going to find us and so it was only nec-essary to know just when, we would have to make a fort from wagons and whatever terrain was handy and hope we had plenty of bullets.

We creaked along for a while and then we got up to a crest and I looked back north and there was a red glow on the horizon.

It was real reddish and it was growing.

Probably the German train, I thought, and the fire's in the dry grass, and the wind's from the north, and so it's headed our way.

CHAPTER 31

The Indians knew their land and winds and seasons better than we did, and they warn't above using wildfire to fry up a nice mess of white men. If the fire caught good and the wind carried it well, we would have a couple problems, the first getting burnt up and the second moving at all. We was grass-powered, and the oxen had a three-part day. Pull eight hours, graze eight hours, and chew their cuds eight hours. No grass, and we was stuck, for the beasts would get weak and we would have to start abandoning the wagons.

Cope was having none of that, and his first thought when the red flames crested the horizon was to save his rocks, as though the fire would bother them at all.

"Do something!" he screamed at me. I sat on my horse

thinking how much I would just like to put a bullet in the son of a bitch's forehead and be done with it all.

We was close to some places that was nothing but hardpan and only a few blades of grass on it, and so the teamsters moved the wagons and the stock up to it and we pulled the wagons in a circle and put the stock inside. When the fire run past and the night come I expected that the Indians would attack and try to steal horses, or anything else come to hand.

Cope's precious specimens was left down in the old camp, the Indians wouldn't bother with them. He ranted and raved and demanded until he run out of wind and then he just sulked. His daddy did not whip his ass enough when he was a little boy, so he mostly still was one.

If you've never seen a prairie fire before, you will never forget what they are like after. The flames was forty feet tall and they bloomed red and orange and billowed gray smoke and threw embers on the wind in front of it. There was a good breeze shoving this one along and it roared past below faster than a good horse could run. I saw a couple antelope overtaken and when the fire passed they was just black logs in the gray ash.

The fire roared on south and the wind blew clouds of sour ash over us and we choked and the stock gagged and stirred, they wanted water and the water was full of ash and when they drank it they would just be thirstier. The little springs that fed the dry creeks here were stout and would flow clear soon, but for now all were clogged and black.

We had a pretty good defensive position, and I thought it best that we stay there the night, even though the animals was miserable and hard to hold, it was better than where we had camped, which had too much good cover for Indians sneaking in. They don't need much.

The ashfall slacked off near sunset, and there was only about an hour of light left when Sir Henry whistled and I run up to the rock he was setting on and looked north and there was an Indian riding toward us, eagle feathers on his lance and headdress and his right arm over his chest, sign for parley.

Sioux.

I rode out alone, and we met maybe two hundred yards from the wagons.

It was Long Runner, who I knew pretty well, a Minneconjou.

"Ah Kelly," he says. "This is for you."

He hands over a thong with about thirty tongues on it, and they wasn't from buffalo.

"I thank you," I says. Though the German party hadn't been with us, shame to an Indian is a general thing.

Long Runner wheeled his horse and left.

So there would be no attack.

Reasonably enough, they had cut the tongues out of the German party, for wasting the buffalo. I didn't blame them for it. Indians have their laws and habits just like us and I suppose they got them because they worked.

I rode back to the wagons and announced we could go back down to the camp.

The teamsters would have to go up and cut wild hay in the pocket meadows where there was water, and when they had enough we could maybe go back down to Laramie. I'd send scouts south to see if the fire left any grass and where.

Folks was quiet. A prairie fire is a natural disaster and living through it, or just even watching close by, will shut up the gabbiest folks.

We was all smudged and smoked from the fire, and them as had consumption was coughing and coughing—there were many folks come west for the dry air and was better, at least till something like this came along.

Cope come by all beaming—he was changeable as a little kid, too—since he realized that we'd have to stay and that meant he'd have more specimens time we left.

Early the next morning the teamsters took four wagons and went off to cut hay, and they found a good patch not too far and was able to come back with enough forage for all the stock by noon. The horses, mules, and oxen ate hearty and drank deep and I relaxed, for if the stock got desperate enough, some of them at least would wander off.

Alys was caught up enough so she rode with me as I went off south to see about the best way to get back. I took some robes and food and a frying pan on a packhorse so we'd be able to stay the night in some comfort. The camp was crowded and it stunk and there was too many people in too small a place.

About ten miles south we seen where the wind had veered off to the east and it took the fire with it and there was still good cured grass, more than enough to graze the animals, so my fears of us being trapped altogether was gone.

Alys said she'd like to get atop the mountains about twenty miles to the west, and I shrugged. Longer I was away from Cope the better I felt anyway. The man was purely beginning to grate on me.

We rode on up to where the trees began and on to a little dell I knew, where there was grass and water and firewood and we et beans and bacon and had lots of strong tea, and finally Alys looks at me narrow and I fished some good brandy out of my saddlebags. The wood burning was cedar and it smelled like incense and the smoke pooled along the ground, which meant there was rain coming on.

Storms up this high could be real wet and so I cut down a fir and branched it and laid the boughs up against the trunk, which was still stuck to the stump about six foot high, to have some shelter. I cussed at myself for not bringing canvas.

I cut more boughs and piled them deep, and of course some rain would get through but most of it wouldn't, and it would keep us from the worst of the storm.

When it come it come hard, lightning crashing down hard. I had hobbled the horses and covered their eyes. They whinnied and complained a while and then quit.

Alys and me had a romp between the thick robes and then lay in each other's arms for a while, trading little stories. The rain was gentling off, but felt like it would keep on till morning.

The horses started whinnying again and I pulled on my boots and took my rifle and Navy Colts and went to see what the matter was.

They kept looking back west, to the trail led there. We hadn't been on it at all, and it was an odd time for anyone to be coming this way, what with the rain and the dark.

I gentled the horses some and moved off quiet and found a place of deep shadow and waited.

Something moved a little just inside the deep shadows where the trees ate the starlight, almost nothing but still it wasn't the sort of thing I cared to leave go, and I waited a long time and then I seen it again, just a shadow moving over another, if I'd been blinking I would have missed it.

I thought I heard another horse whicker to the west, with the rain and the wind rising I couldn't be sure.

'Fore I left Alys I said may be a while before I come back and keep damned quiet; if there's Indians sneaking around I will have to sit till I can see them and figure what to do. I hoped to hell she'd do that.

The storm cleared off sudden and the stars was there and I could see another storm not far off—they come through, sometimes regular as the hours falling away, clear up, storm, clear up, storm, and I have never seen that anywhere but in the Rockies.

I'd been there long enough and began to slip back to Alys, taking care to move in the cover of shadows, wondering if what I had heard had been there, or perhaps if it was Indians they had swung way round to avoid the trail altogether.

I waited in shadow maybe fifty feet from the bower Alys was in, and I could see good, except behind a big boulder maybe forty feet from the fir I'd chopped down. I just laid there waiting, which is what scouting mostly is, finding a good spot and setting, for days if necessary.

Nothing moved, and the next storm come on just as vicious as the one just left. Lightning started crashing around and gave a harsh sudden light, like photographer's flash powder.

A close bolt lit up the landscape, the boulder come out good, and there was a man on the top of it, crouched, and I swung up my rifle and shot and he screamed and fell back.

I run like hell to see if I'd winged him bad, but when I got round the boulder I saw a horse almost into the trees and a rider hugging down close, and then he was gone. I went 'round for sign and there was only the one horse. I found a little blood.

He wouldn't be back, so I went to Alys, and we slept real good.

CHAPTER

32

Before packing us up I walked over the ground around the boulder and followed the tracks of the horse. The Indian had moved from the boulder about a hundred feet to his tethered pony. I swore that I hit him in arm or shoulder, but he was dragging a leg. I shrugged. The light was fast and he had been moving, I could have hit him twice with the same bullet.

Cope, by the time we got back, was anxious to leave, and said we could return next year. He was fussed about something, but then he always was.

So the crew spent that day loading up and the next morning the train slowly pulled out, a good mile long, with ten miles to go for grass.

Me and my boys ranged out, our job after all was to keep Indians from attacking. It was the middle of August and the time seemed to have gone somewheres on its own and I couldn't think of that much I had done since we come up here in the spring.

We was all worn out and bored, so much so that Mulligan actually began to come close enough to be seen. The crazy little man would pop up like a dirty leprechaun and grin and then go to ground again.

The Indian I had winged bothered me, stuck in my mind, and though I said nothing I had a feeling he may have been Blue Fox. The Kraut gunners had pounded the top of the rock to rubble, but shells miss soldiers down in the ground and it wasn't impossible that he had managed to live. We never found nothing but blood and bits, but that all could have come from the horse.

I told only one man, Sir Henry, and he nodded and drifted slow like to a place near enough to Alys to protect her but not near enough to alarm her.

You can easy spot some people just by the way that they move, or ride a horse, at a long distance, longer than you can see a face. Blue Fox was supple as a snake and fast as a rock lizard. The Indian I seen didn't move like that, but if Blue Fox had been bad wounded he wouldn't.

About like that evil son of a bitch. Hard to kill.

We saw no Indians all the damn way to Laramie, and come to town riding ahead of the train. They would take another day or so to come on in. Me and Alys and Cope and Sir Henry and Will and a couple journalists showed up after we headed back come riding into the shabbly little thrown-up railroad town late in the afternoon and me and Alys went to my rooms in the hotel—I'd paid through October—and got acquainted with hot water and soap. Bucket baths just ain't the same, try as you will.

We was refreshed and in clean clothes and having a drink before seeing what we could find in Laramie by way of dinner and there was a knock at the door and a bellboy stood there, with a long white envelope addressed to Alys.

Just her name. I gave the kid a dime and I walked back to her and handed the envelope to her and her face got pale and she ripped it open and then she began to cuss, in English and French and even passable Sioux.

She offered me the letter.

> *Your services are no longer required.*
> *Jonathan Cope*

"That dirty bastard," I says.

"He is that," says Alys. "I'll have one hell of a time getting my personal things back from him now."

And then she began to laugh, and I did, too. Many parcels of drawings had come down to Mr. Adler. Alys was clever, and there wouldn't be anything left in her trunks to make Cope suspicious.

"Jonathan eventually suspects everyone, and I mean everyone, of plotting against him," says Alys. "He had one of his assistants jailed once, accusing the man of stealing specimens, but then it came to light that Marsh had bribed a watchman. So Jonathan had to drop the charges, but the assistant had his career ruined, as though it was his fault the guard was corrupt."

I had known men like that. The whole world was against them. Usually the ones did that out here shot themselves, I don't know why. I remembered a captain of cavalry whose voice got higher and higher as he screamed his suspicions and then there was a shot and we found him in his office with most of his head gone, them Navy Colts have a fierce load of powder, and you stick the barrel back in your throat your whole head explodes.

We ate and then we went out on the wooden walk and moseyed down the street, Alys turning time to time to see if we were being followed, down the two blocks and change to the little jewelry store. I smelled a sharp smell of burnt wood. There weren't streetlamps on that short, poor section, which was butt up against the warehouses and hide yards.

The jewelry shop was gone and there warn't nothing but a hole and some ashes and sour water puddled. It must have burned maybe the day before, at most two.

Alys never batted an eye, but I could feel her arm trembling and she clutched mine tight as we went back up the street to the hotel. We went in and on up to my rooms and when we was inside she raged, stomping back and forth. Then she slumped in a chair and steepled her fingers.

"Could you please see if you can find out what happened?" she says.

I went on down the stairs and out the door and across the street to the Crosstie, and found a couple loafers there who was thirsty and had nothing better to do than catch the town news.

It had done caught fire and the little Jew was passed out drunk and burned to death. The coroner ruled it accidental, there was fires all the time what with the new lumber in the dry air and oil lamps gettin' knocked over.

Time the folks had got there to fight the fire the place was gone right up and they had best try to save the buildings on either side, and they had—they was newer and had asbestos sheets in their walls.

Adler had been buried quick, no one knew him and there was no folks back East anyone knew either. He'd been in the ground for about twelve hours, they'd planted him when we was lookin' down on Laramie from the hill to the north.

I found Alys drinking brandy, her eyes swollen from crying. She had a Spanish cigarette in her hand and another in the ashtray, and a long look in her eye. She'd tried something and it hadn't worked and months of her scheming had gone to nothing.

"Adler tried to help me," she said. "He came here to do that, and they killed him."

"Pretty serious business, science," I says. Men out here killed for gold and they killed for land, but the thought of professors killing didn't make no sense. They was already rich, but not in the things they wanted most.

Of all things that crawl upon the earth, says Homer, there is nothing so dismal as man.

I wasn't going to add my two cents' worth, figuring Alys was the one who lost the most, and so I waited for her to speak.

"Herr Adler was a tutor of mine," said Alys. "Uncle Digby hired him and he lived in the house and he taught me German and French and Italian and the beginnings of natural science. He had retired and Digby had settled a pension on him. He loved me and he came here to help me and now he's dead."

She could change, for sure, remembering the first time that I seen her, shooting Pignuts in the ear and marching him off to dig up her poor brother and boil off the rotting flesh so his bones could rest peaceful back East.

"I want to go home," says Alys. "Luther, will you please come with me? Please?"

I had got drawn farther into this than I cared to be, and when my wife died I got cold inside and didn't want no one in there again and Alys was chewing away to get there.

I had money, and I could pick and choose my work.

I hated the East, the cities made me sweat and so nervous I was afraid I might kill some poor bastard run up behind me or looked at me funny. It was that bad.

She got up and come to me and put her arms around my neck and her head against my shoulder and she wept, her tears warm through my linen shirt. She didn't plead or wail, the bitch, all she did was stand there smellin' wonderful and leaking.

They don't play fair.

"Of course," I says, I expected before she rolled up the big guns and said of course I could refuse and *disappoint* her.

Well, havin' said that I had to go and no mistake.

We was a few days getting things sorted out, and her private stuff recovered from Cope, who wouldn't even talk to her direct, but had one of his flunks observe her gathering her things.

We was waiting on the train from the west, and Alys was taking a long bath in her private car, and so I went down to the loading platform.

Some troopers injured bad enough to be sent east for discharge was lying on stretchers there and the ones could walk or manage crutches was outside leaned up against the wall.

One tall feller with a battered uniform had been burned and his face was all swathed in bandages, only his eyes left open a little, a narrow slit across. He had an arm in a sling and his hand curled up like they get when they ain't moved.

Our eyes met and we nodded and I went back to the parlor car.

CHAPTER 33

When I got back to the car it was still sided off and it seemed we had guests for the journey.

Stefano and Libretta was loading their traps in the car. Oh, good, I thinks, all across America with arias from Eye-talian operas and a fug of bird shit and feathers rising every time we hit a bump.

Stefano beamed when he saw me, from under a giant cage which held a vexed golden eagle staring out through the screen with mad yellow eyes.

"Kell-ee," says the little bastard, "good-a morning."

I smiles and says the same thing and steps up into the car and there's a gleeful yelp and one of them sausage dogs clamps on to my ankle. It was long-haired and I'd never seen one before. The little bastard kept growling hard while trying to puncture my boot.

"Ah, Alys," I says, lifting an eyebrow at the wee nasty beast, "what the hell is going on?"

"Stefano and Libretta needed a ride," says Alys. "They're going to New York."

"Them and their goddamned buzzards and purebred Eye-talian ankle gnawer?" I says.

"It's German," says Alys.

The sausage dog started flailing its body around to drive its teeth deeper.

"First trestle," I says to the dog, "you can bite air till you hit the rocks."

"Lucia!" says Libretta. "No!"

The dog bit harder.

I lifted my foot and shook it a while, which made the dog happy as now it was a game, my hundred-dollar boots notwithstanding.

"Jaysus," I says, "the Krauts got nothing better to do than sit around dreaming up beasts like this?"

Libretta swooped down cooing at the little bastard and she stuck a thumb in its jaw hinge and the sausage dog let go, whining and trying to lick Libretta's face.

Alys looked at me straight-faced, just the barest hint of a smile at one corner of her mouth.

All oil and smiles I saunters over to my lovely and I grabs her arm and lifts some and propels her off to the sitting room.

"It looks really lovely," I says, looking at more cages. "Them pigeons go so nice with the wallpaper."

Three crates of them fat dumb birds what crap all over everything was standing near a window.

I sneezed.

"Stefano was here collecting birds," says Alys.

"No shit," I says, as an eagle screamed back in the guest room.

"He's collecting them for Prince Masoud," says Alys.

I nods. Of course.

"And we are carrying Prince Masoud's falconer and such back to him," I says, "WHEN THAT GODDAMNED TURK COULD RENT A WHOLE TRAIN!"

"He's not a Turk," says Alys, "and I like Stefano and Libretta."

I sort of did, too, but expected I would like them less as I understood more of their lingo.

Stefano broke into song and the birds set up a screechy counterpoint and then there was a yelp and a lot of Eye-talian cussing.

"Oh dear," says Alys, starting to move toward the noise.

"No fair," I says, keeping hold of her arm. "They caught him fair and square and now they get a chance to eat him. You wouldn't want to interfere with *Nature*, now would you?"

Stefano screamed, and I heard Libretta running.

She cussed in counterpoint to Stefano's cussing.

"We need to go and see if they're all right," says Alys.

"They have to be," I says. "Why don't we go when it's been silent for five minutes?"

She punched me in the ribs and strode off and I grinned and followed.

The couple in the guest room was deeply involved in trying to get a golden eagle to let go of Stefano's shoulder. The bird huffled as we come in, spreading its huge wings and cracking Libretta a good one. She cussed and grabbed her eye.

"These here birds," I says happily, "would make a nice *stew*."

Everybody ignored me.

"We could trade the feathers to the Indians," I says. The Indians had fine feelings for hawks and eagles, and had catchers who dug pits in the earth and covered them with branches and hid under them and when the eagle or hawk come to the bait they'd reach up and grab their feet. The most successful had very few fingers left.

There was yelps and *two* happy sausage dogs clamped on my ankles.

Alys was helping Libretta get the eagle to let go of Stefano.

I shuffled off sneakily with murderous intent. There was a big tub of soap and water out by the car, from when it had been washed. I lifted one and then the other goddamned hound carefully as I moved along, and then I got to the tub and lifted my right foot, savored the moment, and plunged the nasty little beast into the washwater. And then I got the other foot in.

Them dogs was so determined that it was a minute before they got it through their tiny Kraut brains that they was underwater and in soap to boot. The little bastards surfaced, hacking and choking. The tub was three foot tall or so and it was a good foot from the water to the rim, and I stood by watching them claw at the wooden sides, occasionally slipping beneath the surface.

I found a seegar in my coat and I lit it and puffed happily.

I was so satisfied with my work I got careless and didn't even hear Libretta sneak up behind me. She whacked me a good one with a chunk of lumber and I sprawled face forward on to the platform and she scooped up them goddamn dogs and held them to her breast and she wiped soap from their eyes.

"Son of a bitch," she says, "you hurt them."

Not much to say to that.

It occurred to me that perhaps it was not a real good idea to be lying flat, as them dogs would be on me soon as the soap was out of their eyes, and I scrambled hastily to my feet.

Then it hit me. I ain't the smartest feller you ever knew, and at times I can be uncommon thick.

"Mulligan," I says.

That little bastard was behind this. He'd been helping Stefano and Libretta get the eagles and he was a cool hand who'd wait a long time for that one shot.

It seemed I was sentenced to a good two weeks of scrawks and stinks and Stefano's arias, which was hard pay for giving that little Irish bastard a bath.

I begun to run around the car, my Navy Colt out, raging.

He had to be here somewheres.

I poked about handy hiding places and then I run up the street to the lowest saloon in Laramie and sure enough Mulligan was at the back and he dropped his glass and shot out the back door with me in hot pursuit.

One of his friends stuck out a foot as I ran past and I went facefirst into the wall and time I got up and outside Mulligan had a real good start, on that big black horse of his. I loosed a couple shots, not wanting to hurt his feelings by ignoring all his efforts, but he was out of range anyway and soon out of sight.

A crowd of friends and acquaintances had come out to enjoy the fun.

I had to laugh, too, and I wondered what Mulligan had done to the other hands scrubbed him down so good when we give him the first bath he ever had in his life.

Bob and Will was there, looking a bit chewed.

"Jake's over at the bathhouse," says Bob. "He done got a package done up nice with a ribbon and all, and . . . well . . . there was a skunk in it."

I nodded.

"Lou was in the whorehouse taking his bath," says Will, "and when he got out of the tub and was drying hisself off he noticed his clothes was gone."

I nodded.

"And his money was gone."

I nodded.

"And you know how Rosie is about money," said Bob.

She had not one speck of mercy for the poor, that woman.

"Let me guess," I says. "So Lou had to make a mad dash for the rooming house. . . ."

Bob nodded.

"But when he got there. . . ."

Bob nodded.

Sir Henry had not taken part, keeping his cold eye on Alys.

And me, I had two mad Eye-talians and a bunch of birds for company for more'n two thousand miles.

I walked back to the railroad station and saw a mess of people standing around one of the piles of boxes covered with a tarp that waited on the right train.

There was a body on the ground and the coroner was kneeling next to it.

Sir Henry. I walked on over.

"Got a single bullet right where the spine joins the skull," says the coroner. "Some little belly gun, hardly made a hole."

Sir Henry, whoever he really was, dead in Wyoming, and about the best hand with a gun I ever knew. But there he was dead, one shot, when he was feeling safe and careless.

"Nobody saw nothing," says the coroner. "Clerk come out

to load some of this . . ." and he jerked a thumb toward the boxes.

Hell, it could have been a ten-year-old kid, all I knew.

Sir Henry had died of the careless.

CHAPTER

34

I'd been a captive in trying conditions, awaiting having my balls cut off by angry women. I'd been held in the basement of Brigham's Lion House and escaped, due to the good agency of Klaas Vipsoek's farts. I had suffered. But being stuck in that damn parlor car with a menagerie of hawks, eagles, and them insane sausage dogs still gives me the whips and jangles.

Animals is animals and they are what they are but I couldn't help wondering if Stefano and Libretta was lacing their grub with hashish. Them ornery little dogs had but one aim in life, and that was fastening on to my ankles. So I painted my boots with pepper sauce and the next time they happily clamped on they both got a funny look in their eye and soon departed howling to Libretta who accused me of being mean to them.

"What about by goddamned ankles?" I hollered.

Libretta ran off a lot of Eye-talian cusswords whilst holding her mutts close to her breast, and them pawing at their eyes which was dumb because the pepper sauce was on their lips and soon they was screaming and rolling around on the floor.

This got the feathered brigade all stirred up and the screams and the shit flew.

Alys listened to Libretta's Eye-talian insults and said none of them was repeatable except she did have to tell me that according to Libretta my pecker was a disgraceful thing wouldn't do for a woman and she recommended further I go and fuck hedgehogs.

"Hedgehogs is in short supply here," I says. "See she's got another suggestion."

There was also this baby gyrfalcon, barely three weeks old and mostly white fluff and bad temper. Stefano let the little bastard out and it looked at me and then twisted its head upside down and screamed and waddled over and leaped and sunk talons into my leg.

I yelped and was about to kill the goddamned thing when Libretta and her sausage dogs dived at me and thwarted the killing blow I was taking with the barrel of my Colt.

Alys was having the most fun of her entire life laughing at me. She came over and blew smoke from her Spanish cigarette in the fledgling's face and it let go and I limped off to tend my wounds. I was dabbing iodine on them when Alys came in roaring with laughter and she informed me that Libretta had said the young gyrfalcon thought I was its mother.

Alys was having laughing fits. I shot a glance at her would have peeled the paint off an Apache but she just choked and put her hand over her mouth and enjoyed herself more.

For some reason, likely there was a bet on amongst the three of them how much of the sausage dogs and crazy birds

I could take before snapping and leaping off the train on a bad curve.

I went to the bedroom and slammed the door and went into the loo to take a piss and some of the pepper sauce had got on my fingers and first my privates was warm and then they felt like they was blistering up and so I started jumping up and down and hollering as my dick caught fire and Alys rushed in to help but my circumstances merely caused hysterics and she was out on the bed paralyzed by laughter. Me, I am scrubbing away with soap which felt worse at the moment and I finally sat in one of her goddamned silk velvet chairs pouring cool water slowly on my aggrieved member, which was doing much better, thank you.

My hollers had also brought the rest of them, all stuck in the doorway, Stefano, Libretta, hot-eyed sausage dogs eyeing my pecker hungrily, and that goddamned little gyrfalcon waddled through the legs and determinedly stomped toward me, twisting its head around.

"Enough!" I bellers. "Out or I'll shoot the lot of you!" and I aims my Colt and they musta known I meant it because Stefano darted in and scooped up the goddamned bird and Libretta ran, clutching her damn mutts and Stefano slammed the door good and tight and I looks balefully at the woman exhausted down to giggles on the bed.

"I'm sorry," says Alys.

"The hell," I says. "You haven't had this much fun since the hogs ate your little sister."

"Oh, Luther," she gasps. "You poor thing."

This here solicitude made me real suspicious. I was a tad bit gun-shy, what with everything.

Seems that things can't possibly get worse and then they

do, the gods got their fingers stuck in the affairs of men places you never dreamed of.

It had always give me an attack of the curious as to just why Stefano and Libretta hadn't been attacked and killed by the Indians, what with their habit of wandering around alone and by the bye carrying enough grappa in the wagon to keep a fair-sized camp drunk for a month.

As I sat there trickling water on my pecker there come from the zoo in the guest room the most god-awful screeks, frawps, and miseries I ever heard. It sounded like a passel of cats was being slowly gutted by Comanches, who, above all other tribes, study on and take pride in their torturin'.

Alys had to roll over on her face with this and sob into the comforter.

Opera. Mad birds attacking and shitting. Sausage dogs whose single aim in life was my ankles.

Now a violin.

"If you thinks," I says, with as much dignity as I could summon given the circumstances, "that I am going all the god-damned way to Boston with them guests of yours and their disgusting pets, do think again, as I'D DRUTHER JUST GET OFF NOW."

The train was going about fifty I supposed, miles per hour that is. If you've spent your life on horseback it was a downright terrifying speed. I looked longingly out at things that would break my neck and end all this fun.

Alys snuffled and tried to compose herself.

"I'm sorry, Luther," she starts.

"You ain't a bit sorry," I says, "and I might point out that you do have an interest in my member and its unfortunate accident."

Alys choked.

The burning had stopped, and other than the goddamned violin I was more or less back to normal. So I pulled up my trousers and buttoned my flies and straightened my collar.

"I'll meet you in Boston," I says. "I got a terrible temper and the thought of murdering the lot of them makes me feel all warm and cuddly inside."

"But Luther," says Alys, "they're delightful."

"Better yet," I says, light dawning, "since you no doubt plan to have Stefano and Libretta and their vermin as guests at your poor Uncle Digby's, why don't I just get off at the next station and go back to Wyoming, as it is safer and very quiet."

Alys changed just like that. Soon as she knew I was serious she was all regrets and tears and promises.

Them women when they think they gone too far turn to apologies and coos. It generally works, so I can't blame 'em, but in this case I was damned I was going to spend the next week bein' gnawed and follered by some dumb bird thought I was its mama and be driven mad by Stefano's musical efforts. I longed for a nice quiet pitched battle someplace, preferably with cannon.

Alys had typical woman's practicality. We was once out with shotguns hunting sage grouse and three was scooting along the ground thirty yards in front of us and I was crouched to swing when they flew.

Alys blasted the running birds and when I complained she looked at me like I was a half-wit and said well, I thought this was to be our dinner.

She draped herself on me and kissed me and of course we ends up in the bed and we has a nice romp and how grateful I was to know damages to my parts had not been permanent.

"I'll talk with Libretta and Stefano," she says.

I grunted.

"Really," she says.

I grunt.

"Poor Luther," she says.

I nodded.

"He needs some peace and quiet."

I nodded. A lot.

So we got up and I made my way up the train to the saloon car, which was full of fat drummers and cigar smoke and I had a triple whiskey looking out at the green fields—we had crossed that line between not enough rain and enough rain and it was clear to the eye. I was glad for not enough rain, it would keep the farmers here.

After I had my nice sulk I walked back through the cars to Alys's and things was quiet. Alys was looking vexed.

"The servants got off at the last stop," she says, "without a word. Even Mrs. McGinniss."

No fools they.

"Libretta offered to cook," says Alys.

"How 'bout fried fowl," I says. "Never have tasted eagle."

Whatever Alys had said stuck, for the vermin was caged and draped, the violin stayed in its case, the sausage dogs was stuck in a portable kennel, and Libretta cooked up Eye-talian food which I will take any day over that overblown Frog stuff.

We was in Chicago only long enough for Libretta to shop and then we was hooked up to an express.

CHAPTER 35

Alys's Uncle Digby was a kind man. A generous man. Brave, courteous, and exquisitely mannered.

"I'm going to kill him anyway," I says to Alys as we sat in the cab in the porte cochere, watching a pinto elephant up-root a nice tasty tree.

"Stefano. Libretta. Vermin. Prince Masoud. That goddam-ned elephant. I want to go home where I can be killed and scalped in peace," I whines. Digby's house was monstrous, and I figured that Stefano and Libretta could be walled off in it someplace, but if Masoud was a houseguest, too, what with his harem and guards and elephants and horses, well, that damn house wasn't *that* big.

Digby come out all happy to see the two of us, and Alys got down and hugged her uncle. They really loved each other.

"Quick," I whispers to the cabby, "to the train station! I'll give you a double eagle!"

The cabby turns and looks at me a moment.

"Sorry sorr," he says, "but the lady thought you might want to do that and she amply ree—moonerated me to guard again such a possibility."

"I'll double it," I says.

"No use, sorr," says the cabby, "she also pointed out that if you wasn't gentleman enough to stick it, you wasn't gentleman enough to pay me neither."

"Rot in hell," I says pleasantly.

"Beggin' your pardon, sorr," says the cabby, "but that is the kind of woman any man would kill to keep."

Digby and Alys quit grappling so I come down off the coach and I shook hands with Digby whilst Alys beamed.

"I laid a bet with her you'd escape," says Digby.

"Not a chance," I says, "and you know it."

"Well, well, come in come in, I've had a light supper laid on and you must be tired from your journey."

"Oh, no," I says, "it was most restful, what with being attacked by dogs and them kind of birds eat other critters and it was all full of the high culture what with Stefano sawing away on his goddamned fiddle and you wouldn't have a half gallon of laudanum? It's time to end it all."

"Oh," says Alys, "how he suffered."

Another elephant trumpeted out in back. Digby had about forty acres behind the mansion and a carriage house and a lake and what-all. Plenty of room for Masoud, if he stuck to his tents.

We went on in and back to the orangerie stuck to the house, all wrought iron and glass. There was them ornamental citrus trees in pots, with lemons, limes, oranges, and grapefruits on them and there was a supper on a glass table—first one I'd ever seen, just a thick slab on black wrought iron, a frame and legs feathered like one of Stefano's goddamned birds, claws holding brass balls at the feet.

Masoud's two tents was back there screened some by trees. There was journalists in packs the other side of the high wrought-iron fence and a few preachers waving Bibles and bellering, I suspected, about the heathens and their ungodly ways, which meant Masoud's yellow tent, every man's dream.

I must have kept my eye on that tent too long for Alys hauled off and kicked me hard in the shins and I yelped and come down to earth.

"What?" I says, collapsing in a chair.

"What," says Alys levelly.

Digby was staring hard at something on the ceiling that was so terribly interesting he couldn't rip his eyes away from it.

"I'll give you what," says Alys. "It was the long strings of drool hanging off your mouth when you were looking at the yellow tent, my foot just ran away with itself, so to speak."

I made a note to inquire of Masoud if he might need a broke-down scout in his home country, which was safer, I suspected.

"The prince is a fine fellow," says Digby. "Cambridge man. So I pretty well had to invite him to stay."

"Fine," says Alys. "Luther and I had this conversation in Laramie, and I expect to have many like it in future."

Hell of a thing when your woman understands you.

"Ol' Masoud's got the right idea," I says, courting death. "I doubt his shins is banged up."

"Oh, God," says Digby. "Run, Luther."

"Indeed?" says Alys. "I take it you feel that women are better thought of as chattel goods."

"I was just funnin', Alys," I says.

"I," says Alys, "was not."

This is one of them conversations, I thought, that ends only the one way. God knows what she'll do, but she'll do it.

Then a sight I purely could not believe occurred out on the back forty.

Mulligan. *Mulligan* was there, riding a big white horse and looking almost clean.

"Jaysus Kay-rist," I says. "What is Mulligan doin' here?"

"Who," says Digby, "is Mulligan?"

"He is a smelly little bogtrotter whose head is mostly adenoids and a right fine scout," I says, "and he don't like civilization at all, which is why I am surprised to see him here."

Alys stared, too.

"Masoud must have hired him," says Digby.

"Why?" I says. "Mulligan is fine where he belongs, I can't see an earthly purpose for him here."

"He's coming to supper," says Digby. "You could ask him then."

I was gratified to see Stefano and Libretta carrying cages off toward the tents. I hoped them dogs was in one of them.

I stepped out the French doors and went down the flag steps and made my way across the lawn toward where I'd seen Mulligan, and when I got past the screen of yews there he was, on that big white A-rab horse looking like a monkey playing cowboy. The A-rab horse was flighty as they is—too much fire and nerves for me, I like my horses tough and calm—but them A-rabs go like the wind and you ride 'em right they cover more damn ground than you'd believe.

Milligan spotted me and he come over, that horse dancing, and he slipped down with the reins and he dropped them and damned if the big horse didn't just sort of dance in place.

"What the hell you doing here?" I says, not wasting time on pleasantries.

Mulligan grinned, showing his brown stumps of teeth.

I was able to comb out the fact that he was here because Masoud had offered him a lot of money to come.

"I figured that," I says. "But why here?"

"Blue Fox," says Mulligan. "Them Krauts didn't get him."

My thought, too.

I says then it was him killed Sir Henry, and I described how we found the lord in the boxes, one neat little hole in the back of his head.

Mulligan nodded.

"You know how he is," says Mulligan. "He'll kill you last, after he kills the lady and whoever else comes to mind."

Cold worms twisted in my gut. There was no damned way that bastard could have lived through the barrage that them Krauts laid on the top of his rock.

But he had.

"But why Masoud?" I says.

"He done told me he feels responsible," says Mulligan, "since his gunners was the ones guaranteed Blue Fox was dead. He's got spies, too, and one of them reported seein' Blue Fox, just for a moment in the window of a passing train. His face was scarred bad, but it was him."

The soldier I had nodded to on the platform.

Sir Henry wouldn't have paid no mind to a cripple in uniform.

"He wouldn't come here," I says, mostly hopeful.

"He ain't supposed to even be alive," says Mulligan, "so I expect he'll go where he likes."

I seen Masoud stride out of his tent, followed by the huge guards, and they headed for us.

"I'll have to tell her," I says, thinking of the man I wounded when we were up in the mountains. He must have barely got up to walk, and he'd come for us, and failed, but he lived, and he would come again.

"We got to kill him," I says.

Mulligan nods.

"That we purely have to do," he says.

We'd damn sure been trying. Blue Fox was more ghost than man. But he was lethal.

And he could slide around the East and not stick out that much, there was tens of thousands of wounded veterans and they wandered all over. No one would find Blue Fox unusual, and his scars would make folks sympathetic.

"This is the goddddamnedest business I ever seen," says Mulligan. "But we're in it and there ain't no way out but to kill him."

No, I thought, there wasn't.

Masoud got to us and we spoke a few words and then all of us headed for the orangerie to talk it over with Alys and Digby.

CHAPTER

36

Even with all of the room in Digby's mansion, them goddamned little sausage dogs hunted me with insane glee. I could
be in the damned dining room and get up to load some more
bacon off the sideboard, and there would be a couple happy
yelps and they would be clamped on my ankles again.

The pepper sauce worked good on the boots but it worked
so good it shriveled and cracked the leather.

I was setting in the orangerie with Digby and Alys one afternoon having a nice drink when the little bastards shot out
of a pile of trimmings the gardener had piled by the door and
something in me snapped. I picked up the machete the gardener had left and I tore after the dogs, hollering war cries
and determined to behead them before doing more serious
damage.

"Bruto!" hollered Libretta, as she took a well-aimed swing at my forehead with a hand-carved pick handle and laid me out cold on the parquet.

I awoke with black shimmers in my eyes to see her cooing at them damned dogs, whilst clutching them to her breast. She looked a lot like paintings of the Madonna, with a couple of demented sausage dogs standing in for the infant Jesus.

Time I struggled up to my elbows Alys and Digby was there.

"I am going to kill them," I says. "I will not rest till I have both their miserable hides. I have had enough."

Libretta wailed like a grieving mother.

"We need to go to Philadelphia," says Alys. "Maybe the dogs will find a new best friend while we're gone."

I was helped off to bed and cold compresses were applied to the goose egg rising on my skull.

"You can't kill the dogs," says Digby. "It would cause no end of trouble."

"Yes," I says.

"They're dear people," says Digby. "A little eccentric."

"Eccentric," I says.

I fished one of my belly guns out of the dresser drawer and checked the loads.

"I'll see what I can do," says Digby, noticing the insane gleam in *my* eyes.

Anyway, I did not see the damn dogs again and we got ready and loaded up the private car for the trip to Philadelphia. Digby had a day's worth of business in Washington, and we was to go to that festering goddamned swamp before Philadelphia.

I knew a lot of folks in Washington and did not trust any government run by my *friends*. Knew 'em too well, you see.

"Grant's in the White House," I says. "And Kelly's not been

seen." The last damn thing I wanted was a private commission to go off and poke around at risk of my precious neck to give good old U.S. a report. He was a funny, sandy red man, not tall, not wide, and looking at him he'd pass for a harness-maker, which is what he'd been after he left the Army. He didn't talk a lot and he was much misjudged, not having much flash and swagger.

But one of our neighbors up in Oneida had been with Grant at Vicksburg and then with him after Lincoln appointed him to lead all the Union forces.

Both times, our neighbor said, about a day after Grant took command everything started to tighten up. Officers did their jobs or they was sent packing. The troops was well supplied.

The feller told me this was in the fortifications built to defend Washington, and he was on guard duty one night when Grant and Lincoln his own self come walking along the firestep.

"The South is the Army of Northern Virginia," says Grant. "And I will take every soldier I can muster and go and destroy that army."

Which he did.

He was shrewd and tough and I really dearly wanted to avoid him, along with about forty other folks seemed to know an uncomfortable amount of my history.*

"Matter of fact," I says, "why don't I just stay maybe in New York and meet you on the way back."

"Several reasons," says Alys, "beginning with New York has ever so many whorehouses ever so much nicer than Rosie's."

A man's worst nightmare is havin' all his friends under-stand him so good.

*See *Kelly Blue*

Digby had made the arrangements with the railroad, and the sheer ease and speed with which we made it to Washington should have set alarm bells off in Mrs. Kelly's boy Luther's mind, but I was being fucked to a standstill every damn night by my lovely and voracious companion and about half-drunk all day with Digby's fine old cognac. I was used to sleeping light and having a gun to hand out where my worst worry was some Indians working off their boredom but it was a lot more dangerous here and I knew that but forgot.

I was sound asleep when we come to a stop in the capital, my dreams perfumed by Alys, and all warm and comfortable in the bed and my ankles hadn't had a dog attach itself to them for two whole days.

Alys shook me awake and said a couple of Digby's friends was coming for breakfast and wanted to meet the famed scout, by which I supposed she meant me. There was several messes of tripe purporting to tell the tale of my heroic life (one spent fleeing by preference, and I took solid pride in the fact that my scars was almost all on my backside) with a lot of flowery speeches and even the Indians soundin' like they gone to good private schools and was fine British gentlemen bound by honor and good manners and all that crap, which was an interesting way to present folks didn't think like us at all. Hell, I even didn't think like us—it was why I was still alive.

All innocence I shaved and got dressed and flicked a few bits of lint off my lapels and I sauntered on out to breakfast and I should have lurked in the passageway a little and paid careful attention to the voices.

But I didn't. When I come out there was two absolute horrors just a-settin' there and I gave off a yelp and turned to flee but Alys was blocking my retreat.

"Luther," says John Hay, "how nice to see you again." Hay

was one of them fellers destined for great things, and he had been Lincoln's secretary whilst in his mid-twenties and now was doin' God Knew What here, but I could be sure it meant no good to me.

The other was General George Crook. Crook was an honest and brave man and therefore dangerous. Once when he was asked by some congressman what was the worst thing about fighting Indians he had replied that the worst thing was making war on people that were utterly in the right, while we were utterly in the wrong. This was not the reply the congressman was expecting, and Crook found himself posted to a fort someplace well past the ass end of nowhere in jig time.

"Who," I says, "was fool enough to let you come back to Washington?"

"Grant," says Crook.

I done a quick sum and the total looked extremely bad for Luther Sage Kelly.

"Nice to see you boys," I says. "I am suffering from a bad and festering wound. My mind is broke from years of terror and suffering in the service of my country. I get fits time to time and begin shooting at good friends, cause I think they are plottin' to get me killed. I got plenty of money and I don't want no more medals. My doctor assures me that only a life of luxury in a nice safe place will save me from the madhouse. I have become addicted to opium and whiskey and . . ."

Hay fishes out his wallet and counts out some bills and hands them to Crook, who tucks them in his pocket without counting them.

"Alys," I says, "these bastards is going to try and get me killed and you must help. Try a bribe, quick."

"Luther," says Crook, "you sure disappointed me. You forgot to mention you are the sole support and comfort of your aging mother and orphaned nieces and nephews."

"That, too," I says.

Alys is having fits of the giggles, of course.

"I resign my commission," I says.

"As an attorney," says Hay, "I would advise you not to threaten to resign a secret commission, because the mere mention of it is a traitorous act and hanging the penalty."

I thought a moment about how much I hated lawyers.

Crook laughed his generous and booming laugh.

"In a world of tricks," he says, "I can always count on Luther."

"No," I says.

Alys is leaking tears. Her and Hay.

"We but bear a message," says Crook.

"Let me guess," I says, "that it comes from some sawed-off drunk used to have a batch of stars on his shoulders but has moved up in life."

"Your old friend the president merely wants to have a drink with you," says Hay.

"Digby is at the bottom of this," I says.

"Of course," says Alys.

CHAPTER 37

Nothing much had changed at the White House since I'd been here a year ago with Sitting Bull and Gall and Red Shirt and Spotted Tail and the others, though it seemed longer. I suppose it does when life is so very interesting.

Grant was a simple soldier at heart, and he hated pomp and all the efforts of them wanted to make the presidency more royal. When he was a general he wore a private's uniform with his stars stuck on here and there, and officers hadn't ever met him would walk right past him, figuring some underling all sashes and gold braid had to be him. He was truly modest and seemed to take on his tasks with fierce single-mindedness. He was also utterly honest, which is not all that much use in Washington. Most folks here would have apoplexy if they told the truth, it was that unnatural.

I remembered him asking Sitting Bull what had impressed him most about the wonders of white civilization, after the chiefs had been taken on a tour.

"Little children working," says Sitting Bull. Grant nodded. He didn't blush about things he couldn't change, but Sitting Bull was right, in more ways than he knew.

Digby was already there, tricked out in a colonel's uniform, and like Grant he wore a simple private's government-issue woolens. This on a man who had the finest tailors in England for his everyday wear.

The privates, case you was wondering, was the ones did almost all the dying. Few officers take that enough to heart.

Hay, Crook, Grant, and Digby all knew each other well and they had a quiet ripple of jokes run around and through the conversation, and since I was fresh meat most of them was at my expense. Alys had got left, much to her annoyance, even though Digby explained there was matters of State to discuss and protocols demanded only them as ranked could hear it.

"Since I'm so junior to everyone," I says, being a mere captain, "why don't I go and get a newspaper or see the hogs been fed proper?"

"Luther," says the president, "knowing your objections to anything I might want of you, and your skill at vanishing, you may find NO in these words with a modest effort."

"I'm wounded," I says. "Just a little walk outside and I will be, anyway."

"Your concern for the carpets is admirable," says Grant. "Now shut up and listen."

Hay trucks on over to an easel got something on it, like a big map, and I did have a slight fit of the curious as to just where these bastards was going to send me so I could get killed next.

Hay flips off the fancy bedsheet covering the map and it's of Central America.

"No Spanish," I says. "Can't hardly manage a word of it and so obviously you'll need someone else."

This heartfelt observation was ignored. Hay stuck a pointer on a big lake in Nicaragua.

"We will soon require a canal through Central America," says Hay. "And one possible place is through Lake Nicaragua and so on through the mountains—very low here—to the Atlantic."

"So dig the son of a bitch and when you're done I'll go and have a look-see," I says. That canal had been an idea for a long damned time and for my own money one malarial swamp is a lot like another.

"The shortest distance is through Panama," says Hay, "but may be costlier. In any case we must forestall the British from insinuating themselves into Central America."

I was feeling relieved. There had to be about two thousand other fellers they could blackmail into this. Surely I was not the only man fit for this job.

"So the expedition seeking the fossils in these limestone mountains would be our best possible means of surveying the route."

Foss-iles. A dim and vicious light came on in my little mind.

"Digby," I says, "do I smell a fine, lovely, and perfumed hand in all of this?"

"Eau de Montreux," says Digby. "It's all she wears."

"How could you?" I says, looking terribly pained.

"Luther," says Digby, "men generally have a weak character, and so Alys is merely providing one of better mettle to you."

That did it. I started into cussing and give off a long and

extensive aria covering all the treacherous backhanded dishonest and etc. of present company and absent wench.

I referred to certain dismal events in which I had part,
none of them anything I wanted anything to do with whatever.
I damned the Army, officers, and ended by roaring that I
purely hated the government, any government, and I was prepared to . . .

"Hang?" says President Ulysses S. Grant.

Damn him, he cut right to the argument and won it, like
always.

"Nicaragua in the winter," says Digby. "It ain't so hot."

I could be a long ways away by winter.

I could be in goddamned Mongolia by winter.

"But we still need to take Alys back to Wyoming," Digby goes
on. "She's very much wanting to introduce me to Washakie."

Even Grant perked up at the mention of the old monster's
name.

"A fine feller, I hear," he says, looking wistful. They was
mighty scarce here in the capital, for sure.

This was no good at all. Blue Fox, for some insane reason,
was determined to kill me after he'd killed Alys, and there
he'd have a much better chance. Digby and me had had a
quiet talk and there was hard-eyed fellers in the shrubbery
after that, and other places.

"You're ordered to Wyoming and Nicaragua," says Grant,
"and Colonel MacMahon is your commanding officer." He
looked at Digby, and he looked at me.

"Feel free to hang him if it suits you," says Grant, looking
satisfied. "It would please so many of my constituents."

Hay hustled us out, there was a delegation of fat senators
coming down the hall bent on some chicanery.

"We've one other feller to see," says Hay. "He heard you were in town and asked if you might drop by and he wanted to meet Digby as well."

Now what?

Hay had a carriage waiting and we got in and the driver took off without orders and he pulled up to this dismal red-brick building, the sort of place has government writ all over it. We got out and Hay led us in past some secretaries and he nodded to a man at a desk in front of a large double door and he knocked once.

A deep musical voice said come on in.

"Don—Eee-Gwah-Gho-Ghe-Wah-Diddy," says Ely Parker.

"Don—Eee-Gwah-Gho-Ghe-Wah-Diddy," says this tweedy feller, all spectacles and earnestness.

"No," says Ely Parker. "Don-Eee-Gwah-Gho-Ghe-Wah-Diddy."

They recited this gibberish for a few rounds and then the tweedy feller scuttled off and we could hear Don-Eee-Gwah-Gho-Ghe-Wah-Diddy faint off toward the front door.

"You son of a bitch," I says, light dawning.

Ely Parker was his white name, and when he was Keeper of the Western Door of the Iroquois, he was Donegawha. He'd served with great distinction in the Civil War, and as aide to Grant he had written out the terms of surrender signed by Grant and Lee. His copperplate penmanship was beautiful.

Hay roared with laughter a while.

Digby looked a little puzzled.

"That feller in here was, I'd bet my liver, a pro-fessor. Ely here done instructed him on the proper pronouncement of his name in Iroquois," I explains.

"Gawd," says Hay. "How the papers will fly and the debates burst into flames."

Parker put his boots up on the desk and lit a cheroot.

"Grant me my amusements," he said. "That pest had been after me for six months for a diction lesson. Of course, all of the time he could have gone up to our reservation and asked anyone, but no, he has to bother me. The director of the Bureau of Indian Affairs. Of course the bastard really wanted to get an appointment as agent for his brother."

Now Digby roared.

"I'm leaving anyway," says Parker. "I've had enough."

He'd got tired of the corruption and the insults from Indian-haters, and so he'd go to being a civil engineer, and he was one of the best in the country.

"Good to see you, Luther," says Ely Parker. "And give my best wishes to the friends you brought last summer. They'll need it."

I nodded. Oh, yes, they would, but they would mostly die anyway.

We all went to Willard's for a drink and we told a few stories and then we went our ways, me and Digby to the hotel where Alys was now.

We didn't say anything at all to each other on the way.

CHAPTER

38

"May giant leeches drain your blood and rodents new to science gnaw off parts and the hell with you both," I says pleasantly.

"Now Luther," says Alys, "neither Digby nor I committed all of the crimes you stand convicted of. By the way, what did you do?"

"I had an attack of the patriotics," I says, "encouraged by treacherous swine such as yourselves. I got absolutely no interest where that damn canal gets dug. I just don't. Every time I get my ass caught in the gears of empire I regret it. I am old and battered and wise. I just know this is going to end up with me dead. Which will cause no end of mirth in the White House. Not to mention here."

"You're whining," says Alys.

"I say," says Digby. "Just how old are you anyway?"

"Twenty," I says. "I joined the Union Army at fourteen and then I went West and it has been a hard few years. Time I'm thirty I will have not one tooth in my head and cataracts from contemplating my fortunes."

"I'm twenty-nine," says Digby.

Alys was somewhere in between but being a lady not a bit interested in pointing out where.

It was on the tip of my tongue to say something really nasty to her, but that wasn't fair. She was right. No one had been stupid enough to do all them things but me, never mind they was the sort of things at the moment you know you have to do and later you wish you'd stayed to home and been a nice safe clerk in a dry goods store.

Cope's exhibition was to open in a couple of days, and I hoped we could get the hell out of Washington, D.C., before Grant and that monster Hay dreamed up other useful services for me to perform on the nation's behalf. I was sure Hay would be president someday and then I thought, no, he's too smart for that, he'd rather just run whoever has that god-awful job.

Digby was just a tad uncomfortable with being part of the screwing of Luther, not enough to complain, mind you, but he warn't really snaky enough to enjoy what had been done.

In his boots I would have, and there you are.

I sulked a while till I got bored, and then Alys says brightly that perhaps we'd all like to go and look at all the trash piled in the Smithsonian. I'd heard of it, it was a national attic and anything perfectly useless ended up there for the delectation of scholars present and future. A place whose heart and soul was all thick with moths.

The biggest reason I did not want to go to Nicaragua is that about anything south of the Rio Grande ran on slavery, and they was smarmy enough not to call it that, but there was a loose patchwork of huge plantations and ranches and the common folks was worked to death, overseers and whips and dogs to run down them as left, and if you're going to have a country like that you're going to have fellers won't stand for it and so there was more or less a steady bubbling of revolt which meant bullets flying which meant danger and personally I would take the West, where the jungles wasn't and them Indians had to pot at you from farther away which gave better odds.

Also there was a lot of maniacs gone down there from here to try and take these little countries over and though none of them had yet succeeded I recalled they'd all been shot and so us gringos wasn't much loved.

It was no news to me that Alys was a conniving little minx, and I had to respect her skill at it. I cared for her a lot more'n I'd admit, even to myself.

We had a good lunch and then we set off to see the Smithsonian, which was a-building and the mess was stupefying. Boxes and crates and professors hollering and there was a few halls done up but the War had slowed things down there and they never did catch up.

They had a display of fossils, mostly from the Cincinatti hills, and they ran to little wigglers lived in the ocean. Alys found them fascinating and so did Digby, but I could have been some happier playing cards with cheats.

We come back to find there was an invitation from Hay, to come to a costume ball that very night, with apologies, but Alys yelped in delight and rushed off to find some things to wear.

Me and Digby looked at each other and said at the same moment a simple mask would have to do.

Alys come rushing back with no parcels and we both lifted

eyebrows but she said she'd recalled she'd packed her harem outfit and she would just wear that.

"THE HELL YOU WILL!" Digby and me roared at the same moment.

"Not that one," said Alys. "I have a modest one."

We witheld judgment until she put the thing on and it was simply dazzling without being a bit lewd, or wouldn't have been if that minx hadn't been the one in it.

She had a brocaded jacket and gold-cloth pants and a skirt over that and soft boots of red leather and a little conical hat and veil.

Digby rummaged around someplace and come up with a pair of men's black masks, and we each tucked them in a pocket.

The ball didn't start until ten, so we rested up, or at least Digby did, and his driver and carriage took us to Hay's pile, one of them wedding-cake things, all brightly lit. It was a modest place with room for about five hundred people in the ballroom, which had been decked out with expensive trash supposed to remind us of the *Arabian Nights*.

We come in escorted by a couple flunks in fezzes and white gloves and the place was already fairly well packed. I seen a blue turban across the room which had Masoud under it and his thugs was done up in customary white: other than Rosie's he seemed unable to piss without company. They was near Hay, who like us wore just a black mask.

There was a big orchestra in formal dress and a conductor on a little stand waving a baton and fast music going and the cream of Washington society was there all dancing and leaking avarice and chicanery.

It occurred to me that a few barrels of powder under the floor in the right places would solve many of the nation's problems, but I hoped maybe that would happen the next time when I warn't here.

There was booths set up along one wall had fortune-tellers in them and Alys laughed and dragged me off to one, a fat old thing with hairy moles and a dirty caftan and she stank of that damned patchouli oil always makes me sneeze.

We waited while she gabbled at a couple in the two chairs in front of her and when they left, all smiles at the good fortune headed their way, we sat down and Alys stuck out her hand and the woman looked at it and she frowned. She shook her head and pushed Alys's hand away like it was hot.

Then she motioned to me and I stuck out my paw and she peered at it.

"You are confused with someone else," she says. And she grabbed a cloth and wrapped it around her crystal ball and she waddled off and was gone, right out the doors, once looking back at us and her eyes rolled.

"What the hell was that all about?" I says.

Alys laughed and said Hay was famous for his jokes.

Heads had turned when she come in and in truth she was the most beautiful woman there, and Digby, eyes full of pride, asked for a dance and I watched the two of them whirl around the floor and right away people pulled back and left them room and they was graceful together. Digby still moved his left leg a little slower but he had an acrobat's grace and a couple of times Alys threw back her head and laughed at something he said.

The music stopped and a tall slender feller in a long coat, yellow, with a pale blue turban wrapped not only round his head but his face, too, cut in and Digby bowed and the music began again and the stranger and Alys whirled and then I got a feeling in my gut like I'd been kicked.

Blue Fox. He was here, and he was out there with my woman in his arms.

I kept calm and I sidled to Digby and whispered and damned if rather than run to the floor he didn't whirl and go to Masoud who was right behind us, and the giant A-rab bent down and then his head snapped up and he and his guards moved slowly toward the floor.

The music was winding down and Masoud was close to Alys and the stranger, but he had his back to Masoud and so when the music stopped I saw Masoud gently slide between Alys and the stranger who I was sure was Blue Fox.

Blue Fox staggered back a little then and one of the guards swung his sword and the turbaned head fell away from the boneless body and blood shot out of the severed pipes.

People close screamed as the blood hit them but past that the crowd just tittered, seeming to think that it was part of the entertainment.

Masoud bent graceful-like and he grasped the turban and he walked back to me and Digby, the head in his hand.

We follered him to a side room and he slowly unwrapped the cloth and I gasped.

It was Blue Fox all right, even though he had terrible fresh red scars from the shelling he'd took.

The guards appeared carrying the body which they'd wrapped in a carpet, and they unrolled it and searched and found one of them Eye-talian spring knives, has a long thin killing blade comes out when you press a button.

Hay joined us, cool as ever, though his guests were still yelping out on the floor.

"An assassin," says Masoud. "Sent here by my enemies."

Hay looked at us.

"Of course," he says. "I will announce just that."

CHAPTER 39

"You really can't do this sort of thing!" says Hay. He sounded real vexed. Well, having a head and a body the centerpiece of the entertainment at your costume ball was something Washington hadn't seen before.

"Oh, hell," I says. "If you just sort of let Masoud's fellers run amok in there, the nation would be a much safer place."

I was looking over Blue Fox's body. Under this long funny yellow coat he had ordinary clothes on. A flick of the knife, out the door in the confusion, take off the coat, and saunter away. There was always gawkers around, looking at the mansions and especially tonight. He could have been gone in under two minutes and blended right in. He even had a fresh bandage to wrap his face in if he needed to.

A servant was mopping up the trail of blood that led out

to the ballroom. After a moment, the crowd went back to admirin' each other. They'd have gone on doin' that if the roof fell in on 'em. They was that sort of people mostly.

"When you plant this bastard," I says, "make damn sure his head is far away and buried deep, where he can't find it." Crazy Blue Fox might have been dead, but he was damned good. I didn't know I could have beat him.

Hay bitched for a while until Masoud gently reminded him that he and his staff had diplomatic immunity and could pretty much do as they pleased. And knocking the knob off Blue Fox pleased him, he added.

John Hay, Esquire, nodded and he went off and I heard him announce to the throng that the unfortunate occurrence was a matter of Turkish politics. You know how them Turks are.

The buzz cranked up and so did the orchestra and other than them folks had their costumes ruined by spurting blood no one seemed to much mind.

Alys peered over my shoulder at Blue Fox's corpse and carefully scrutinized the bastard's head.

"A resourceful man," she says. "We must give him that."

Alys had little dark speckles on her pretty clothes, and her heart, too, there was something hard in her and if she had any fear I'd never seen it. I thought I knew what she wanted, but then I remembered Spotted Tail, so long ago.

Women are lawless, he said, and only a damned fool of a man would ever think he knew what they *wanted*.

"Someone put him up to this," says Digby.

He looked at Alys and she looked back and they both nodded, just the once.

"He was always crazy," I says. Even the Cheyennes was afraid of him some, though he was one of theirs.

"In my country," says Masoud, "assassins are best mad, and sent to kill full of hashish. They know nothing, and so cannot reveal who really sent them even under the most terrible tortures."

"Jonathan isn't clever enough to be that evil," says Alys. "If Blue Fox was someone's agent it would not have been him. He has no more guts than a damned June bug."

"It does not take courage," says Digby, "to hire the likes of Blue Fox. All it takes is money."

He had little patches of white on his face, where blood had drained in his rage. I'd seen them patches on other men, and they was the sort would charge hell with one bucket of water. Some officers would give orders and hide, but I knew Digby would have been right at the head of his charging troopers. Not way out in front, just right where he'd pull them along and all of them crazy and happy to die.

There was a knock at the door and in come some men who was cops and trying not to look it. They had those hard eyes come of seeing awful things, and Hay took them aside and they talked in low voices and then one of them stayed while the others went off.

A couple of orderlies came in through a side door with a cloth and a stretcher and they hauled Blue Fox off; one of them looked at Digby and give a sharp salute and Digby returned it. One of his old troopers, I suspected.

"If we've been here long enough not to offend by leaving," Digby says to Hay, "perhaps it would be best we retired now."

Hay snorted and nodded.

"Grant sends his best," says Hay. "and as soon as I can decently leave I'll go to him."

Masoud and his henchmen drifted out to the ball, they all walked like their feet barely touched the ground, all coiled and ready. I thought of where he come from. Rich he might be and powerful, but at any moment a knife could find him.

America wasn't a bit behind in the matter of civilization. You could get knifed here, too. I thought on that.

"It was me he was after," I says finally, "and Blue Fox being his own self, he was going to kill Alys first. It was a game to him. It ain't like a Cheyenne. I expect he learned how to think like that at Dartmouth."

I was in a funk, all the fight had drained out of me, and all I really wanted was to be in a cabin someplace where there wasn't nobody, and watch the seasons a while. I knew several in the West and wished heartily I was there.

"We have to see all of this through, *Captain* Kelly," says Digby, all colonel now.

I nodded.

We went out together and made our way round the mansion. It had begun to rain, a cold one from the ocean, and the gawkers was still there, dry—they'd brought umbrellas. Digby spotted our carriage and we got in and rolled back to the parlor car. I took off my coat, and Alys laughed.

"My hero," she says. I looked down. I had one of my little belly guns stuck in my waistband. Well, you never know.

"How grateful I am," says Digby, "that you did not use that."

The belly gun wasn't accurate at more'n about fifteen feet so it was no use to me anyway, not when Blue Fox was waltzing Alys right up to death. I still couldn't believe how fast the guard had swung his sword—he drew it two-handed with the point down and swung it like that—so fast I still was puzzling on how he managed. Well, Masoud would surely have the best.

We had drinks and cheroots and Alys her Spanish cigarettes and it wasn't no time before the car jerked a little, a yardpuller was moving us out to a train. Digby hadn't been out of my sight, so I suspected Grant. He didn't look like much, as I said, but he had a long damn arm.

"Masoud wished to join us in Wyoming," says Digby. "Under the circumstances, I told him we'd be delighted."

I laughed. Well, with the damned A-rab and his pinto elephants and flunks bearing the best of Abercrombie & Fitch, the Sioux and Cheyennes would leave us the hell alone.

Yellowstone Kelly, Gentleman & Scout, leading a goddamned comic opera after bones so long dead they was stone.

"Well," I says, "I'm all for it. The Sioux and Cheyennes will be laughing so hard it will spoil their aim."

I'd be ribbed for the rest of my life, what the hell.

A whistle blew and we bumped into a coupling and the steam hoses ran the brakes hissed and a smell of hot metal and rubber rose from underneath the car. We began to move, slow, so the train was a fairly long one.

We was all drained, and so not much was said. Alys went off to bathe and me and Digby sat looking at each other a while.

"It don't make no sense," I says, "for me to be slogging through Nicaragua. I never been there and don't know the ways of the country and you'd be better off you had a local guide."

"We'll hire them, of course," says Digby. He was looking off out the window and altogether too innocent.

"Without provokin' a duel," I says, "this would not all easily lie at the feet of that blond wench in there?"

"More whiskey?" says Digby.

I fumed. I was being dragooned into going off to a damn jungle because the president thought Digby and Alys would like that. It warn't *fair*.

"Travel," says Digby, "is broadening."

No use in talking to him about it, the one I was going to chew on good was perfuming herself at the moment.

I liked Digby, and distrusted him, too—oh, it warn't that he had a dishonest drop of blood in his body, it was he was so damn dutiful and noble he was likely going to get killed and me with him. He was actually a good deal more dangerous than an idiot like Custer, at least in the matter of Mrs. Kelly's son Luther.

I went off soon to clean up and sleep, and Alys was already in the bed, lying on her side, her hair still damp from the bath.

When I slid in beside her and breathed deep, about to let go in the matter of how little I appreciated all this, she turned and clung to me and she sobbed and shook and shook and sobbed and she leaked so many tears and sounded so frightened she fetched up manly twinges in me, which I guessed was the whole damned idea.

When she would quiet down I began to say NO NICARAGUA but all I got out was about half the NO.

She wailed and blubbered and wound herself around me and I give up.

Then she laughed, a small giggle.

"You wouldn't *disappoint* me, Luther?" she says.

I swear I'd have wore the hide off her butt if that damned Digby wasn't in the next room.

But I was beat, and I knew it.

CHAPTER 40

Long-dead critters like dinosaurs and woolly mammoths and such was all the rage in Philadelphia, which figures.

Society ladies wore hats with little cloth dinosaur puppets on them and the papers was full of breathless stories about the great Cope and his discoveries in Wyoming.

Cope looked out from the engravings, with such a noble expression on his face he needed some cherubs with trumpets to stand on. I thought I'd mention this to the editor, should I run into him.

His exhibition at the University of Pennsylvania was a society event, and he actually sold tickets to it, fifty dollars each, in the name of disinterested science.

Digby had got tickets, of course, and that afternoon we queued up with the bored rich and filed into the hall. A couple of flunks been with us in Wyoming started when Alys and me come in, but we had them tickets and they didn't know what to do and then we was in and it was too late.

Cope hadn't had time to do much with the specimens he'd sent back, so they was piled here and there still in the plaster, with drawings on easels beside them to let the eager throngs in on what was behind the uninteresting lumps of plaster and rock.

Alys let out a little gasp when she come to one drawing. There was a pale space down in the right corner with some numbers on it, where her name had been rubbed out.

"Adler?" I says.

She nodded grimly.

So here were the drawings she'd snuck out of camp, some of them anyway, now the property of Professor Jonathan Cope.

There was mounted specimens in the hall, too, the biggest a woolly mammoth about fifteen feet tall, the whole skelton wired together and sitting on a steel frame poked up here and there from the wide long plinth it stood on. The tusks was dark brown with yellow streaks and I thought that the West seemed to have been getting tamer for the last thirty thousand years or so. There was also a monstrous bear, much bigger than a grizzly, flat-faced and well supplied with teeth.

Other than the little gasp Alys made no other sound, she just clung to my arm and looked stony-faced at her drawings, both the ones she'd let Cope have and the ones Cope had stolen.

Digby saw friends and he chatted gaily with them, never once letting on how angry he must have been. Not the time for it.

Alys steered me to an exit and Digby was right behind. The appearance was the thing, and having arrived we departed. All

Alys had to say was that after the fossils we would gather in Wyoming soon were exhibited, these bastards would get theirs.

We stopped in New Haven and looked at Marsh's collection, too, and Alys was startled to find some of the drawings she had tried to smuggle out there, too.

"I never thought," she said later, "that the two of them . . ."

This made no sense at all to me, and it's things make no sense that you look for on dangerous ground. Marsh and Cope hated each other, were jealous of every advantage the other gained. It just didn't fit.

Back in Boston Digby wound up his affairs, and Alys saw to replacements of what she needed for the expedition.

I'd long since gone to travelin' with the least I could get away with. Most of that stuff offered by the merchants is worthless anyway, and making time across Indian country you pack just enough to keep you alive. Every ounce on the horse may be a large matter, you just never know.

We had a couple dinners back in the big tent of Masoud's, and I noticed that there seemed to be no sign of him packing. He had plenty of flunks, true, but to move all this was a huge job. The elephants was gone, though, and gardeners was replanting the trees and shrubs that they'd eaten.

I sent a telegram to Lou and Jake to get ready.

Masoud said that Mulligan had already gone. Well, he'd find us if he'd a mind to.

One morning Digby caught me standing outside and he nodded off toward the maze of barbered yew in the backyard and we went there walking slowly.

"Alys wants to be known as a scientist," says Digby, "and that's damn hard for a woman to do. What with the petty jealousies and the ways of the academic world. There are few enough positions as is."

I'd just seen an editorial in the paper by some professor of anatomy said that women's minds were weaker because their brains was smaller and too much learning could derange them. He cited cases of women once hard at work who'd gone mad and been put in asylums as proof.

"Thing bothers me," I says, "is that *both* Cope and Marsh had her drawings, the ones she was trying to smuggle out."

Digby nodded.

"I would expect money is the culprit," he said. "Neither Cope nor Marsh has the stomach for murder, but they don't care how the knowledge and the specimens they want are got."

So that was it. They offered rewards and there was plenty of men in the West would kill for a ten-dollar gold piece. And if the offer was big enough you'd get top talent, easy money, and who gave a damn about some rocks? Rob a bank or a train and you'd have hard men after you. Bushwhack some feller had a dinosaur bone out well past the law's reach, and no one would be the wiser.

"They're both independently wealthy," says Digby. "Most professors are at the great schools. It's another means the wealthy have of keeping control of the country."

I looked at him curious.

"The best students come to Harvard, Yale, the others," said Digby, "and the best aren't necessarily from moneyed families. But this is a means that assures vast abilities may rise. Otherwise they'd be plotting revolution. You know that the rich worry constantly about revolution? Most of them have done nothing to arrive where they are, and the thought that it might all be taken away gives them nightmares."

I could see where it would. I'd had my share of rich fools to guide, and once a damned idiot when we was flat in the middle of trading shots with a party of Cheyennes offered to go out and parley and see what they'd take by way of money to go away.

I damn near let him do it. Now, them Cheyennes didn't know what money *was*, for one thing, and they had no place to spend it if they did have it. It was a long moment before I told him to keep his head down, I doubted they'd be interested.

"I gather that the specimens Alys found when riding with you are exceeding large," says Digby.

I nodded. The biggest of them extinct bastards was a good seventy feet long, and a ton a foot wasn't too low an estimate. A Democrat freightwagon could carry a ton. Seventy wagons, teams for them, the lot, for one dinosaur.

And they was a lot farther north than where Cope and Marsh had been. It was a good twenty days by wagon if they took no time off and there was no interruptions, and there's always interruptions.

"Be hard to get them out before the snow," I says.

"When does it snow there?" says Digby. I'd forgot he'd never been West. "Well," I says, "you can have a blizzard anytime, but the heavy snow comes in December. Or if it's a warm winter it may not come at all. I been six feet under in August there, it's a strange place."

"Could we find men to guard it over the winter?" says Digby.

I shook my head.

"Be safe enough just left," I says. "Washakie'd look after it, and then early as travel could begin in the spring, why then they'd have the summer and all to do it. Probably that's what will happen."

"Do you know honest men?" says Digby.

"Some," I says. "They's rare."

Digby laughed.

I was completely lost, and had no idea where in this barbered hedge we happened to be. Digby sat down on a marble bench.

"We could go to Nicaragua in December, then," he says.

"Shit," I says.

Digby laughed.

"I'm afraid Grant has you by the neck," he says, "and so do I. I'm still a colonel, detached duty. That means . . ."

"Oh," I says, "don't bother explainin'. I *know!*"

We each had a cheroot and then we got up. Digby led us out in about three turns. I'd be in there yet.

Alys saw us and she waved and come out through the French doors.

"My niece is uncommon fond of you," says Digby.

Digby's voice was soft as always, but there was a good bit of steel in that last.

I looked back at the maze.

CHAPTER

41

The East has seemed unreal to me, even when I was growing up in it, and ever since the day I had taken my friend Gus Doane's advice—he was my commanding officer in Minnesota—and rode for the sunset without waiting to be mustered out, the West was my home. I belonged there and I didn't much of anywhere else.

When we got under way to Wyoming, I relaxed some. Blue Fox was dead, it was fall—the best of seasons, and I knew the dangers there. The East was packed with people, and I couldn't read them or the land. It had become a foreign country.

Alys brightened considerably, and she seemed to have shrugged off the loss of the drawings and Herr Adler, or they was buried some. She was tough and determined and that carried her on.

Digby asked thousands of questions, it seemed, and they was good questions. He wanted to know what was, for instance, the list of truly important things to keep in mind when traveling in that high cold dry country.

I told him good clean water, adequate clothing, and a camp could be defended if there was enough guns, or had a lot of ways out if there wasn't.

He wanted to know how Indians fought and I said very well and they was masters of ambush and attack, resonably enough since they had to get every rifle and every bullet from traders who sold dear for robes and furs. Their favorite spots was out in the Plains in country looked all innocent when you was far away and when you got to it there would be draws and coulees, deep enough to hide men and horses, and they would try to rise up when you was on a bald patch and drive you into another band hid in the ground behind you.

"Them damned newspapers," I says, "is always gassing on about what savages they are, and then on to how stupid they are. Well, they are losing their whole world and they are outnumbered and they didn't ask us how to make war and they're plenty smart. And out in the country they only got to be smarter than you the one time."

Digby showed me a brace of pistols he'd carried in the War, British they was, with a stubby shotgun barrel up top held a few ounces of buckshot and a five-shot cylinder below and barrel for bullets. They was heavy, which is an advantage shooting from a horse. Mean-lookin' guns. German, of course.

He asked me about some of the characters I knew like Buffalo Bill and Hickok and Bullwhip Annie, who was this big woman worked as a teamster and who could outfight, outcuss, and outshoot most men on the frontier. The papers was full of Calamity Jane, who was drunk most of the time, But Bull-whip Annie was a Christer and a teetotaler and when she was shooting at Indians she'd touch off a round and then quote the Bible, favoring St. Paul.

Being sober, she tended to hit more of what she aimed at than Calamity did, and the Indians called her Sharp-Eyed Woman and hugged the ground when she unlimbered her buffalo rifle.

Once a passel of drunk nasty hide hunters sneaked up on her intendin' to rape, but found themselves full of bullets, some of them provided by Indians, who divined their intentions and just did not like seein' a warrior of Annie's merits despoiled. Annie whacked the nuts off the ones still alive, while the Sioux cheered. I didn't know what portion of the Bible she'd quote at such a time.

Digby laughed softly.

"Custer is out here somewhere," he says.

"Ah," I says, "Goldilocks. Now there's an idiot going to get himself killed and a lot of troopers with him." I would not myself go more'n half a mile away from town with the bastard—he was just a cold killer, stupid and aggressive, and he killed women and children real easy in his heart.

"I know him," says Digby. "Properly guided, he's useful, but God help troops if he's the officer commanding."

Digby asked me to review the things he'd brought—like a soldier he'd laid them out on a small tarpaulin on the floor of his room. High boots at lower right, the pistols in the center, his saber, a pair of binoculars in a black-leather case with bullet scars on it, a small kit with needles and bandages, and coffee boiled down dry and chopped up so when you put it in water it made coffee and no grounds. Ammunition pouches, a light blanket and the ground cloth and a repeating rifle, one of them revolving carbines gets off nine shots in about seven seconds.

"Very good." I nodded. "One other thing." And I told him that compasses was untrustworthy out here and he should learn to tell where he was by where he'd been, easy in the West with the mountains and all.

Alys brightened considerably when we crossed the Rain Line and the West rose up in sagebrush and grass where there had been trees and corn. Most of Nebraska was still empty, but you couldn't see it from the train, for the farmers come and the closer they was to the railroad the better for them. Or it would have been if the fellers who owned the railroad wasn't so good at fixing freight rates high enough to let the farmers barely hang on for another year but not low enough so that they could put anything by.

But past the Rain Line there was cattle, and few of them could be seen from the train; everything was gnawed down by the railroad for the cattle had to be shipped, too.

We stopped in Cheyenne for a couple of hours and we three got out and walked around to stretch our legs and damned if a mob of fools in red coats and white breeches didn't gallop past behind a mixed pack of hounds and terriers. They was after a coyote who led them on, wholly unworried. Coyotes is smart, and I suspected in time they would learn to draw the toffs into bands of Indians and damned if that didn't happen not a half hour after they'd passed.

There was the sound of rifle fire a few miles north and it quit quick enough and Digby looked at me and I looked at him and we busted out laughing.

"I am sure," says Digby, "that the coyote survived."

In about fifteen minutes a bunch of men mobbed up on horses and rode off toward where all the ruction come from and we heard no more gunfire. In half an hour or so they started to trickle back, long faces on them and the smallest men with a body over the saddle in front of them, limp and boneless.

A troop of cavalry finally headed out after the Indians, but they never could catch them except when they was stuck in winter camp. Then if they could sneak up they'd kill mostly old folks, women and children, and count it a victory. But they never did even once catch the warriors by just ridin' after them.

Red Cloud had said to me once that fighting the whites was so very easy. The blew a horn, he said, when they woke up, when they ate, when they rode out, when they were ready to charge, and so the Sioux could go on playing mumblety-peg or scratching their arses and then mount up and be gone.

We was headed back to the parlor car when there was a bugle off to the east and damned if it wasn't Custer and his unlucky troops parading in after, I guessed, once again finding no Indians at all except old people ready to die anyway. The ancient Sioux when they decided they'd had enough of life would sometimes stay in camp and keen insults until the troopers cut them down. The interpreters was Metis—them Frenchy-Indian mixed bloods from the Red River of the North country, and knowing what the oldsters was up to they'd faithfully translate until some brave soldier split the old person's head in half with a saber.

I was feeling real sour when I mentioned this, and Digby looked sad and said he doubted if most of the soldiers cared anything at all for any of this.

That shamed me. Oh, I hated what was happening here, but Custer and a few others was almost unique in their murderousness and the officers and men of the Army hated the whole damned business and it was not right of me to tar them all with Custer's behaviors.

But you get a bunch of scared-to-death boys shooting and it sort of takes on its own life, that bloodlust, and it ain't confined to any particular Army or people. Just the lousy human race.

"We'd do well to act the way the British do," says Digby. "When they run the Union Jack up the flagpole the natives have rights and standing in the courts. It ain't perfect, but it has to be better than treating mere tribes as nations and disregarding the treaties as soon as that can be done."

"America is money," I says. "We worship it, and when there is money to be made nothing else matters."

We got to Laramie in the early evening and my rooms was still mine, though when I took Alys to them I smelled perfume and so the hotel had kept an eye peeled for me while renting the rooms out, but they'd kept a close eye on my things so I couldn't really complain.

Alys was tired and said she'd sleep a little so I went on down to the lobby and found Digby and we went out and I showed him the better saloons.

We was standing at the bar having a snort in one of them when a drunk bellered that there was gold a-plenty in the Black Hills.

That meant the death of the Sioux. They was a great people and I was sad, for they had been true friends when they wasn't trying to kill me.

"You were here when it was good," says Digby.

I nodded.

Yes, I had, and now it was to be chawed up like the whites had done everything else.

Wyoming was full of stinking-water springs. I supposed it would not be long till there was resorts there, where fat idiots could take the waters and mud baths.

Couldn't say I thought it was an improvement.

CHAPTER 42

Digby stayed in the parlor car and me and Alys in my suite of rooms, so as to not be too much in each other's pockets. I was just weary from the trip East and I spent most of the next two days dozing and even missed having lunch the second day with Digby and Alys, though they promised fresh oysters which is a food I love above all else.

So there I was sleeping when there come this fearful racket out in the hall and a pounding on the door and I come up from slumber ready to kill because the voice belonged to Buffalo Bill and he was drunk as usual.

"Why ain't you in Denver at Big Bessie's gettin' your damn bell rope pulled," I snarls through the door.

"Open up, Kelly," says Bill. "Me and the prince would have a word with you."

I opened the door, glaring at Bill. Masoud and his two guards was right behind this drunken clotheshorse. I thought I saw the barest of smiles on Masoud's lips.

Nothing Buffalo Bill liked better than an audience and I seen him perform to a deaf-mute once as there was no one else about he had not completely worn out.

Having a prince of Araby to play to would likely keep him going till Masoud got tired of him. I wondered if our friendship was deep enough so I could quietly propose that Masoud's guards behead Cody, but I expected I would not get far. Ah well, where are your friends when you need 'em?

Bill was in new clothes, a fringed beaded coat, white duck pants tucked into thigh-high cavalry boots, a creamy new Monarch of the Plains Stetson hat, and jewelry. Lots of jewelry. He was favoring silk waistcoats and sashes these days.

"No ostrich plumes." I says, looking at his hat.

You can't insult the man, he just don't hear it, and God knows I have tried.

"Together again!" says Bill, throwing an arm around my shoulders.

Now the only time we'd ever been together was when we was tied up in the Hitchfoot Hotel behind a saloon once. The owner was one of them smart sorts and he cared deeply that his customers not die on him, at least till they was broke, and me and Bill had got grass-grabbing drunk and passed out and I woke up with my right foot tied up to an eyebolt in the wall. I was lyin' on fairly fresh sawdust only puked in a little.

The barkeep had figured out that his customer, having drink taken and likely to die of exposure or an enterprising skunk gnawing him to death, could be kept safe from harm and when said customer was sober enough to reach up and untie his foot he was sober enough to stagger back into the saloon and spend more money.

While we was so inconvenienced Bill give me the full story of his life, as I frantically scrabbled and clutched at the rope to get away from his flowery lies, and after that session I had vowed never to be caught outcountry with him. He was brave and no denyin' that, but bravery is common where brains isn't and dyin' a noble death was not something I aspired to. Even if I did have my own paragraph in Cody's latest pack of lies. Hear him tell it he done defeated about every great warrior the Sioux, Cheyennes, Arapahoes, Apaches, and so forth had in mortal combat before picking his vanquished enemy up off the ground and handing him a Bible to comfort him in defeat.

I could think of about a hundred Sioux I knew would make very short work of him and resolved if I could arrange for Bill to meet them, it was sort of a public duty.

"We shall ride with our brothers, the horsemen of Araby," says Bill.

"What happened to the elephants?" I says.

"They all died," says Masoud. "It was foolish to bring them, but it was thought nothing less would do for me to ride."

I thought of Masoud at Cambridge, in his student gown, riding his damn elephant off to class.

"The press is fascinated with our quest," says Bill.

"Excuse me," I says to Masoud, and I swung and caught Bill on the point of his chin and he crashed into the sideboard and slid down and blinked at me.

"The press," I says, "is to stay away from us, if you mean to come along with me."

"It's the American story," says Bill, getting up.

"He don't come," I says to Masoud. "Can't trust him."

"I have never lied to you!" whines Bill.

"That ain't the problem," I says. "Now why don't you just mount up and head for Big Bessie's."

"But Luther," says Bill, looking all stricken, "we's friends."

"Damn it," I says to Masoud. "I am the one got to get us in and out alive and I do not need ol' Bill here speechifying when silence is our best bet."

He had been done in by fame. I had seen it happen to others.

Masoud nodded, and he went to Bill and spoke softly and Bill brightened a little. I assumed he was being paid off.

Bill give me a hurt look and walked out and Masoud burst into laughter, rich and roaring. I had never so much as heard the prince chuckle before and assumed he didn't do that sort of thing.

"Afternoon, Luther," says Digby from out in the hall. He come in, and the grin told me everything.

"I ain't never had an enemy do much to me," I says, "but my friends is a whole other matter."

"Had you goin'," says Digby. Him and Masoud was real thick.

"He leaving for Denver?" I says. I had an interest in it.

"No," says Masoud, "he's to stay here and announce our discoveries to the press. My harem has been sent home, so he will have to make do with Rosie's, but I somehow think he'll manage."

"You actually think he'll stay put," I says. I had visions of Bill at the head of a regiment of reporters thundering north. Pay him and top him up with good whiskey and he would, too.

"If he stays here," says Masoud, "his expenses, including Rosie's, will be met, but he only gets paid if he does not leave until our return. Should he follow us, the agreement is null and void."

"We couldn't just kill him?" I says hopefully.

Masoud shook his head.

"Schoolchildren would weep," he says, "if their hero died."

"Well," I says, "I hope the poor little bastards never get to know that son of a bitch."

"He means well," says Digby.

My mother used that phrase, by which I believe she meant that though the damned fool might get us killed he had no malice in him. I never will understand women, especially the Irish ones.

"Means well!" I snarls. "God help us all."

Bill seemed to be safely pinned in place so I shrugged and let it pass.

I heard Alys come up the stairs and she was cussing like a blacksmith got a mule standing on his foot. It was eloquent and heartfelt and I heard her mention Marsh and Cope and their mothers and offspring in passing.

Digby grinned.

Alys swept into the room carrying a few newspapers, and she stuck her pretty finger on some articles said that both Cope and Marsh had announced the discovery of a huge meat-eating dinosaur.

"All the time we've been gone," she says, "their paid prospectors have been digging and sending back specimens. God damn them."

Digby looked at one of the articles carefully and he nodded and finished it and he held up a hand so Alys might stop cussing and it took her a moment to wind down but she did.

"It seems that this beast," says Digby, "is indeed quite large but if I recall the one you found has a skull seven feet or so long and this one is about four."

Cope had provided a sketch for his find, a mean-looking bastard all teeth and head.

Alys calmed right down.

"You're right," she says. "It's not the same."

"I think," says Digby, "perhaps it would be wise to go and exhume your giants, and then allow Luther to arrange for the transport next year. We could pay men to guard the place through the winter."

I heaved a sigh of relief. Pay enough money and you can get men to do anything, but that didn't mean that a blizzard wouldn't wipe the teamsters out and leave the wagons full of the sort of riches Cope and Marsh would pay very highly for.

"That can be done easier than the other," I says. "I've mentioned it before."

Alys didn't like it. I could see her point. Here was what she wanted most in the world and to get it out and safely locked up was real important, and she wouldn't rest easy till it was done.

"How far is it?" says Masoud. "I have good horses. I expect to travel simply."

"Ten to twenty days for horses," I says. "Depends on the weather and the Indians."

"Wagons?" says Masoud.

"Fifty or sixty this time of year," I says. I went on to explain about the gumbo mud forms when it gets wet. Dry land turns to grease and a man can't walk too far before the mud on his boots stops him cold.

"I want to go now," says Alys.

"Just as soon as we can," says Digby.

CHAPTER 43

"No," I says.

"But Kelly," says Masoud, "you recommended it so highly. Surely you had a good reason."

Play a little joke and it comes back to haunt you.

Masoud, that A-rab son of a bitch, had the Abercrombie & Fitch Highly Revolving Duck Plucker loaded up and ready to go, in a cart drawn by a pair of A-rab horses, which is not what I'd choose for a draft animal.

Digby was standing next to the thing, idly spinning the wheel. The little rubber fingers wiggled, reaching for a duck.

"You have some use for this we don't know of?" says Digby. He was grinning, like you do when you find a good friend tossed off a horse.

"All right, all right," I says, "I was funnin' a little. Masoud was about the strangest dude I ever encountered and he was waving that damned catalog at me so I . . ."

The cart was all gilt and ivory and ebony, probably worth enough to buy a large ranch and the cows for it.

"I will take it," says Masoud, "as a memory of our first meeting."

I threw my hands up.

"I'm honored," I says.

"No doubt," says Masoud, "as I am."

Time might be gettin' short for us, and so we was packing and getting ready for the ride. Jake was hiring three other men and would come later with two wagons and enough grub and blankets to live the winter through. They'd guard the fossils till the late spring, when a train of wagons could come to remove them and ship them down to the railhead.

Buffalo Bill galloped past, white hair streaming in the wind, all fringe and beads. He was a hell of a horseman when he was sober. I figured he was displaying his gorgeousness so we'd relent and let him come with us.

I knew him well. Too bad. Oh, I liked Bill, he was one of the kindest men on earth, but ever since the penny dreadfuls had made him famous he was impossible. Fame does that to folks, I have often noticed.

"How 'bout we take a photograph of that there Highly Revolving Duck Plucker?" I says. "You could hold it up when you felt it was necessary to embarrass me. Work just as well."

"Forbidden by my religion," says Masoud with a straight face. "Photographs are graven images."

You always knows when your friends are up to something when their faces is straight and they are solemn as owls. I didn't have any idea what was up, but there was a stink of conspiracy about that would fair knock your hat in the creek.

"Okay," I says, "I got it, and you fellers best mind your backs as the best defense is an offense and bein' offensive is something I practice. Not perfectly, as I find myself with you two bastards headin' into Indian country to gather rocks, but hell if I didn't try."

I'd hired on a muleskinner and his five best friends to pack supplies to us. A mule could carry two hundred pounds or more a long damn ways and though there would be wagons moving supplies as far north as fast as they could, the broken country could hold up a wagon for a damn week where a packer with a string would move easily through. There was rain here, of course, not a lot, but it often came in great soaking storms, and there was countless coulees and gullies cut by flash floods.

There was a couple of flunks in uniforms specially designed to announce they was the Keepers of the Highly Revolving Duck Plucker. The crest on their turbans was a duck with a bare ass and the rest feathered and a blur of what initiates would recognize as speeding rubber fingers.

"An awful expensive joke," I says.

"My subjects give me my weight in precious gems once a year," says Masoud, "on top of the oppressive taxes they pay."

"Must love you a lot," I says.

"Oh, they do, they do," says Masoud.

I shrugged. That goddamned Highly Revolving Duck Plucker was going to follow me the rest of my days, and there was no helping that. Then I thought it might spare me the vaudeville circuit, which a lot of my friends was on, a hazard of them penny dreadfuls. Being so corrupt, you see, I *can* be bought.

Then I had one of them flashes of inspiration I get just often enough so I stay alive.

"We could make a gift of it to the Sioux," I says. "It's just the sort of handy thing they like."

"Oh, really?" says Masoud. "What a brilliant thought."

I looked at that six-foot-six bastard with the gob of silk on his noggin and I put on my most solemn face.

"Why, yes," I says.

Masoud nodded. There was never even a flicker across his face, of mirth or devilment.

It had been right rude of me to suggest to the gullible prince this ridiculous implement, but I'd done it and he had me and damned if I was going to let on now that I knew he'd let me make a fool of myself and he warn't prepared to forget it.

The Highly Revolving Duck Plucker ran out of use as a conversation piece and we went back to the lists of supplies, double-checking everything. There was, for instance, an entire twenty-mule pack train for whiskey, two kegs to a mule, except three which had better stuff in patented india-rubber bags with spigots.

Digby knew soldiers and he knew men, and the other thirty-four kegs was there to assure the three with our booze got through.

Them muleskinners stank like distilleries, and with a steady diet of dust and mule kicks I couldn't blame them. The West was a place back then where about four out of five men was more or less drunk more or less all of the time. We didn't have much by the way of pecksniffs. But they'd be along. They always are.

We finished the lists about four in the afternoon. Alys had come for the last hour or so, all her sketching materials and journals in a couple of leather trunks, small so they'd fit on a horse.

She looked at that damned duck plucker and let out a bellow and that finally touched off Masoud and Digby, and they bellered. I had to laugh, too.

Well, it was pretty damn funny.

We would ride out in the morning, me, Alys, Digby, Masoud, and a mixed lot of rascals, some of them mine, armed to the teeth and known to the country, and Masoud's thugs in their robes and scimitars and them long rifles called *jezzails*. Other than the costumes they all looked pretty much alike.

The lists was checked and the skinners was doing final checks on their tack and they'd load up before dawn and we'd leave then. Digby and Alys and me went up to the better saloon for a drink. Masoud begged off, since he'd invited us to supper and needed to go and look over the food. Though he was generous with booze to his guests, he never drank, and said he followed Mohammed's rule. No pork. No alcohol.

Jake was there and Lou and Whinny and we drunk a toast to Sir Henry. Blue Fox was dead all right, but it didn't help. Sir Henry was an odd and murderous duck, but we had a lot of them folks, and all we asked of them was that they keep their word and Sir Henry did.

Digby was immediately accepted, and I thought what a hell of a colonel of cavalry he must have been, for he put on no airs and he bought some drinks, enough to be sociable but not so many as to leave the boys feelin' obligated. They was not inclined to like the rich much—as a group they're pretty awful you will admit—but it turned out Whinny had been a sergeant in another brigade and he'd heard of Digby and so pretty soon they was refighting the whole damn war and so I tipped my hat and said good evening and Alys took my arm and we walked out to the warm night. It would be cold soon enough, and usually was even in September after the sun went down, but that evening the air come up from the south and it was damp enough so your skin didn't feel parched and stretched.

Alys wanted to walk down the boardway to the spot where Adler had his shop, and so we sauntered on. A bullbat clacked past overhead—there was a couple of gaslights now—and the bird was gorging on the moths attracted to the glow.

The hole where the little German's shop had been was cleaned out and there was lumber piled there, so someone was going to build a shop. Laramie was growing and it would a while, anyway, the West was a place for druggists and dry goods merchants as well as cowboys and the vanishing Indians.

We'd seen and turned when there was a shot and it hit me, just a shallow furrow across my shoulders and it missed Alys's neck by not much. The wound burned like hell and I had left my guns in the rooms, but Alys had hers and she had it out and she was blazing at an alleyway across the street while tugging me on. We dived behind a water trough and it warn't long before a lot of folks with shotguns and rifles showed up.

Digby and Masoud and the boys was some of them, and Digby got them white flecks at his eyes and the wings of his nostrils.

The fellers searched but found nothing.

Whoever it was had taken the one shot and gone.

Digby cleaned my long shallow wound carefully and put ointment on, so it wouldn't crack and bleed as I rode. I'd ridden with much worse.

We would leave in the morning.

What bothered me was I didn't know if it was me or Alys the bullet had been meant for.

CHAPTER 44

We passed the burned station on the way, about four that afternoon. It was like it was, and the graves had been dug at by coyotes, but they was deep enough so the bodies was still down there. It ain't always the case.

There was a spring five miles past large enough to water the stock, with grass in plenty. Even though the fire had come close enough, on the prairie the grass grows faster after a burn. The Indians had long known that, and they set fires because it brought game. They knew their country.

I rode a long circle around, but saw no sign there was anyone been camped waiting on us, just a few piles of them rocks Indians put up on boulders so they can peek through and not have their heads show.

I was full of heart, even with the gouge in my back. I loved it here, the huge sky and the air so clear you could see miles.

Toward evening I come on some antelope, and I shot one and gutted it and carried it back to camp, where Masoud's cook made chops out of it in about three minutes. Then he boned them and rolled the chops in garlic and herbs and grilled them. They was delicious.

We was traveling light, no wall tents, just tarps, and even Masoud had an ordinary canvas, though the precious rugs was brought and comfortable down-filled blankets. His guards stood all night like statues and slept on their horses by day.

The next morning we went on ahead, while the skinners packed up and made the air blue with encouragements to their stock to behave, which is not a mule's natural intentions. Other than the noise, the skinners was gentle with the animals and rough as the men were they liked their beasts. Also, you abuse a mule it will accept that and wait, years if necessary, for that one kick that can kill. They are smarter than horses.

The weather was fall and perfect and the alders and cottonwoods had turned color and prairie chickens broke from the cover near us and Masoud swung an expensive shotgun and brought down bird after bird. I'd have been leery of shooting from the back of a horse, but the big black A-rab he rode didn't even twitch.

Masoud had threatened to take that goddamned duck plucker right up to the last minute, finally ordering the flunks to stand down and take the damned thing back to the big tent. I was part relieved but worried since lacking that I expected Digby and Masoud to come up with other annoyances.

We come up over a rise and saw buffalo below and I shook my head. We didn't need that much meat, and the skinners still had the roasts of beef they'd left Laramie with, partly cooked and rolled in rock salt. They would keep up to two weeks if the weather warn't too warm. After we got short enough of grub we could kill a fat cow, but I knew the warning Red Cloud had given me stood. I remembered the tongues of the German party on the thong.

Whinny was off looking over the country and I saw him wave from up a hill off to the west and so I rode on over to see what he wanted.

There was a couple of dead men behind the hill, they'd been staked out and had fires lit on their chests. Enough of their clothes hadn't burned so we could see they was wearing suits, for the love of God, and I gathered from the busted pencils and blank paper scattered about they was newspaper reporters.

I looked round the ground and figured maybe eight bored young Cheyenne warriors off on a horse-stealing lark had happened on these two fools and done this and wandered on.

The coyotes and birds and skunks had been at the corpses good, so Whinny and I shrugged. We had better things to do than plant idiots, there was country to see before sundown and our charge was the living.

What they was doing here I couldn't guess, but it often happened that pilgrims like these would just up and wander off thinking they was somehow exempt. The lucky ones, and there were a lot of them, made it through and they never understood how you could come on a war party you'd have missed if you left your last camp a couple hours before or after.

We went back, each carrying another antelope, in time for Masoud's cook to work his wonders again, and as we come in I seen we'd been joined by a goddamn preacher and three sallow assistants.

The fool ranted a while about saving the souls of the Sioux

and how it was our Christian duty to assist him in getting far enough north so he could pester them perfectly happy folk before winter set in.

This lunatic then looked round for heathen to convert, and his pale blue eye landed on Masoud and he fell to his knees calling on the Lord to help him save the Savage Turk.

The Savage Turk listened politely to this rot a while but when the preacher tried to come close enough to whack him with his damned Bible the guards flicked up their scimitars and cut off the exhortations in mid-howl.

"I am quite happy with Allah," says Masoud civilly enough, "but just today Digby remarked that he felt his soul was in peril."

The preacher then took off after Digby, who finally pulled out his Navy Colt and said his soul was in fine shape now shut up.

I didn't feel we needed to have our sleep broke by this fool's bellerin' to Jesus all the damned night so I told him he'd done worn out his welcome and to take his traps and flunks and go away, far enough so we didn't have to hear him calling on the Lord.

" 'Sides," I says, "them Sioux been long familiar with Christ. A couple hundred years ago Father Brulé come to spread the word. Now, he wouldn't make medicine to help the Sioux steal horses or get scalps in battle or nothing useful, but they was impressed by the single-mindedness with which Father Brulé pursued their souls. They held a council and did adopt him into the tribe, sort of."

The preacher looked at me.

"They are not completely lost, then," he says. "I thank you, my friend, and I shall pray for your soul."

"Neither is Father Brulé," I says, "since the Sioux et him.

He is even got a memorial back in Minnesota the Sioux gave him. It's called Place-Where-We-Shit-The-Blackrobe, a day's journey away from where the feast was held."

The fool goggled at me for a moment like a turkey seen something it can't figure out, cocking his head this way and that, and then the whole damned camp broke out in howls and bellers of laughter and men was slamming each other on the back and the preacher and his flunks went all pale and they got back on their horses.

They didn't have but a couple pack animals, and overloaded at that, so they'd run out of grub in a week or so and then they'd either starve to death or run into a war party.

In a final burst of genius I rode after them and pointed the way to the two somewhat charred journalists, as folks who could use a good sermon over them before being buried.

That was far enough away so we'd be spared, and them two fellers the Cheyennes had killed was past having theological disputes.

Masoud's cook had a big pot of stew bubbling and the smell of onions come off it, and then it occurred to me we hadn't packed any, and I tried to find out from the man where he'd got them.

Masoud finally come over and he translated, and it seemed this feller had found a whole patch of wild onions not far from the spring and he'd dug them up and they was in with the antelope now, cooking right nice.

I told Masoud they was likely death camas, the two kinds grow right together and one is a root and the other a poison. So we dumped the mess in a little hollow and covered it over with stones and when we come back the cook was setting there by the fire and a big pool of blood under him. He'd been shamed, hell, he'd almost killed his prince. He'd jabbed a dagger into his throat and cut the jugular and then he'd sat there till he died.

"I forgave him," says Masoud, "but it wasn't enough."

He looked real sad.

"Lots of folks out here don't know the country end up eating them camas and thinking they are wild onions," I says. "I found most of an emigrant train dead or dying once. They had scurvy and they thought the wild onions was a godsend."

I was sure as hell going to miss the cook, but damned if Jake didn't try his hand and he managed to make antelope in little chunks on skewers of willow and a couple Dutch oven loaves of bread and that with some dried fruit was pretty good.

We was tired and turned in early, the light was failing now and every moment we had was useful.

I was to sleep in Alys's arms and along toward dawn there was a tug on my shirt and I whirled around and had my gun coming up and I smelled Mulligan, who had been far enough away from his bath he had his own stink back.

I slipped out and saddled my horse and Mulligan led me away from the camp, over the hill four or five miles away where the two journalists had died and the preacher and his flunks was to camp.

"They come about two maybe, by the Dipper," says Mulligan. "One warrior for each man, I guess. Just used war clubs; they was too close to you to do any torturin'."

The four had been brained and scalped and mutilated, as usual.

Mulligan had watched it, of course, but there wasn't a thing he could do.

CHAPTER 45

Us folks who was paying for and runnin' the expedition could travel light and fast, but we was held by the mule train and the need for the protection of the skinners and packers. You never really could know what the Indians was up to, and it was a mistake to think that the chiefs was dictators. The tribes ran somewhat on the advice of people like Red Cloud and Spotted Tail and Bull Shield, but it was finally just advice and the young warriors was like young men pretty much anywhere, all fire and few brains. Wars depend on having ample supplies of stupid young men who know they're immortal.

We could roam some, as long as if we was attacked we could draw the others in hearing our gunfire. Digby had enough sense to know this, and if he could keep Alys from going that extra half mile it might mean the difference between life or death. It was hard for her, when she'd spot a layer of that yellow-brown rock that the fossils was usually in and want to go look and it was just a little too far.

Mulligan would slip into camp likely wriggling between the sentry's legs for the sport of it, and he kept me up on who was near and passing by. I'd get up and make up some cold grub for him and give him a twist of the cheap tobacco we had as a gift for the Indians and he'd be gone. He didn't come I would worry some, that my best ears was threaded on a thong somewheres, but he'd come in a day or two and allow as how when he had nothing to say he would not say it.

Without wagons we could move pretty fair, and if the trail was open and didn't have too much by way of good ambush spots had to be checked before the long train could file through, we could manage thirty miles most days.

I never had liked them A-rab horses, thinking they was flighty and easily winded, which was true, but you had to ride them some different than our stock. They was fast and needed a rest exactly every so often, and Masoud and his men know that and once I began to follow their rhythms even my horses worked better. I felt a little foolish, but Masoud said that his people were people of the horse and had been for thousands of years. He rode like he was part of the animal, for sure, more graceful than a big man should be.

But then when we was about eight days out we come right to a bank of clay that had been stone before it rotted and there was bones weathering out of it and Alys gave off a whoop and she was down off her horse peering at them and clapping her hands.

They was a mixed bag of camels, horses, and, so help me, hippopotamuses. With one long terrible fang used to belong to an overgrown mountain lion. Mountains lions aren't given to attack people, but I was right glad this one was extinct. That fang was a good eight inches long.

I thought we might make camp there, but Alys said the bones was from critters that was known to science and nice enough but what we was after were the two monsters that Washakie had shown us, locked together in the stone.

Alys said that them two hadn't died together, that they was killed somehow and their carcasses was in the water and when they bloated up they floated off to a sandbar on the ocean she said used to be here. If they were on land something would eat them and if they was out to sea something would eat them, but at the river's mouth nothing could and so they was buried many millions of years ago.

I couldn't quite believe all of this, for we was a good mile above sea level, but she assured me the earth moved around a lot given enough time. She pointed at Africa and South America on a map and said they was stuck together once. Well, they did fit like that.

Like any boy raised by doting parents I had had parsons try to scare me into good behavior and they was always ranting about how God just made up everything one week, but this was a lot more marvelous than having some Thing men dreamed up. It seemed right.

I could see why science was thought to be enthralling. The secrets of the world was being unraveled.

We went on the next day and a couple Shoshones out scouting buffalo come to camp. I knew them as Washakie's people, and they said he was still camped on the Wind River and waiting on us. I give them some tobacco and they asked for whiskey. I refused. The old chief knew well what firewater did to his people, and he would be angry with me I poisoned these two youngsters. Oh, they'd get it somewheres else, but I couldn't stop that.

At night the wind would quarter around to the north and it smelt of pines and snow. It would be winter already up high, and could be winter down here anytime. You never can tell. If we wasn't hit by the blizzards the old-timers talked of in '46, when there was eight feet of snow and blizzards for weeks and the sun never came up without two sun dogs, one to either side, we could have even up to three weeks or a month there and still get out before the deep cold, which seemed to come in January, the month the Indians call the Moon of Exploding Trees.

One morning the sentry started hollering and I went off to the noise and he was pointing at a lone Indian off on a hilltop a couple miles away, and I squinted hard and made out the long white hair and the full formal dress of the great chief of the Shoshones, Washakie. He carried a rifle and nothing else, and the man's force was enough even at that distance to put a scare into the young skinner standing guard.

Washakie was far too smart to fight the whites, and so his people was spared the slaughters more belligerent tribes brought down on themselves. He knew he couldn't win, and that was that and so he did what he could.

Not long back some of his young men called him an old woman for not letting them take revenge on some miners who let their hogs root up the camas meadows that was the Shoshones potatoes.

Washakie disappeared for a month and he come back with seven scalps taken from the Blackfeet and Crows, and he had to be over seventy when he did it.

Having made his impression Washakie walked his horse slow down the hill and toward us, taking his own damn sweet time and every eye in the camp on him. Well, a passel of howling warriors in paint was one thing but this tall straight old man was even scarier, just alone and coming on and not a care.

We watched fascinated and Washakie dug his heels into his horse's flanks and come on at the last at a gallop, riding like he was on a stuffed chair, loose and easy, and he rode right up to Digby and Alys and he stopped the horse cold and slid down, graceful as a cat, and he grinned at them. Alys threw her arms around him and she kissed the old bastard and they beamed at each other a moment and then she introduced him to Digby.

I went over and watched the old goat turn on the charm. Alys and Washakie was beaming at Digby and she rattling away about what a wonderful man the chief was.

"But," I says, "I have known the chief for many years and . . . he cheats at cards."

Washakie gave me a bored look.

"Kelly," he says, "loses at cards, which is worse."

Masoud had been watching all this and he come over with his two guards who was never more than a sword's length away from him.

Washakie looked at the prince of Arabia and them two knew each other, master in their own lands and no mistake. And then the damnedest thing—Masoud bowed. A courtesy, I figured, from one prince to another.

This odd scene was then interrupted.

There was a yell from back down the trail and I turned and saw about the last damn thing I cared to see here and now.

Buffalo Bill, the Great Scout of the Plains, was riding hard toward us, on one of them big damned white horses he favors, so he'd stick out.

His fringes was flapping in the breeze and he was standing up in his stirrups, and had a lance and pennon, with what I guessed would be his own personal coat of arms, this from a farmboy raised amid the hogs and chickens in royal Iowa.

Cody sure looked the part, that is if you wanted to draw the attention of every pair of eyes could see you. Difference between Cody and Washakie was Washakie could dress modestly and act the same while poor old Bill had to be got up like some actor in vaudeville.

I looked at Cody again.

He was rocking back and forth a little.

Drunk. Well, like I said, we mostly was back then.

Cody kept on coming, his hair a-flying and that little pennon snapping in the breeze.

He thundered through the pack train behind us, making a few of the mules buck, and the skinners added heartfelt cussing to the noise of his passage.

Cody kept coming on, and it occured to me he might be drunk enough to trample anyone in his patch, so I sort of took Alys's arm and tugged her back and Masoud come to the same conclusion and so did Washakie. Digby, too.

When Bill got close he pulled his horse up, so he could do his patented rearing act on the big white gelding.

But his timing was off and the horse stopped dead and Cody flew over the animal's head, turning in the air and crashing down on his back hard enough so the bushes quivered nearby.

There he was, out cold.

"I could just cut his throat," I says.

"The poor man might be dead!" says Alys.

Cody let out a frightful snore, sounded like a walrus with a bad sinus infection.

"Ah," says Washakie, "our good friend."

Masoud shook his head, but he was smiling.

CHAPTER 46

We'd eaten the loads off a couple of mules so the skinners rigged up a pad and we hung Bill over the mule and tied him on so he wouldn't maybe fall off and hurt something. He was sleeping right peaceful and my original suggestion, that we just hang him upside down from the neartest cottonwood was met with them sort of stares tell you that you're bein' unsporting.

"I thought he was your friend," says Alys.

"Oh, a bosom chum," I says, "and he'd understand he woke up hung by the ankles. Why, if I presented him an opportunity like that, well, he'd take it."

It was about noon and Washakie said if we rode now, we'd make his camp by dark. The skinners could come along in the morning, but for tonight there was a dance we was to be honored guests at and besides I knew Washakie was bored and wishing to charm folks some. And here he had lovely Alys, Digby, and Masoud. Me, he knew better.

Digby and Masoud wanted to take Bill along, but I said no, we had to travel and it suited me not to have that son of a bitch until tomorrow, as he was so potted he'd still be drunk when he woke up.

So it was just me and Alys, Digby, Masoud, and his two guards, and Washakie.

Washakie led and then when we was maybe a couple miles from camp the trail widened as it went straight across a plain and I rode on up ahead and got near the old chief who glanced back at the folks following and then said something that made me damn near fall off my horse.

"Blue Fox is near," says Washakie.

That was impossible. I'd seen his head. I watched the guard swing his sword, it could not be—and yet the face I had looked at was mostly red scars and healed flesh.

I swore and swore.

When we stopped at a spring to let our horses rest for a few minutes and drink I went to Digby and Masoud and told them.

"He's vowed to kill me," I says. "And crazy as he is he'll kill Alys and try to kill you before he kills me. The man's insane."

Masoud looked a little uncomfortable. I didn't want to embarrass the prince, but I nodded off and we walked a hundred yards away and I asked what was he fussed over.

"The man who tried to kill me at the ball was known to us," says Masoud, "a man from a sect sworn to kill all of my family."

I was enraged.

Masoud looked at my face, and he held up his hands.

"It pleased you to think it was this Blue Fox," he says, "so we let you think so."

"Digby know?" I says.

Masoud shook his head.

"I am sorry, Kelly," he says. "It seemed of no moment at the time, and of course on the journey we are well protected."

The country around that had been so lovely only moments before now only held menace. I had no idea why Blue Fox was so damned intent on killing me, and I couldn't for the life of me understand why this had all started. I had killed few Cheyennes, and that in honorable combat, and no one in that damned tribe held a thing against me but Blue Fox.

I looked rapidly round trying to see places where a sharp-shooter could set up. Damn, damn, damn.

"My young men are to either side of us," says Washakie, "so you are safe. But you must guard and well."

"Blue Fox," I says. "When did you hear this?"

"I *saw* it," says Washakie. "He was riding north and I came upon him and he cut from the trail, driving his remounts before him. There were fresh scalps on his saddle."

"Just him?" I says.

Washakie nodded.

"The Cheyennes wish him dead, too," says the old chief. "He came on some young women by the Platte River, and he killed them. He is mad. He is dangerous."

I looked at Washakie.

"My horse was tired," says the old chief. "I would have chased and killed him, but he had fresh horses and I only one."

Digby and Alys had joined us and so we let the matter drop. No use in spreading panic any farther than me for now. I was good at what I did, but Blue Fox had the advantage. He was mad, and sometimes that makes men more animals than men, with an animal's sense of night and cover.

We mounted up and went on, and I recalled a place where the trail led through a long defile barely wide enough for a man and horse, a good quarter mile and then it opened again, but there was all sorts of places to hide up and wait. That's what a hunter does, wait, and if Blue Fox was up top and us below he would be many miles gone before we could pursue.

There was Washakie's young warriors, and I hoped they knew their damned job.

"We will go around that place," says Washakie. He could read other's minds, I was sure of that.

I nodded. We were in his country and perhaps he was great enough to outfox even that mad Cheyenne. Blue Fox scared me more than any other man I have ever known. He would scare anyone. He warn't human.

And now he was so far gone his own people would kill him if they could find him.

"Mulligan is out there somewheres," I says suddenly.

Washakie laughed.

"He came to see me three days ago," he says. "We played chess."

"So does Masoud," I says, remembering the board by his divan in the big blue tent.

"Ah!" says Washakie, happy at last.

In an hour I could see the gap where the hills reached down close to the plain and the trail was choked off, and Washakie went east on a narrow trail and past a few buffalo wallows and then we began to climb up a strange slanting gangplank of rock, clear to a pass where we could see many miles to the east and west.

On the south side of the narrow place we'd avoided I suddenly saw the bastard, rising up out of the ground and then ducking behind a long slab of rock and then he came out mounted with three horses I recognized from the parson's party. Blue Fox must have killed the young warriors. He was pure evil now.

He moved off south, pushing the remounts ahead of him, and then I saw Mulligan riding like he meant to cut him off. The little man come to a place of vantage and he slid down and run up this pile of rocks, carrying his buffalo rifle and he laid down up top and waited for Blue Fox to reappear.

He never did. There was no damned way he could have got past Mulligan, he had gone to ground there, and then I saw Blue Fox and he had doubled back and was going to cut his own trail and move off east.

It was too damn far for my voice to carry and so I put a cloth on a stick and waved it frantically, which gave me something to do, but Mulligan had his mind on Blue Fox and would soon know the bastard would be heading elsewhere.

"Get these folks on, would you?" I says to Washakie, and I mounted up and headed back down toward the plain we'd just rode up from. I pushed the horse, he was a good one and used to mountain travel and he made good time and when we got to the bottom I pulled up to scan the horizon and looked behind me and there come Digby.

He might be a fine soldier but this was pure killer's work and he'd likely be more trouble than help. I was ready to tell him to go back when he waved his hat at me and come up.

"Alys was going to come," he says. "I said I would, and she agreed to go on with Washakie and the prince."

That was that.

"Stick close to me, do what I do," I says. "We got maybe one chance get that bastard."

I recalled the land we were headed for and remembered a blind canyon actually had a trail up to the rims; we'd have to lead our horses but the climb wasn't much, maybe fifteen minutes and we could then try to cut Blue Fox's trail. He'd be ahead but not by a lot, there was a couple deep coulees he had to cross that would slow him some, too.

We rode like hell and found the canyon and I shot up it, my horse runnin' like a rat up a drainpipe, and when I got to the trail I swung down and took my horse's reins and began to climb. It was steep and the shale there slippery and broken, and you'd put a foot down on a rock and it would scoot off. Bad enough for me but horses hate bad footing, and mine was no exception, but without me on his back his balance was better and so we made it up. Digby had trouble and had to blindfold his and so we lost fifteen minutes and by the time we was moving again I knew Blue Fox must have maybe three miles on us.

We crested a ridge and saw Mulligan and he saw us and he gestured he was moving west, to cut the trail if Blue Fox went that way.

In half an hour we looked down at the muleskinner's train and I sent Digby down to round up Jake and the others and send them after.

There'd be a lot of us, and that was the only hope.

Digby went right then; he knew what he was about.

CHAPTER 47

We finally made it to Washakie's camp two days later, and Blue Fox was still very much alive and damned if we knew where. We'd fanned out and the boys knew their business and Mulligan was as good as anyone, but the advantage was Blue Fox's in that broken country. We found his tracks, and he'd double back and circle wide and never quite show up where we could put a bullet in him. Then a storm had come up and he was gone out into the Plains and his tracks washed away. He might as well have sunk in the ocean.

Much of this didn't make any sense. There's nothing puts your enemies at ease more than them knowing you're dead. I'd been careful not to offend the Sioux and Cheyennes, and had an eye peeled for their young warriors out making mischief, but that damned Blue Fox could have picked us off he had a mind to, could have shot one or two and fled, and come back, and since he was dead I at least would have been sure I was dealing with someone else.

It was puzzling. I puzzled a lot.

Washakie had rolled out the best for Alys and me and Digby and Masoud, and him and the prince was engrossed in chess games and the old chief allowed as how Masoud could stay all winter if he liked. Washakie would like.

But that warn't why we were here so shortly after me and Digby got to the camp we packed up and got ready to go on to the two big dinosaurs Alys coveted.

"It will make me at one swoop one of the world's leaders in the field," she says.

Why she gave a damn was beyond me. She was rich and could go pick bones anywhere. But she hated Cope and she hated Marsh and she wanted to do one better on 'em.

I recalled my Uncle Angus, who'd been a trapper and had his fingers sawed off by a Sioux, he was playing dead and I knew him because he kept right on playing dead while the warrior got his rings and his fingers on his left hand. Angus was a wry man and when I was twelve or so I had said I wanted to join the Union Army and win medals.

Uncle Angus nodded.

"Ambitions you have, laddie," he says. "Weel, ambition is a bushwhacker and ye'd best make of yourself a small and moving target but ye'll not listen to me. One day ye'll wish you had."

I thought he was an old fool.

The skinners had had some rest and the mules had eaten good grass and the place we was heading was about two days, three if the weather turned bad.

Washakie said he'd come along, with some of his young

men. He wanted Blue Fox dead, too. I saw him praying just before we left, and they was war prayers, for strength and cunning.

Even Washakie was worried, and that man never worried. Why, when he was young—he'd been a leader since birth, I gathered—his buffalo-hunting party come on some Crows and they all got ready for a scrap and Washakie calls a parley and offers to fight their best warrior, winner take all. If they did it that way, he pointed out, there would be sorrow in only one lodge rather than in many.

The Crows agreed and sent their best warrior and Washakie killed him and then cut out his heart and ate it. Most of Wyoming warn't mapped yet, but all of us knew where Crowheart Butte was.

We left early in the morning and a fog was low on the ground and it had teeth, we was all bundled. The fog muffled sound some and I found myself with Washakie riding in the cloud, we could see the track but anyone who wandered off would get good and lost in fifty feet. But the trail was wide and well traveled.

Washakie was lost in thought and he would time to time look up as he was thinking, and finally he nodded, and he turned back to me, one hand on his horse's rump, and said my name.

"Uh?" I replied.

"Blue Fox is doing white man's business," said Washakie. "I don't know what, but there is nothing of the Cheyennes in this. That lie about him killing the women is Bull Shield, he is jealous and wants to be chief. He spreads those rumors about many."

News you don't want to hear comes any way and you got to listen to it.

My mind went to Cope and Marsh right off, but though I knew they'd not stick at having their men shoot each other, it still seemed a long stretch for them to want to murder a woman over some fossils, when there was so many in Wyoming. Or kill me, for the doing of it. The bones was what they wanted, and it seemed a high price to pay.

The sun come up and burnt the fog away and there was the desert again, and the grass and the antelope fleeing, white rumps bright as bleached shirts.

Beautiful it was and very cold with menace.

Then it hit me. Blue Fox hadn't shot at anyone, because if it was Cope or Marsh or the pair of them—and they'd scratch each other's backs or cut each other's throats like any other pair of disinterested scientists—they'd want those bones. I whirled around and rode to Alys, she was with Digby.

"Them drawings was stolen," I says. "Were any of them of the fossils where we're going?"

She nodded.

I didn't even try to get her to go back.

"You knew this all along, didn't you?" I says.

She cast her eyes down.

"I was hired on," I says, "but that's all. And you may go to hell, Miss de Bonneterre."

Nothing I hate more'n bein' used.

I'd begun to love her some, she was a lovely woman and had great fun and laughter in her. But she was just as cold and determined as them two goddamned professors, and that was that.

Never trust the rich, my Uncle Angus used to say, for they got rich for a reason.

I was furious cold now and if that damned Mulligan had come out of the landscape and I could have talked him into doing my job I would have headed for someplace and not looked back. But I was here and no helping it and as furious as I was if I left I would have broke my word. That ain't a reputation a man can afford out here.

My fury run down to ice and I kept well away from Digby and Alys and Masoud, too, hell, all I knew now he could be in it, too.

Digby finally come riding up and he asked to confer with me in private and I couldn't think of a good reason not to, so we rode on up a side hill and sat there until the others had gone on out of earshot.

"I don't understand," says Digby. "Alys is crying, and you look like you'd shoot her if you got a chance."

So I told him and he looked down at his saddle horn and said he'd no real idea, but he supposed it was so. Alys was determined to be well-known, and as a scientist, and she was as ruthless as any, if a bit more gracious. Or just smoother.

"I'm sorry, Luther," says Digby. "I never thought of any of this."

She'd always be the little girl he was the only family to in all the world.

Digby was an honorable man.

"Is it so bad," he says, "to want something like that? Women are routinely insulted, thought to be featherheads. It's made her angry since she was a little girl. She didn't want to go to finishing school. She didn't give a damn about making a good marriage."

"I don't mind wars," I says, "but I purely hate not knowing what and why I am fighting. This ain't a great question, Digby, like the War was. This is ambitious people."

They all was. Buffalo Bill wanted fame, and I knew he would get it. He wanted that more than anything.

Me, all I wanted was to roam this country and then lay up somewhere with good whiskey and an orderly and well-run whorehouse, to rest up. I didn't ask for anything more. But others had decided some things for me. Like it or not I was a captain in the United States Army, and I knew I'd be called whenever there was a bit of nasty work I was best qualified to do.

"I should have stayed home and rolled pills," I says, "or become a damn lawyer."

Digby laughed.

"Alys wants her bones," he says. "Perhaps that will be enough for her."

I shook my head. I never seen anyone that determined who would ever be filled up enough; it summoned up a hunger that never would be glutted.

We made camp that night in a pleasant grove of aspens near a clear spring, with grass deep and all cured standing in what was once a beaver pond and was now a meadow. You find a flat place in the mountains, likely them beaver made it. Their ponds fill up with mud and go to grass.

I camped off, sulking, and I was back to my half drowse at night, hearing everything. I heard her coming and I feigned sleep and she slipped into my robes and out of her clothes and she held me close and she wept and wept and begged my forgiveness.

She wore me down, the damned wench, all perfume and sweet flesh. I never been able to resist women, it has caused most of my troubles.

Buffalo Bill caught up with us right after dawn. He'd been raving the first couple of days and then sick. Now here he was again.

I looked at the folks I was with.

They *were* my kind of people and that made me feel sad, and after a while I laughed.

There's always folks smarter than you, Kelly, I says to myself, embarrassing as that is.

CHAPTER

48

That evening we come to the place of big bones, the two monsters in the stone, and Digby and Masoud and Alys looked and she explained and waved her hands. They was all excited and I left them to it, but that night after supper I pulled the three of them aside.

"I come to find," I says, "that I am not well thought of, enough so I at least know what you all are up to, I will quit and be gone and you can die here all I care. You understand?"

They all agreed, even Masoud, who I didn't suspect at all. He could hardly give a damn if some professors thought highly of his paleontology, what with having everything in the world at birth and he'd just come because it amused him.

He come on to me later when I was out listening to the

night sounds and marking the places Washakie's warriors was hid, to spend the night listening and looking for Blue Fox.

"I did not know," he said.

"Fine," I says. "Apologies if I insulted you."

"In my country," he said, "we have many of these fossils, but our scholars are uninterested. One day soon others will wish to come. I do not care to have our fossils plundered, as they have so many other things. I am rich, but my people are very poor."

Alys come into my robes late, she had been excited by just the getting here, and stayed up jabbering with Washakie. Between looking at Alys, which was a pleasant task, and Masoud's chessboard the old man was right satisfied.

Alys made no more pleas to have me forgive her, since I already had, and now she knew how far she could go, which is a very dangerous spot for a feller to be in. They always find out eventually and that's that from then on, trust me.

The next day Alys fell to sketching the bones in place and putting little daubs of white paint on the rocks and a number, so she'd know exactly where what fitted when this was all uprooted and shipped and there she would be with a puzzle.

A few million years or so and now you poor bastards are just an inventory, I said to the bones.

I had my way the West would have been forever untouched, other than my carting off enough gold and jade to live comfortable.

"Feller's got to think of his declining years," I says to Alys. "Whiskey and whores will go up in price, like bribing congressmen and common groceries. Man's got to look ahead."

My shin paid for that one.

"I've never paid you false, Luther," says Alys, "and that's the

God's truth. I thought you *knew* those drawings had been stolen, too."

She had me there. I should have.

Buffalo Bill rode on back to check the skinners and get some whiskey. Bill was in his own way an honest man, and I liked him, maddening as he could be.

Bill, just nicely lit, come in late the next day and the lead skinners not long after, and about half of them arrived and the other half camped three or so miles away when the dark come on. I had them build a corral for the stock to hold them at night—an Indian will cut a rope quiet, they have more trouble with a stout pole fence. I had thought to bring nails, and since very few Indians got pullers, I figured we'd have most of the stock when we needed it later.

Whinny and the boys went to putting up a cabin, just big enough to live in and not so big it would be hard to heat. They'd go off and cut cottonwood—oh, the wood would rot out soon but it would last the winter, all they needed, and it began to take some shape quick.

The skinners had brought little miner's picks and shovels and they was put to work digging up the bones. The rock was pretty well busted and the stack of specimens grew quick.

When they'd got most all out of the ground they could set black powder charges careful and cracked the larger pieces down to a size would fit in a Democrat freightwagon. A ton of rock is about the size of two sacks of spuds. It looked like it would take eighty wagons to haul what we'd dug away.

It went on like that for a couple of weeks, and I thanked the fates that had busted the rock up so nice. If we'd have had more to blast and shape down, it would have taken a good deal longer.

I ranged out each day, looking for Blue Fox's sign, and didn't see a damn thing, and neither did Mulligan or any of Washakie's young men. If he was around, he was keeping damned quiet.

I thought maybe there was just too many of us in camp, and it was likely Blue Fox would wait till we was headed back.

White man's business, says Washakie.

Finally, the day come when I knew that we had to leave. I could smell the weather changing and though I had smelled snow when the wind was from the mountains, this wind had a smell of storm to it, too, and it would be here in a day.

Alys looked at me like I was mad, and so did Digby, for the day was hot and bright and the sky washed blue without a cloud in it. But Washakie backed me up and so after just enough argument to keep her hand in Alys began to pack.

It was a week earlier than I had hoped, actually, but there had been a great deal of work done and what wasn't finished now would be easy enough to do in the spring.

The muleskinners was delighted. They weren't much pleased with the mining trade, and I ticked off the grub and such we'd need for the trip back and we piled everything else in a little shed Whinny and Jake and the boys had made, up on stilts of pine so they could get in when the snow was deep.

Some of the skinners wanted to leave right then, and make ten or so miles before sundown, but I held firm—we'd all go in a group and that meant they had to wait until the rest was ready.

"We'd best travel all night," I says, "and swing some east, maybe far enough to come to Cheyenne. The lower we are the less we got to fight the snow."

It was such a bright and beautiful afternoon.

Alys had saddled her own horse and she swung up on it to

check and see the girth was tight enough, and I was standing beside her.

There was a sound like a slap on wet flesh and Alys threw her arms up and fell boneless down into my arms, dead.

I screamed.

I set her down and when I did so Digby rode up and he looked off and pointed at something and he shrieked, a sound of such grief and rage I hear it still. He kicked his horse forward and I swung up on mine and followed after, but I had to stop and adjust the bellyband. So he was ahead, and I thought I saw a faint white cloud of powder smoke a good half mile off.

Digby was a good four hundred yards ahead when the gun fired again, and the slug took him in the belly and shattered his spine and he fell off his horse every which way and time I got there he was gone, too. He tried to speak, but his eyes just clouded.

I screamed again and I fired a few shots at the place I had seen the smoke, a long range for my saddle Sharps, I had to aim ten feet above the place.

Then there was another boom, a different sound than the one killed Alys and Digby.

I rode as fast as I could toward the spot, some rocks all piled up by God knew what, and I was givvering the whole time and damned if I can recall what it was I was saying.

I rode in a dream, things moved so very slowly, a bird flew past in front of me and seemed to be swimming in clear syrup.

In time I come to the rocks and I went on up.

Mulligan was there already, and the little man was crying.

We walked together on up and there was Blue Fox, finally dead, Mulligan had hit him low in the back as Blue Fox was lying down and the bullet had gone out his left shoulder.

I rolled the bastard over, but he really was dead this time, and though his face was some scarred it was nothing like the man I thought he was killed by Masoud's guards.

Mulligan was bawling, and in between sobs he said he'd been two days tracking Blue Fox and had come up on him from behind as he was taking aim, and Mulligan sighted and was about to squeeze the trigger when a breeze moved a limb in his line of sight, just for a second, no time at all, and then Mulligan heard the shot and then nothing.

He'd rushed to the side to get clear and laid down and was ready to fire when Blue Fox shot again and Mulligan's slug hit him seconds after, he'd not even had time to start wriggling back away to run.

Mulligan sat on a rock holding his head in his hands and sobbing.

I looked at the rifle Blue Fox had used. It once had been Sir Henry's, the Creedmore with the ivory stock and the brass telescopic sight on it, that Sir Henry had blacked with some acid so it wouldn't glint.

I went through the little that Blue Fox was carryin', and found nothing but some tobacco and a knife and a pencil but no paper. His horse didn't even have saddlebags. He must have camped near; I would find it.

There was men coming up every way that they could now, but I just looked straight ahead.

I come to the camp. Buffalo Bill had put a blanket over Alys.

He could be a good friend.

CHAPTER 49

As annoying as Buffalo Bill could be, you knew him for a good man if you happened to be a friend of his and got in trouble.

I was sitting on a rock stunned and felt my blood had drained away. My arms were too heavy to lift and my legs were quivering.

Bill came and he tipped my head back and poured whiskey down my throat. Then he threw a blanket around me and he just sat there and waited, and every once in a while he'd give me another dose.

"I will never know," I finally croaked, "just what this was all about."

"White man's business," says Washakie. I hadn't heard him come.

I nodded. Yes.

White man's business.

I may have sat there an hour or two days, I can't say, but finally Bill said we ought to bury Alys and Digby. We were too far from the railroad to take them and if they was planted deep and well covered, then their bones could be got later if anyone cared to.

We found a good place in a little knoll and the skinners dug deep graves and we buried them wrapped in blankets and then piled rocks four feet high on top of the cut earth.

Weren't any of us prayerful sorts except Washakie, and he said gently he could see to it later. I was grateful.

The weather was turning cold, and so we left, riding ahead of the mule train, and Washakie cut off to head back to his camp. I would see him in the spring, I said.

"No," he says, "it will be three years from now."

I nodded. Washakie could see beyond time, and if he said so that was how it would be.

Masoud and his guards, Bill, me, and Jake headed overland, with just jerky and hardtack and some coffee. We would ride day and night, and we drove remounts with us, I wanted only to go somewhere I could be drunk and safe at the same time for a year or two.

Not having anything to hold us back we come into Laramie in five days and change, the last day through some light snow. It was blacker to the north, and I hoped the muleskinners was able to keep going. This time of year if they stopped we might not find them till spring.

I was in a state of funk so deep that Bill wouldn't let me out of his sight, for fear I'd get a twitch and shoot myself.

Masoud asked me to come with him as he was planning to go East and then home, but I said hell no, and I did have to wait until the mule train got in. If they was more than two days late, I'd have to round up some fellers and go after them.

Masoud nodded. We was at Rosie's, at her table in the back, the girls left us alone, neither one of us was much in the mood. I drank and Masoud sipped thick black coffee. Bill stayed just sober enough to keep an eye on me.

The mule train got in about the time I expected and no one lost, so that was that and I didn't care a goddamn who ended up with the blasted fossils—they cost too much.

"Don't never want anything too much," I says suddenly, looking up from my glass.

"Yer gettin' better," says Bill. "For a few days there you didn't say anything near that stupid."

I come up off the chair and tried to smash his face in, but he just held out his hands and pushed my fists this way and that and I run down as fast as I had blazed up.

"I'm sorry," I says.

Bill shrugged.

My hotel rooms still smelt faintly of Alys's perfume and there were some of her things there, and of course the damned parlor car sat looking back at me every time I went out.

I might have sat there in a black fog the whole damn winter but for one of them things always happens to me when I am about out of patience with the earth and all that's on it.

I was sitting at Rosie's about drunk enough to go and take a nap when this boy come in, in a blue monkey suit with a lot of brass buttons, and he hands me a telegram. Yellow envelope. One of them. I have never opened one without wishing I had just put the damned thing in the fire. I got up to do just that, and the boy cleared his throat.

"Begging your pardon, Mr. Kelly," he says, "but there was

another telegram said to tell you if you burned that without opening it there was no use as you'd get another and if that didn't get opened there'd be consequences."

"That son of a bitch," I says.

"Son of bitch?" says Masoud. He was playing chess with Bill. I opened the goddamned thing.

KELLY   ORDERED WHITE HOUSE BY 1 DECEMBER   GRANT

"He has to find me first," I snarls, throwing the telegram on the floor.

The kid fished out another telegram. He handed it to me.

PICK THAT UP   GRANT

I had to laugh. No fool, our president.

Masoud pointed to the telegram and raised an eyebrow. He had such good manners he wouldn't demand to know. I handed it over.

"Oh, jolly good," he says. "We can go together. I am to see the president before I depart."

"Anything about me?" says Bill.

I shook my head, and Bill slumped a little. He'd never met Grant and wanted to.

"What day is it?" I says.

"November 19," says Masoud, "in your calendar."

Eleven days. Barely enough time to get there, allowing for a day or so holdup some place, which usually happened.

"Fine," I says. "Let's go."

The ease with which I found myself installed in one of Masoud's three coaches should have set my ears to quivering, but

I was still in a funk and not thinking well. If I had been, I could easily have slipped off into the winter and made myself good and scarce. Washakie kept a good lodge. I could have made it in time.

Masoud had summoned up his very own locomotive, so we didn't have to endure the delays common rich parlor-car owners got. We had our own train.

I sat in the saloon glumly looking out at the brown land going past, and the damned farmers seemed to have moved a bit farther west since I last come this way. Wouldn't be long till my West was all pissants and preachers.

When we got to Omaha and crossed the Missouri on the ferry that carried the locomotives—there wasn't a bridge yet—I began to perk up a little and thought once again I couldn't be held accountable for desertion if I didn't know what my orders was yet, and so whilst our train was being off-loaded on the far shore I took a quiet sneak toward useful obscurity.

I looked back at the train and saw no one looking and ducked down and scurried quick toward a handy alley.

I stopped dead. There was a couple of them giant A-rabs from Masoud's retinue in it, and they neither moved nor spoke, just kept their hands on the hilts of them swords, and so I put my hands palm up and shrugged and I trudged back to the train.

This finally started me in to thinking, and now I wasn't going to run.

Oh, no. I was going to take them two lovely little belly guns and I was going to change my appearance some and I was going to kill both Cope and Marsh, the bastards, and even if they didn't really know where their damned money had led they was responsible. The connection to Blue Fox was there, mad though he was, and there was someone must have known that, must have at least suspected what the end could become.

One of them really strange snowstorms that's half a blizzard and half a thunderstorm blew up just like that, and the air got wet and stank of St. Elmo's fire. I'd been in them in mountains and seen my horse's ears and head dancing with electric blue light, seen it crawl over my gloved hands like a live thing. It was a harmless thing, but weird.

I got in the coach and sat with some whiskey looking out as the black clouds rumbled and the snow fell and the sleet lashed the windows and slipped down like fiery tears.

I had to kill the pair of them the same time, for if I got one it would sure warn the other. So I needed to get to a debate, one thing I could count on was those pompous bastards and their silly quarrels that cost so much blood and death. They needed them, it was all their life.

Now I had something to do and I would do it and if I hanged, and I damned well might, well, fine.

Alys had got inside me and once again my heart was torn and like before I had gone all cold and calm and needed death I dealt to make me whole and warm again. That was what Jim Bridger and Washakie had seen in me.

The storm got furious and the winds pushed the car on its springs and the lamp chimneys rattled in their brass holders. The flames went up and down as the car did. I couldn't see more'n five feet out the window.

I had some more whiskey and I pecked at some cheese and meat and chewed real slow.

Blue Fox had slipped through disguised as a wounded soldier, and I could do the same thing if I was uniformed, bemedaled, and my face touched up with collodion, fake honorable scars. Getting the uniform and medals and such was nothing, old soldiers sold what they had, the government was slow to pay them for their blood. And the thanks of a grateful nation.

I'd do it alone. I'd speak to no one.

When they were both dead, I would be some satisfied.

It would have to do.

CHAPTER

50

Masoud come in later, moving as he always did, silently, his feet in soft boots with soles thin as glove leather. Not havin' to walk on anything rougher than his subject's backs, the wear was slight.

"There is nothing out there you should be looking at now," says Masoud. "We will play cards."

Flunks set up a table with best green felt and chips and cards appeared and my goblet was refilled and I got up and went over and slumped in the chair, feeling some better but worn-out.

Masoud shuffled the deck with practiced ease and set the deck over to me and I felt them just for show and lifted up half and there was the black ace, the spade.

"Very good," says Masoud.

"What game?" I says.

"Five card draw," says Masoud, "since you don't seem a man who would enjoy whist."

I nodded and dealt and Masoud bet and I matched. There'd been no mention of money, I had little and he had so much he didn't have any idea of his worth.

"Apologies for the guards," says Masoud, "but I was asked to see you safely to Washington. There was some worry you might slip away."

I nodded. There sure was.

"You should come to my country," says Masoud. "Much of it is like your Wyoming, spare and bleak, the people there are fierce and loyal and they ride like centaurs. They live on their herds and flocks and come but once a year to trade their meat and cheese for grain and goods the villagers make. Otherwise, they live in tents and move with the grass and the seasons."

"Well," I says, "it's a nice idea, but I am afraid U.S. Grant is going to shoot me off to Nicaragua."

"He might," says Masoud, "but if I were to mention to him that I would appreciate having Yellowstone Kelly an honored guest, he could perhaps find someone else."

"If he could find someone else," I says, "then I could go back to Montana this time. They was friends of mine, and I'd sort of like to see no one for a while. I know places there."

"Four tens," says Masoud, which went well over my three queens.

We played a while.

"I meant no offense," I says. "My heart's black and needs air and country."

"We have both," says Masoud.

He didn't bring it up again, he had most excellent manners and I thought it kind of him to offer me the journey. I like them far places and folks who don't wear boiled shirts and talk always of money.

"What happened to your people at Digby's?" I says suddenly. We had wired the terrible news, but I knew of no family they had, not even the name of the lawyers would oversee and take their slice.

"Took ship already," says Masoud. "Did you know that Alys left something there for you? She asked me to keep it and give it to you in time if anything were to happen to her and Digby."

I looked up sharp.

"She *knew?*" I says.

Masoud nodded. "They both did, Kelly. In this world nothing is ever safe, and they both knew their deaths would solve a great problem for Cope and Marsh."

"You knew about Blue Fox," I says, "and did not tell me. They knew, too, and if I'd known, I could have maybe done something."

Masoud shook his head, once.

"What is written will pass," he says. "Our lives are in the Book and we may not escape them."

I threw my cards down.

"If I'd have known," I says, "I would have made it damned clear to those two bastards that . . ."

"Of course," says Masoud. He lit a cheroot.

I suddenly flew hot with rage, at Digby and Alys for playing me like a fool, and all for nothing. My face flushed and I turned and looked again out the window, but it was coming on dark and there was nothing out there not hidden by the night.

I would go into that night let it cloak me, and hunt.

"I am content," says Masoud, "to let the will of God, Allah, prevail. It will anyway."

"I ain't," I says softly.

"Foolish," says Masoud. "You will break your teeth for nothing. It is written, Kelly, and no one can see down time."

Washakie could. He would see me in three years and that was plenty of time to kill Cope and Marsh, even with a side trip to Nicaragua thrown in. Hell, that would take a few months. Better that way, Cope and Marsh would be off guard. Not that I couldn't see about a pair of shots before we left. The military don't move fast, for sure.

I wished Sir Henry was still alive. The two of us could have done it, and he'd have jumped at the chance. But Blue Fox killed him, too.

He'd killed a part of me as well.

My mother used to tell me to enjoy my youth, for life will maim you and then kill you. I could go see her, I thought. I had a large family, it went damn near end to end of the town, brothers that was lawyers and other objectionable things. And she wouldn't let me slip in and out at night.

Hell with that, I thought, I am in no damned mood to make nice and won't be for a while, and when I am I'd best be a long damn way from the East a while.

"Kelly!" says Masoud. "There is nothing out there you should look for. You are ill. I shall summon my doctor."

He clapped his hands and the chamberlain appeared, all hunched over, and Masoud said a few words and off the man went and in two minutes a fat, white-bearded little A-rab, some greasy rice still on his robe from the supper he had left so suddenly, appeared. An assistant clanked in, carrying a yoke with bottles and oddments hanging from it in strings of clanking tinkling glass.

Masoud said a few words to the little man, who was facedown on the carpet, and then the prince stood up and glided off, silent as a cat hunting.

Folks the world around expect different things from their quacks, and so I awaited the bedside manner.

First the little fellow packed a pipe with a black gum had white threads in it and he lit it and offered it to me. It smelled sweet and dangerous. I shook my head.

The little doctor looked angry. He clapped his hands and them two monsters usually was waiting to behead them as came near Masoud come up out of the carpet and lifted me off the floor and one held a dagger across my throat and the little doctor stuck the stem of the pipe in my mouth and I sucked rather eagerly, since this warn't going to end till I'd been cured.

The smoke wasn't harsh, just thick, and after three deep puffs the little doctor took the pipe back and nodded to the monsters and they peeled off my shirt and flang me down on a divan and then here come the little doctor with the assistant clanking and various oils and ointments was applied here and there.

My head fell off my neck just then, though since I was flat on my back no one noticed. I expected the room to whirl as it rolled off the divan and across the room. The aromatic stinks I'd got on my chest and face was cloying and I choked a little, but the doctor stuck some burning grass under my nose and the stinks left and the room stopped spinning.

I had an instant of feeling myself, and then I fell into a deep pit, down into dreams. I could go on for days about them, they happened fast but was full of the past, recent and far, and the last thing I remembered was Alys waving at me, dressed in the transparent silk harem pants and bustier, as she walked through a spring wood.

How long I slept I don't know, but when I woke it was bright out and we was clanking across farm country heavy with snow, the cows looking stupidly at the train.

I sat up.

Masoud was sitting at a table, with a roast lamb and rice and some sort of greenstuffs. If you're rich enough, you can have salads in winter.

I was starving. I sat up and felt all right and I made it to a chair and fell on the food with all the grace and charm of a starving grizzly. Masoud leaned back to escape the sleet of lamb bits and rice kernels I was throwing off.

"Where are we?" I says, when I'd et myself to a standstill.

"Virginia," says Masoud.

I sank back, almost ill from the huge mess of food I'd wolfed down.

A flunk handed me a goblet of whiskey and a lit cheroot. I sank back, and thought about collecting my wits. I hadn't a lot of time to slip away, what with Washington that close by. I noticed I was wearing a heavy silk robe and soft slippers. I goggled stupidly at them.

The whiskey was scotch, I thought, smoky and pungent. Wyoming was a long ways from this good stuff. I liked it better even than smooth Kentucky bourbon.

I had a good slug and then another and a warm bloom grew in my belly and the cheroot tasted mighty fine.

I stretched and yawned and my fingers began to tingle and then my toes and then my lips.

My head swelled and I started to fall. Strong hands carried me to a bed.

I slid down into that deep sleep.

There was incense burning somewheres.

CHAPTER 51

I been drunk enough plenty of times so when I woke up I didn't know where I was or how I got there, and usually I was in some nice whorehouse smelling of women and lamp oil. Couple times in a jail cell, too, nothing much to that.

But when I come up out of my deep sleep I was real sick to my stomach and I rolled over and began to heave nothing at all into a bucket some soul had thoughtful-like placed there. This exercise lasted some minutes. I was groggy, and it took a while for me to realize I wasn't light-headed or feverish. I focused my bleary eyes on the room I was in. It was small, and I was in a bunk had a rail on it and I stared stupidly at the shelf over a little washbasin was stuck to the wall. A book on its side slid to one end of the shelf and after a moment when my stomach began to ripple and heave it slid back to where it had been.

I looked at a funny round window up in the wall over my head. It had a brass grip on each side and so I grabbed on and pulled myself up and I looked out dumbstruck.

Gray seas was rolling meanly and a sharp wind cut white spray from the tops of the waves.

Kelly, I thinks, this is the goddamned end. Your good friends, them turds, has you on a boat.

On the goddamned ocean.

Never been on a ship before, or the ocean, but I had read all of these books and I damn well knew that Virginia warn't cut in half by no large bodies of water.

I was naked, and there was my clothes, all fresh and clean, on a chair had a clotheshanger built into it. I got dressed and pulled on my boots and someone had stuck some sort of sandpaper on the bottoms.

My little belly guns was not in sight. Good thing, too.

I tried the door but some kind soul had locked it from the outside.

"Masoud, goddamn you you heathen son of a bitch!" I roars, pounding on the door. "I am a United States citizen and . . ." and it occurred to me that the government I proposed to complain to was no doubt behind my present straits, specifically a short red-bearded seegar-smoking ex-general son of a bitch who I had at least trusted far enough to send me to goddamned Nicaragua, where I could have easily bided for the couple months it would take to tramp across the jungle, before returning here to kill and scalp Cope and Marsh.

Neither of them deserved to live, god damn it.

I cranked up my volume and called Masoud a bunch of

really inventive names, pounding on the door all the while, and when I run down and gave a final dispirited whack with the palm of my hand it swung open on to a passageway and there stood Prince Masoud, looking tall and bored.

"If my minions knew the hundredth part of your insults, he says," I would barely be able to keep them from slicing you to chops and feeding the sharks. I don't mind the insults, Kelly, my good friend: in your country they are a mark of esteem and friendship. I especially liked the bit about me fucking pigs. Pigs are thought an abomination in the eyes of Allah, and should the least of my servants hear such an atrocious lie, they would be honor-bound to slit your throat. So shut the hell up and yell about Grant."

I yelled about Grant for a while. That treacherous . . . and so forth and so on but like Washakie the bastard was both a shrewd judge of men and smarter than me.

Masoud nodded happily, agreeing with my every slander of good old U.S. Grant, the Man who won the War.

"You regard him highly," says Masoud.

"I do when the bastard don't stick me on some damn ocean liner," I says. "I don't think I'm going to like England."

Masoud clapped his hands and a flunk came with a goblet had some potion in it. I drank it down and my stomach quit heaving.

"Come, Kelly," says Masoud, "and please keep your head always lower than mine."

Remembering his absolutely humorless guards, I hobbled along, ducking down when we had to go down two steps. Masoud was so tall I didn't have to duck much, even if he was standing a good two feet lower.

We went through some doors all blue and gilt and sparkling

with gems to a huge stateroom all done up in the manner of style I had seen in his big blue tent.

Masoud motioned me to a divan and he settled on his, a good three feet higher. The chamberlain come in and crawled over.

Masoud said a few words and the man backed away, getting a little higher for each foot he retreated. When he got to fifty feet he stood up and backed out of the room.

There warn't anyone else visible. But there was a lot of silk curtains around, and servants and them huge bodyguards right there, I was sure."

"Nice stateroom they give you," I says. It reached across the whole liner. I could see portholes on both side of the giant mess of silk and enamel and odd carved furniture.

Masoud just nodded.

A flunk appeared and filled my goblet with whiskey. I put my nose to it and sniffed suspiciously.

"Nothing in it but whiskey," says Masoud. "We no longer needed the opium and syrup of lotus."

"Needed?" I says. "Oh, I see, so you could shanghai me."

"I suppose," says Masoud, "I could arrange for you to work as a stoker. Do you like the thought of shoveling coal into the boilers better than lying here, and sometimes playing cards?"

Light dawned.

"This ain't," I says, "no British ocean liner or anything like that."

"No-ope," says Masoud. He'd been practicing his Wyoming.

I launched into a long recitation of Grant's oddities and character flaws and various dire acts he had no doubt committed as a farmboy in Illinois, and heavy on the ducks.

"How you admire him," says Masoud, grinning.

"This is your yacht," I says.

"Indeed," says Masoud.

"And what," I says, half-knowing, "am I doing on it exactly?"

"You are to be the new military attaché," says Masoud, "to my court."

"You're the sultan of Turkey?" I says.

"Heavens, no," says Masoud. "I am a mere prince of a vassal state. I myself am a Kurd, but many of the Kazakhs are ruled by me also."

"Military attaché," I says. Other'n gettin' shot at, I had little military experience. And, I thought happily, no uniforms.

"Grant," says Masoud, "asked me to give you your orders when I felt you could be persuaded to read them." He handed me one of them piss yellow government envelopes just never, ever has good news in it.

> *Major Kelly,*
>
> *You are to proceed to the court of Prince Masoud al-Diloof and serve there as sole military attaché, with an eye to trade possibilities. If the prince wishes you to assist his forces in drill or tactics* of peaceful nature *do so.*
>
> *Grant*
> *Commander in Chief*
> *by JH*

"They were concerned that you might try to kill the professors," said Masoud, "and wished you farther away than Nicaragua. You need time, Kelly, to let those worms die which are eating your intestines. All is written in the Book, and I have found in life that swine such as Cope and Marsh are best left to live their lives. They will do more evil to themselves than you could yourself dream of. It is what we carry within us, Kelly, the world is but a dream. . . ."

Things flooded back, and tears welled up in my eyes. I had loved Alys and Digby, too, and now they were gone.

I was all set to sob when I got sudden-like distracted and I looked down at my boots in horror.

Them sneaky little sausage dogs had crept up and dashed out from hiding and they was clamped, one upon each ankle, uttering little Kraut cries of happiness.

I made a grab for a tall brass coffeepot, long and slim and heavy, and I got it and swung it up two-handed but Masoud reached over and grabbed it before I could smash the little bastards.

Libretta appeared out of nowhere, waving a large cleaver, and explained in broken but adequate English what would happen to my parts if I ruffled a hair on the little shits.

Stefano burst in next with some demented bird on his fist, a big white-and-black hawk.

"Kell-ee!" the little guinea bastard chortles.

"Kell-ee, we have saltimbocca tonight!" says Libretta.

"SNARL MUNCH SNARL GRRRR. . . ." added the sausage dogs.

"Shit," I says.

"All life is written in the Book," says Masoud.

CHAPTER

52

When I finally staggered back to my room and got inside there was a package there, in a soft leather briefcase, yellow-brown and waxed and used. It was a thing of Digby's probably, I thought, and I choked up and wondered what Alys had put inside it and I thought for a while before I undid the three leather straps that held it shut.

There was a book, and a little pocketknife all brave with gold filigree on ebony for the handle, and when I opened it the blade was chased and scribed, a hunting scene, and a woman swinging a shotgun after a flight of birds. And a ring, a heavy gold one with a black stone in it, that fit the middle finger of my left hand.

The book was a privately printed one, excerpts from journals Alys had written, the last three from her summer trip in Wyoming, when she was working for the disagreeable Cope, him of the deadly ambition and the money to poison and destroy lives. In the name of disinterested scholarship.

I would have to read it, I knew, and I left it closed, and knew I would not sleep until I had, at least the last three entries.

I will keep them still, save for this. She had gone for a walk with Washakie, and they had seen an owl, and Washakie had said something in Shoshone and closed his eyes, and the owl had flown.

". . . I felt something cold round my heart and that feeling that someone had stepped upon my grave, and so I demanded that Washakie tell me the truth, that I could bear it, but if he was my friend he was not to keep it from me. He said I was soon to die, and I somehow knew that he was right."

There was more.

". . . do not wait for me for there is nothing behind the curtain, go on, my brave and funny scout."

I thought back and remembered now a couple times Washakie had looked at me, his old face impassive, his black eyes unreadable. But he was my father, more than any other man, and it was a measure of his love that he would let me find out in time, for those who fight fate and lose are worse off than those who simply do not know.

Damn, I cursed, she could have stayed and . . .

No. She would not do that. I could see her point. In Wyoming she could die by assassin, if she stayed in Boston it would be a goddamned trolley car.

I have no God and neither know nor in truth much care what happens after death, I will find out in time.

A book, a knife, a ring.

There was a knock on the door, a soft one, and I opened it and Masoud's chamberlain was there, and he handed me a folded piece of ivory parchment. There was a wax seal on it. The chamberlain floated away.

I broke the seal and opened it and there was a brief note, in a lovely flowing hand.

Kelly,

We shall sail through the Dardanelles and thence to a small port on the eastern shore of the Black Sea, and go overland to the Caspian and cross it to the south and so go on to my lands.

I am a religious leader as well as a prince, and once returned, I may not again offer you alcohol, or pork—the latter I am sure you may live happily without.

The excellent Stefano is a skilled distiller, able to make his filthy grappa out of anything which comes to hand, and were I you I would keep him close, as he has skills and the equipment to keep you from thirst, which you folk in America's West seem to fear more than any Man or God.

Grant and Hay requested that I keep you as attaché until I and my soothsayers are convinced you will do nothing so foolish as to kill or attempt to kill the Professors Cope and Marsh. They regard you highly and expect most valuable services from you in the years ahead.

The package entrusted to my care has not been opened and contains only those things which Miss de Bonneterre put in it. Digby did not know. Perhaps someday we may return and bring their bones back to Boston, or perhaps they will sleep more peacefully in the little dell you found.

Any request which I may grant, you have only to ask.

MASOUD

Well, that was that. The little journal from Alys was enough. There was whiskey in the cupboard below the little washstand and I had some and I opened the porthole and smelled the sea. The roll wasn't bothering me, though I expected to wake in the night all heaving and miserable.

I closed the porthole and nodded at myself in the mirror. I looked aged now, the wind and rain and dust and blood had cut deep lines around my eyes, we all have them out there, even young children, from squinting at the distances.

For the first time I noticed a velvet pullrope and I gave it a jerk and in about sixty seconds there was a soft knock and I opened it and there was an A-rab in a blue uniform, with a white-billed cap.

I began to flap my arms and make noises sort of like Stefano.

The A-rab looked at me gravely.

"Sir," he says, "I have English."

"Well, I says," I would like to see Stefano and Libretta, them two Eye-talians with the mean birds."

"He is consultant falconer to the prince," says the feller, "and she is an honored guest, the more so because her veal piccata is so splendid. When you are ready, I shall lead you there."

I nodded and followed along, and he led me down a passageway.

"Wait a minute," I says. "You got any really hot pepper sauce?"

"Not with me," says the feller, "but I will fetch some."

"It's for them damned dogs," I says.

"Ah, yes," says the A-rab. "Very brave of heart are they. And you are sure you wish to risk the wrath of the woman? She is most fierce in protecting her little beasts."

I thought of the cleaver.

"Perhaps, sir," says the A-rab, "some oil soap would do as well. The attendants who have to go in there find it does discourage the dogs most readily, without making them yelp."

I nodded and he immediately brought forth a small bottle and I dabbed my ankles with it.

"I would do as much again," says the A-rab.

"I take it," I says, "you are experienced in these matters."

He nodded.

Armored against them tiny little monsters, I gave him back the bottle and we went on. I could tell we was getting close from the mixed stink of bird shit and fermenting fruit and Eye-talian cooking and heavy on the garlic.

Stefano and Libretta had a nice suite, or it had been before a whole lot of big cages with eagles and hawks of many descriptions screaming at the stranger in the doorway had been added.

I stepped in when Libretta waved at me and them two hairy little bastards leaped out and clamped on and let go and hacked and spat most gratifyingly. Libretta scooped them up and crooned to them.

"It seems," I says, "that we are entering one of them places don't like booze."

"Yah," says Stefano.

"Well," I says, "what are we going to do about that?"

"Not to worry," says the little Eye-talian, "long as you are not drunk at a meal given by the prince, his people will pay it no mind."

I had never knowed he spoke good English, always distracted by them damned sausage dogs and Libretta fingering that cleaver.

"Castrato!" she'd say. "I use the flat side, too."

Just then this damned eagle I just noticed stuck a foot out through the mesh of its cage and opened its fist and the damn foot was bigger than any bald eagle's I'd ever seen. It didn't look like any eagle I'd ever seen either. It was bigger, and had a funny helmet of feathers.

"What is that?" I says.

"Harp-eee eagle," says Stefano. "Eats monkeys. Lives in Brazil."

"Interesting," I says.

Stefano held out his arm. There was red healed wounds on his wrist, that looked like bullets had done 'em. He pointed to the harpy eagle flexing its talons.

Libretta put down the sausage dogs, who growled and looked glumly at my ankles, but didn't bother charging.

"Anything I can do to help our grappa still, here?" I says.

"Stay the damn hell away from it," says Stefano. "You Irish use potatoes!"

"Ah hell," I says. "They use malted grain."

"Grain is for pasta and bread," says Stefano. "In Italy, we are eating good veal and drinking fine grappa, you are still eating each other. Potatoes. You Irish should be . . . excommunicated."

"Fine," I says. "I don't think they got potatoes in wherever the hell it is we're going." I looked at the A-rab purser. He shook his head.

"In our land," he says, "we do not grow potatoes."

Libretta gave me a nice peck on the cheek and a hearty hug and so I went back out.

"The prince up?" I says.

The steward on duty nodded.

"He rises to pray very early, sir," he said.

I thought a moment.

"I'd like an audience," I says, "on a small but pressing mat-ter."

The steward led the way.

I looked through a porthole at the black and waiting sea.